SCATTERED
Petals

SHIBANI GHOSE CHOTANI

PARTRIDGE

To order additional copies of this book, contact
Partridge India
000 800 10062 62
orders.india@partridgepublishing.com

www.partridgepublishing.com/india

CONTENTS

For women

The bold and the conscientious spirit, magnified with goodness, much larger than you will ever know.

Acknowledgements

I am indebted to many people in helping me bring the book *Scattered Petals* into the light. The inspiration and support of my wonderful family and friends have been imperative to the outcome of this book. They have my endless gratitude.

I want to thank my mother for her unrelenting inspiration at every stage of the writing process and my father for his unwavering enthusiasm to see the book in print. My thanks to my brothers Siddhartha and Harish for their steadfast support.

My sincere acknowledgement is to my editor, Ann Minoza, for her patience and understanding to guide me through the various steps of the editorial process. I am grateful to her for the many questions she answered and helped me take care of the challenges along the way.

I would like to thank the team of Partridge Publishers for their advice and assistance: Jules Hernandez, Emman Villaran, Marvin Easton and Vanessa Dean. I am thankful for their gracious support.

Last, I would like to thank my husband, Gopal and my daughter, Eva, whose patience and insightful thoughts deserve my unshaken gratitude.

From the Heart

I n six months, Min-Seo established herself comfortably in the third-floor apartment of the quiet French town. The petite twenty-four-year-old Asian girl with black shoulder-length hair, a peachy white complexion, dark eyes, and an outwardly soft-spoken persona integrated into her newly married life in a fairly similar manner to how she would have lived in her hometown a suburb of Seoul where she was born and had spent most of her life. But, everything changed on the day when her husband, Ji Soon, was confirmed for the post-doctoral research fellowship from the French technical institute located an hour from Paris.

Min-Seo never imagined a life outside her country, not till that day. It became instantly apparent that she had to habituate herself to the unexplored foreign life thousands of miles away since she was going to accompany Ji Hoon. Her heart clenched at the thought of a new place, and immediately, she sensed apprehension and feelings of wariness in her mind; she had no knowledge of French language and she was uncertain how much her fragmented English would be of use in a country that prided itself on its pleasing and elegant native language.

A girl of simplicity and composure, Min-Seo had lived a sheltered life in her country and after arriving in the French town, she most always refrained from socializing, she felt a kind of certainty not having to speak to people. But, there was no question about Min-Seo having a withdrawn persona, as a matter of fact, she had never lived a socially disconnected life. Living with her two older sisters and parents, she knew what it was like to socialize with a community of friends and extend herself to people of all ages irrespective of their different interests. By all means, she had the comfort of her own native language, her own culture. But, after arriving in the French town, an unsettling feeling clung to her; she could not communicate as she wished to. Every so often, she tried to get by in social situations with gestures or with broken English phrases, often receiving uncertain responses from people who would try to comprehend what Min-Seo was trying to express, but shake their heads and utter the English word 'sorry' and walk away. Despite this, Min-Seo yielded to those disheartening encounters quietly, not exerting herself to unsettling thoughts; she did not want to demoralize herself. Without letting time pass, she enrolled for three days a week in a local French language school in the town.

The French teacher, *Monsieur* Kernavais, stood in front of the class and introduced Min-Seo. "We have a new student— *Mademoiselle* Min-Seo." As the faces turned towards Min-Seo, the French teacher continued, "Please introduce yourself to your classmate." Min-Seo looked at the faces of each student as they spoke their names. She heard the countries they were from—Spain, Italy, Holland, Austria, Norway, United States, Egypt, Japan, India, China, Thailand. Each name sounded unique, foreign to her ears. In her whole life, she had never come across people from so many countries. Instantaneously, a classroom full of foreign students galvanized her, sparked optimism that she had not felt so far. *What was I thinking!* In that moment, she realized there were people who were as novice to the French language as she was. She was not alone.

There is a drawback when you focus on yourself and think you are the only one. Min-Seo reassured herself.

On the days she did not have classes, Min-Seo revived her photography skills, strolling through the town and taking pictures of archaic buildings, churches and monuments. Some days, she quietly sat on a park bench, absorbing the undemanding pace of life in front of her; there were pedestrians who leisurely walked by greeting *'Bonjour'* or a man who gave an acknowledging nod as he briskly walked past listening to his hand-held transistor radio. Every so often, she would wondrously watch a Renault or Peugeot race rapidly through the narrow street, with young men frolicking cheerfully inside the vehicles, crossing every line of obedient behavior. She could feel the profuse forthrightness in the way people lived. She realized there was a different kind of life that she needed getting used to. Afterwards, when she had an extra half hour, she would walk into the *Délicieuse* Bakery to see what kinds of bread varieties were displayed inside the glass cupboard. The bakery lady noticed and smiled at her every time, saying, *'Bonjour, Madame!'* Min-Seo would reply with *'Bonjour!'* She was hesitant to stay longer, in case the lady would initiate an engaging conversation in French; she had seen the lady do that with other customers.

I could never carry on a conversation! The thought would immediately occur. Then, she would gesture a good-bye wave and exit the bakery.

On certain days, she passed in front of the town hall, it was the statue of Joan of Arc that dazzled her every time; the young French woman with moral courage and physical bravery who led the French army to victory in the Hundred Years War during the late middle ages. She thought about the period in which the warrior woman lived, when leading an army was considered unthinkable for a woman. Now, she saw the statue in a different light, perhaps from the irresolute feelings vacillating within her—the mighty woman on the horse stimulated her. An unwavering character of courage that transcended fear and self-doubt.

The brick buildings with iron-railed balconies and square windows served as the married students' accommodation. The one-bedroom, one-bath, kitchen, and living room unit of Min-Seo and Ji Hoon was an austere place; natural light streamed through the white voile curtains onto the low rectangular wooden table, around which lay the round-shaped satin cushion pillows, creating a decorative sitting area on the floor. A tall shoji screen separated the sitting section from the kitchen. The screen was a gift from Min-Seo's older sister that she brought with her to decorate her new home in France, and it aesthetically suited with the oriental arrangement that she had created in the apartment. A veranda extended from the living room, looking down into the green lawn with a walking path and a few beech and maple trees. Every so often, the occupants of the building took the path to the bus stand or to the institute center that had the library, book shops, cafés and a cafeteria.

Min-Seo's husband, Ji Hoon, twenty-nine years of age, was a man of fewer words. He spoke when he thought his views were worthy of contribution. His average command of English most always outranked his disinterest for learning French. He inferred the meaning of French words through whatever little English he possessed, though, it would be even a miracle to hear him utter a few words in English. Despite this, he managed to create his own expressive means with a unique mixture of French and English phrases when needed.

He maintained the same routine every day, having twenty minutes of morning meditation, followed by drinking a glass of orange juice while scanning the headlines of the local French newspaper. He most always dismissed the opportunities to do anything leisurely with Min-Seo after the long hours of mental work conducting scientific experiments at the laboratory. There is nothing more imperative than work; it was what Ji Hoon believed and devotedly followed in his daily routine.

Min-Seo conceded to the fact that Ji Hoon was the sole provider in the foreign circumstance; therefore, she accepted the disadvantages of being a dependent in a foreign country while being grateful for the trouble-free life she had in return. She took care of the household chores, prepared meals with fresh produce from the market, and kept in touch with her family in her home-town. Most days, Ji Hoon came home to have the hot lunch that Min-Seo prepared, exchanged a few words while he sipped green tea and looked through the mail. In the few hours Ji-Hoon was home, Min-Seo never brought up heavyweight topics of conversation; she showed him the picture postcards of stunning French castles and the glittering city life of Paris she was mailing to her relatives. He nodded smiling, feeling appreciative that Min-Seo was settling herself in the new country as well as being mindful of remembering their families. He signed his name at the bottom of the postcards; Min-Seo added the details with insightful messages in Korean. When Ji Hoon returned to work, Min-Seo took the bus to the town center post office to mail the postcards.

Any kind of errands outside the empty apartment was inspiring for her; they were the best part of Min-Seo's day. She cherished the thriving life in the busy quarters of the town as she strolled down the narrow streets. She saw women standing at street corners engrossed in conversation with other women, people shopping for varieties of cheese and baked food inside the small shops, customers waiting in line to buy the crisp grilled chicken being prepared on an open rotisserie flame, young women experimenting with new hairstyles inside salons, and even elderly women sitting on benches and talking adoringly to their perfectly groomed poodles with fancy collars. She even saw groups of young students engaged in light-hearted discussion in outdoor cafes. They appeared to be from foreign countries, but they spoke French willingly, even if they did not sound like the native speakers. There was a kind of charm in whatever people were engaged in. Min-Seo wished she was part of this invigorating life outside her home.

Isn't it why people experience other cultures—to breathe another kind of air?

In those times Min-Seo felt an emotional separation between herself and the life around her. She was eager to mingle, but she sensed the barriers she had to overcome. A part of her was hesitant to step over what seemed to her an invisible divide.

On two nights a week, Min-Seo accompanied Ji Hoon to the research lab to give herself a break from the four walls of the apartment. While Ji Hoon monitored experiments in the lab, Min-Seo walked through the corridors of the science building, reading the events posted on the bulletin boards. She saw the names and photos of professors and read the dates and times of their lectures. She thought the topics were substantial, just looking at the French words; she never studied technical subjects. Even the incomprehensible subject matters energized her.

How gratifying it must be to sit inside a lecture hall and understand the subject matter in a foreign language! She sensed a deep appreciation for those foreign students who attended those lectures at the French institute.

On other nights, Min-Seo stayed home and revised the chapters of the French lessons, yearning; she would rather be part of the vitality outside. In those moments, she knowingly didn't seek to share her feelings with Ji Hoon. She thought he wouldn't believe that she harbored such trivial thoughts; he was a person engaged in serious scientific work daily and he did not give importance to emotional feelings that interfered the mind. Besides, there would not be much he could say to elate her dispirited thoughts that she only understood.

Living away from home for the first time, and being the youngest of her siblings, Min-Seo often remembered her oldest sister, Insook and her mother. Her father passed away five years before her marriage, leaving the responsibility of her ninety-years-old mother to the care of her unmarried sister, Insook. Insook was in her early fifties, and was devoted to her work at the local mending shop, where she and two other women had been renewing women's clothes for the last twenty years. With her obligation to both the jobs, taking care of her aged mother at home and fulfilling the orders of the customers at the mending shop, Insook withheld anything else that entered her life. She had become accustomed to one type of living. She knew coveting for a change in the situation she was in, would not be desirable for her either.

Min-Seo's middle sister, Mi Kyong, was a married woman in her mid-forties with two boys. She worked at a beauty parlor in Seoul, counselling clients on the best-suited hairstyles, and she had gained a reputation for the bridal hairdos she created. She visited her mother every Sunday, like a duty she was obligated to fulfil, though, Insook could rarely depend on her on the days she needed to work late at the shop. On those days, Insook relied on the lady who lived downstairs in the first-floor apartment, a retired middle-aged woman who had worked as a nurse her whole life. Insook was pleased with the choice; the neighbor eased her worries.

A person has to make use of the best situation available; sometimes strangers become families. It was how Insook reflected when making the arrangements for her mother when Mi Kyong could not help.

Whenever Min-Seo thought of Insook, a feeling of resentment would overtake her mind. With Insook being older in age, Min-Seo had seen her sister as an ardent and sincere woman all her life. Insook was like her mother; Insook had been twenty-five when Min-Seo was born.

There was not a day that Insook expressed displeasure at carrying the responsibilities of the home, and now with their aged mother, she had adjusted her work schedule, reorganized her modest apartment, and sold off much of her furniture and many personal things to accommodate a physically challenged adult in her place. She refrained from speaking about her difficulties to her sisters; she neither cared for their advice nor asked for their help. She rose early every morning to prepare the porridge and mixed vegetable for her mother, massaged her arms and neck, and bathed and dressed her before she left for work. She returned back at mid-day for lunch, to help her mother with the meal. Some days Insook stayed longer finishing her chores at home, and in those hours, she cooked two extra dishes to give to the lady nurse downstairs; she was grateful to the woman for the help she provided. She confirmed the doctor's appointments for her mother and then spent time reading spiritual poems to her sitting by her bedside. Her mother was at peace living with Insook; there was no place she would rather be.

In those quiet moments with her daughter, her mother spoke of her late husband, consoling herself with words about how she had a good life with him, blessed with three sensible girls, while she closed her eyes and said a little prayer for her family. At times, she asked Insook if she was the reason Insook never talked about marriage. Insook gave her the same response every time, that marriage was burdensome at her age; she had to be prepared to compromise, for which she was not ready. Insook provided confidence with her words that the choice was hers alone. Her mother would listen quietly and never responded back.

But, Min-Seo knew exactly what thoughts hid at the back of her sister's mind. Her sister wished she had found a man who would have been sympathetic to her situation in the likelihood that she had to take care of her mother.

Sisters understand each other's hearts. Insook's life had more unspoken constraints than happiness— The thoughts clouded Min-Seo's mind as she sat on the bed folding the washed clothes. Lately, she had felt irresponsibly withdrawn from her obligations to her sister and her mother, and the more she thought about them, the more she felt desolate with resentment.

When Min-Seo had reached twenty-three years of age, Insook made sure she fulfilled the responsibility of getting her youngest sister married as her father would have wished. Insook was grateful that Aunt Eun introduced Min-Seo to Ji-Hoon; he was aunt Eun's best friend's nephew. Reluctant at first to the idea of spending a lifetime with a man she barely knew, Min-Seo had resisted to agree. Why is marriage important? I could share the burden of taking care of my mother with Insook, I am also one of her daughters.

Min-Seo had thought about the life she could have; unmarried and continuing her job at the bank. She could share the hours with Insook looking after her mother. Even on weekends, she could let Insook have a few hours to herself, doing what she liked, which she never asked for. She had felt annoyed at Insook's persistence to convince her that she knew what was a better choice for Min-Seo—a culturally enriched life with an educated man. She discouraged Min-Seo from patronizing the idea of a single life, she resisted elaborating on details incase Min-Seo questioned her. Insook knew in her heart that it had been a mixed blessing for her, though she would not have chosen to do it in any other way because of her mother. With whatever Insook said, Min-Seo understood that her sister exerted power over her because of her own determined faith in her beliefs.

Insook had made the arrangements for Min-Seo's wedding, hosting the engagement lunch at a restaurant for the groom's family. The wedding was at a church, and later, there was a festive dinner with both families, who had traveled from nearby cities. Insook brought her mother to church in a wheelchair to watch her youngest daughter take the vows of marriage. Afterwards, her mother gifted Min-Seo with an envelope containing a gift check. Hesitant, Min-Seo accepted the gift out of respect for the wedding tradition, though, she knew how much more useful the money would be staying with Insook; her sister had the bigger responsibility. But, Min-Seo knew she could never break such sacred traditions, Insook would never allow it.

The day Min-Seo departed for France, there was no one she yearned for more than Insook.

A painful tug of war played inside her, between the foreign life she was going to live and the obligations Insook was destined to carry on alone. Forcing herself to be strong, Min-Seo kept head turned towards the plane window. She felt intense sorrow, she hadn't felt like that since her father's death. All the time she hoped Ji Hoon did not catch sight of her tear-filled eyes. But, she also knew she had to push her own feelings aside for the sake of Ji Hoon, and for her newly married life with him.

After bumping into Min-Seo a few times in the French language school, it was Celia who came forward at the cafeteria after the French class to introduce herself to Min-Seo. She said she was from Brazil, twenty-five years of age, who was in France to learn the language and teach two levels of Portuguese. Min-Seo immediately understood from her talking that Celia had a better English proficiency than her, with the way she quickly began asking about how Min-Seo was enjoying life in the French town. Min-Seo hurriedly answered back shaking her head, 'No English,' which surprisingly did not seem to matter much to Celia. In fact, she instantly prompted if Min-Seo wished to meet to practice French conversations together.

Min-Seo fell silent for a moment, as if the reality of actually conversing in French with someone just registered in her mind. She nodded spiritedly with a smile showing how thrilled she was for the idea. She came to know Celia was two levels higher in French which she thought was a favorable opportunity to fast forward her own goals in speaking the language. They decided to meet two times a week in Min-Seo's apartment, and Min-Seo relished the pursuit of a one to one interaction in French that she had been longing to do. From then onwards, they managed to communicate through non-verbal modes of gestures and drawings or by uncovering the correct words in their respective dictionaries. Sometimes, they felt amused by each other's creative modes of expressions, and Celia consoled her by saying, 'No worries. It begins like that.'

In that moment, Min-Seo truly felt a soothing sense of alleviation from the uneasiness to communicate in a foreign language. She suddenly felt drawn to Celia.

Sitting together on the floor cushions, with French books and picture cards laid out on the table, it was the time with Celia that Min-Seo most eagerly looked forward to. For Min-Seo, it was more than a conversation time in a foreign language; it was about a friend she had found to socially interact with. It did not matter where she was from. In those moments, she felt like paying attention to everything Celia said and how she talked. She was quickly attracted to the way Celia initiated conversations; the topics she chose about each other's cultures with simple phrases and the colloquial French expressions that were part of the everyday language. Min-Seo did not hesitate to speak, in fact, she felt energetic with the hints of encouragement that Celia imparted in between their exchanges. She felt motivated when Celia emphasized how remarkable it was to acquire the language in its native surroundings—an opportunity to practice the language in actual social situations the person was living in.

"A language becomes challengingly different as a result of influences of other languages. It could display unique features in another cultural setting." Celia described how Portuguese spoken in Brazil has indigenous influences unlike the European Portuguese.

Min-Seo opened the atlas lying on the table and pointed to places, showing Celia that the Korean language was also related to diverse languages.

"Isn't it interesting that our languages get linked to different parts of the world? Influence causes changes to happen, but also shows how we are fundamentally connected," expressed Celia thoughtfully.

Min-Seo listened quietly. She thought Celia brought out a fresher perspective to the topic; she was going to learn things that she hadn't thought about.

Min-Seo went to the kitchen and brought out a small clay teapot with tea made from roasted barley and fermented ginger leaves and ceramic cups to the table. Unlike other days, she had more on her mind than just studying French with Celia. Her seriousness towards everything sometimes amazed Celia; quiet and perceptive, her physical presence would be in one place while her mind wandered far into other thoughts.

"My mother-in-law sent me spices from Korea. She is worried I may not find them in the French town."

"Oh, really! From so far?"

Min-Seo nodded smiling. "She thinks I have a lot of time on my hands. I could try out Korean recipes."

Celia laughed. "But, who will you entertain here with your recipes?"

"I don't know." Min-Seo looked at Celia. "Do you never cook for your friends?"

"Brazilian food? Once in a while," Celia said smiling. Min-Seo stopped for one short second of hesitation. "Don't you miss your country's food?"

An uncertain expression came on to Celia's face, as she was not sure what exactly to say.

"Of course, I do! My country has extraordinary cuisine. But, for now, I want to expand my cultural education. I want to eat like people in France."

"What about your native language?"

"Portuguese? I have my students who are learning my country's language. Other than them, I haven't found anyone." Celia laughed. "But, for now, I am alright with speaking French. You miss out on a lot if you don't speak French, for sure."

Min-Seo nodded slightly in agreement. She was silent for a brief moment.

"You are brave!"

Celia was surprised at the comment "Why do you say that?"

"Traveling alone to another continent so far away."

Celia looked at her face attentively. "You could do it too, you know."

Min-Seo shrugged her shoulders. Celia noticed a shadow of disappointment on Min-Seo's face.

"I don't know."

"Why?"

"Unfamiliarity, I suppose."

"Don't get yourself upset at that. Cultures will vary, but human emotions will not. They will ultimately connect you," said Celia gently.

Min-Seo glanced at Celia's face as she poured more tea into the cups.

"You cannot deny the fact that so much is different– the etiquette, the way people think, expectations of others, what one should or shouldn't do. The list goes on," said Min-Seo.

"But, consider yourself lucky too."

"Sure. That's another way of looking at it," Min-Seo said with a smile.

"Did you not wish to travel to another country?" asked Celia in a friendly tone.

"It's not that at all. There are things I need to take care. It's difficult to explain."

Celia said nothing. She held the small clay mug in her hand and sipped the tea.

"Look at us, we are from two different parts of the world. Do you think we cannot understand each other's feelings? On the surface everything seems different."

Min-Seo looked at Celia's face. Her words comforted her. She liked the sound of her voice, and the way she presented her thoughts. She said she lived in São Paolo and grew up in a close-knit family. She said her family get-togethers were mostly about watching football, discussing social and political issues of her country and relishing a good time with food and drinks. Her persona suited with her energetic lightly tanned face, her long light brown hair and her marble-like eyes. She wore dangling oval wood earrings that matched her crescent shaped wood necklace. Even as she sat comfortably, cross legged on the satin cushion, sipping tea, Min-Seo thought how at ease the Brazilian girl was with the new cultural etiquette of sitting on the floor. As much as Min-Seo was surprised, she appreciated the versatility that Celia conveyed.

"I bet you never drank tea sitting on the floor."

Celia laughed softly. "Would you believe that I have?"

Min-Seo looked at her curiously eager to listen to what she said further. Celia described how she visited a village in Bangladesh three years ago. She experienced eating meals with a family living in the village, sitting on the floor, eating with fingers. She grinned showing her fingers. "Yes, I really ate with these!" She said the family gave her hot tea in an earthen cup after the meal; she was touched by their hospitality.

"Honestly, at the end, the generosity of the heart is what really matters," Celia said smiling.

"That makes all the difference, doesn't it?"

"Surprisingly, you find it, too!"

Min-Seo became quiet briefly.

"I presume you never felt awkward traveling to unknown places and being amongst strangers."

"It is not awkward when you understand they are also people like you, but have different customs," said Celia smiling graciously at Min-Seo.

Min-Seo nodded, mentally picturing the situations that Celia described. Min-Seo had no experience of other cultures so she did not want to say anything.

"Never miss a good chance." Celia laughed.

She narrated about a trip she had planned with a group of five friends to visit Kenya when she was nineteen. But, when all her friends backed out, she did not follow them. She joined a group of unknown travelers for the trip that was her dream. She had always wanted to see Kenya's Maasai Mara National Reserve with its vast array of wildlife, especially when the Wildebeests migration took place from the Serengeti into Kenya; it was something she always wanted to view. She thought she should not miss the chance.

"I was with unknown travelers and local people all the time," said Celia.

Min-Seo leaned forward attentively listening to what Celia said. She gazed at Celia's face in wonder without saying anything.

"I believe that humanity has dominantly good people and as a traveler, I learned to come out of my shell in order to rely on strangers."

"Amazing to hear that! A person should not be afraid or hesitant, right?" said Min-Seo with gentle firmness.

"The ambivalent feelings are normal in a new place. But, you should not allow them to control you. You need to take the initiative first, then help follows."

Everything Celia said impressed Min-Seo. She had the kind of wisdom that allowed her to know everything, along with a fortitude and light-heartedness. She thought they were the qualities that allowed Celia to adapt to the various factors of a new place. Despite, she was not sure if she could be like Celia. She told Celia that how a person grows up, molds the personality and the ways of thinking. There are many influences that form the person one is.

"But, unless the person adapts to the new surroundings with one's thinking and behavior, there will be a disconnect that remains with the life around," said Celia.

Min-Seo thought she had the right words, but they were not as straightforward as she made them sound.

"That's because you are used to something different. There is a whole new view of the world when you step out of your nest. Look at it this way: would you ever have met a Brazilian girl if you never stepped out of your country?" Celia grinned trying to bring a lighter tone to the conversation.

"Probably not." Min-Seo paused. "It's like I am looking for the things that are not in front of me yet there is so much I could still be content with. Strange, isn't it?"

"Well, you know what, you are absolutely right. I think a freshly baked baguette with some *Camembert de Normandie,* accompanied by a glass of *Bordeaux,* are worth considering for yourself." Celia winked, smiling, as she lifted the tea cup as if to make a toast.

Min-Seo nodded softly, giggling, gazing at Celia's distinctive communicative style of expanding to new possibilities.

"Seems like you have found a home here."

"You can make every place your home. Different is not bad. Why should everything be the same anyways? Variety is what makes the living inspiring."

Min-Seo gazed fixedly at Celia's face and sipped the tea from her cup. She had never met anyone who thought like Celia. She wondered how Celia could be the way she was; she was also from another country.

"The truth is, you have to put in effort. Once you have got that right, everything comes easily after."

The words sounded wise. The challenges of a new place should not distress a person. Despite, it seemed like a one-sided struggle to Min-Seo. She was hesitant to elaborate on her thoughts to Celia.

Min-Seo reflected on those days when she went to the *Délicieuse Boulangerie* to get a few croissants. She saw the bakery lady every time. The woman appeared younger than her sister Insook, possibly in her late forties, with medium dark blonde hair, tied at the back with a barrette. Min-Seo found her attractive, her flawless subtle makeup that blended with her soft colored lipstick, they made her look she had not done anything on her face. Even her average height suited with her slender physique wearing the long beige linen apron with two pockets. Min-Seo could recognize the apron from a distance and know it belonged to someone working at the *Déliceuse Boulangerie.*

Every time Min-Seo came to buy bread, she saw the bakery lady busy in conversation with customers, speaking pleasantly in French as she handed them the warm baked baguettes. It was not just business; it was connecting with people to share news of everyday events happening far and near. Min-Seo marveled at how she spoke, the high and low intonations flowing inside her phrases, putting emphatic stress on sounds, the language sounded eloquent and resonated with emotions. She wished she could converse effortlessly; she could learn so much more about the French breads and baking techniques if only the bakery lady paid attention to the fact that Min-Seo was a newcomer and asked about her country and her language. The bakery lady appeared considerate enough to do that, but she did not ask. Perhaps she thought Min-Seo would feel self-conscious and embarrassed. Instead Min-Seo would pick up the four pieces of croissants, pay the lady, and quietly exit the bakery after saying the usual '*Merci beaucoup! Avoir!*' Something always held her back. There was nothing more to their interactions.

Min-Seo checked the mailbox to see if there was mail from Insook. In the last two weeks, there had not been mail from her sister. Today, she was relieved to see the two handwritten letters. They were both written within a few days apart. From the time she had arrived in France, Min-Seo could follow the dates on the calendar to know exactly when the letter from Insook would arrive.

She hurriedly sat down on the bed, opened one of the letters, and quietly read the handwritten page written in black ink. Insook asked about her life in the French town, how much progress she had made in learning French, if she had made friends or if she went to Paris to see the Louvre. She advised Min-Seo to find a local library and read books about the history of France, learn about the historical castles built through the centuries and put effort to speak French. She told her to learn a few French recipes and to use her mother-in-law's Korean spices to prepare dishes for Ji Hoon and her friends.

Those are the kinds of things Insook always says, Min-Seo thought.

Insook wrote about her mother. She had more health issues and needed to make frequent visits to the doctor. Insook had hired a new employee at the shop to fill in the hours she could not work. She needed to be at home with her mother; her mother needed more assistance than before. She was contemplating taking on a full-time caretaker, but Insook did not elaborate on the details.

Min-Seo understood the expectations were unrealistic for Insook's financial situation; it was why Insook did not mention anything.

The French class finished before noon. The French phrase Min-Seo learnt in class kept recurring in her mind. *Monsieur* Kernavais had used the phrase several times, emphasizing, how important it was to put effort in speaking French with the new words and phrases he introduced in class, and not to feel reluctant to use them in real situations. At times, she thought, the teacher displayed an extraordinary honor for the language, as if there was nothing more gratifying than learning French. *There are other languages in the world other than French!* But, Min-Seo instantly brushed off such redundant thoughts that emerged in her mind; she was living in France, she wanted to speak the language.

'*Qui, n'avance pas, reculé* ', *Monsieur* Kernavais repeated the phrase a few times. Then, he translated with his faint knowledge of English, 'Who does not move forward, recedes'. Instantly, the meaning had caught her attention. How true the meaning was, not just for learning a foreign language. For anything one attempts to do in life, perseverance is the key. Min-Seo took a deep breath and raised her hand; she wanted *Monsieur* Kernavais to say the phrase again; she liked the sound of the words. Min-Seo repeated in her head after listening to him.

Walking down the steps to exit the building, she felt a sudden vigor inside her, inspired. She liked how the teacher had expressed the French phrase, looking at the face of each student, speaking with the intensity of emotions. It was why the expressiveness captivated her. She kept repeating the phrase in her mind.

The lunch time ambience on the street added a whole new vitality to her feelings... people crowded inside restaurants; students clustered together at an outdoor cafe table, gleefully conversing; foreign women in their native clothes spoke in French to outdoor vendors at markets;

men sat alone inside cafes, reading the paper while having a *Quiche Lorraine* or a *croissant* with coffee. The two-hour lunch break had a new dimension, a discontinuity from routine work, a time to connect to life's lighter moments.

Min-Seo strolled through the vibrant part of the town, crossing narrow streets, occasionally smiling and saying '*Bonjour*' to elderly women walking with sticks. She came to the front of the town theater. She saw posters with photos of two young women; they read, '*Voix mélodieuses des soeurs,* Daniella André and Camilla Perot, Performance *samedi á 19 heures.*' Min-Seo stared at the black-and-white photos of the two French women, similar in ages to her own two sisters. She had never heard of the singers… not that she knew anything about the French singers or the local artists. She recognized the word *soeurs*; she liked how the two sisters displayed their talents together. Immediately, she thought about Insook and how she had taught her to recite musical verses when she was a young girl; Insook was the reason her fondness of musical tunes had grown with age.

Min-Seo reached the end of street and turned towards the bakery. Today, for the first time, she wanted to be inside the bakery for a longer time than she usually stayed. Was it because she liked the bakery lady's presence, even if it had been brief, and without much interaction in the past? She felt herself saying yes. The woman could be easily like someone from her own country—her aunt, her cousin sister, her friend—except that she was French. Maybe I need to step forward first? Why should I expect that from others? Min-Seo started to feel optimistic about those thoughts.

The doorbell chimed as Min-Seo entered the *Délicieuse Boulangerie*. The bakery did not close for lunch, like most places in town. The French people liked the long lunch breaks.

"*Bonjour, Madame! Cava, aujourd'hui?*" The bakery lady called out from behind the counter as usual. Min-Seo suddenly noticed the lady was talking to her as another customer exited the bakery. She could almost hear the smile in the bakery lady's voice. Then, something happened and Min-Seo quickly unleashed the French words from her mouth, smiling.

"*Oui, cava, Madame!*"

"You know French?" the lady asked softly.

"Petite."

"*Tres peu.*" The lady corrected her. "No problem! What would you like?"

"*Quatre croissants et une baguette, sil vous plait!*" Min-Seo suddenly felt she had the words to respond in French. Hurriedly, she searched for the words in her mind to continue the conversation.

"*Bien!*" The lady handed her a warm baguette. "Take this! I baked it a few minutes ago." She handed over the four croissants inside a paper bag.

"Vous êtes gentile!" Min-Seo said softly, instantly feeling amazed at herself for initiating French phrases on her own.

There were already three people in line behind her as she spoke to the bakery lady. She took the paper bag and moved aside to sit down on a chair at one side of the bakery. Her hope was to talk to the bakery lady after all the customers left. It did not matter how long it took for the customers to leave, she would wait. She sat quietly, thinking, formulating the short French phrases in her mind, she had enough words in her vocabulary; she had been delaying using them for a long time. The phrase, '*Qui, n'avance pas, reculé*,' kept returning to her mind.

"*Madame! Attendez vous quelqu'un?*" The voice of the lady interrupted Min-Seo's thoughts.

Min-Seo quickly stood up. "*Non, Madame*! I want to talk to you!"

"All right. Please tell me." Without delay, Min-Seo expressed her wish to make a few pieces of her mother's special bread for her.

"*C'est merveilleux! Merci beaucoup!*" exclaimed the lady cheerfully as she heard Min-Seo's wish. The lady thanked her smiling, gently patting Min-Seo's shoulder affectionately for the kind offer. She expressed regrets about how little she knew about other culture's food.

"*Je comprendre.*" Min-Seo felt a sudden joy as if she sensed a correlation in the train of thoughts. What's more, she felt the conversation was easier than how she had imagined.

"I will bring for you. *Merci!*"

Stepping outside the bakery, Min-Seo felt the droplets of water on her face. It had begun to rain slowly. The limited sunshine that was visible in the October morning, was now surrounded by the grey smudges of clouds in the sky. She stood for a few minutes under the overhang of the bakery building. The dull tone of the weather suddenly influenced her mood. Thoughtful, she sensed a subtle earthy smell filling the air as if begging her to wait and watch the splattering dance of the raindrops falling. She loved the rain and it had been a good day. There was no urgency to reach home.

The next morning, Min-Seo baked eight pieces of egg bread using her mother's recipe and placed them inside a hot box to take them to the bakery lady. A gratifying feeling elevated her confidence; she felt she was making the connection she had been wishing for. Today was the first time she spoke to Ji-Hoon about the bakery and the French lady who worked there. She expressed to Ji Hoon what she was going to do and asked him what he thought. Ji Hoon looked at her confused giving an amusing grin to what she said.

"Why are you going through so much trouble?" Ji Hoon asked.

"Not trouble, just a friendly gesture."

"Do you think your bread will impress her?"

She understood what he meant. "I don't know."

"What if it is not what you want to hear?"

Min-Seo was quiet for a few minutes. "It's all right. I won't worry about that."

"After all the work you did to prepare?" asked Ji-Hoon surprised. Min-Seo sensed a signal of disapproval from the questions he asked.

"Sometimes you find the French food not to your taste. It happens."

She answered gracefully. She knew everyone had something to say. She preferred to dismiss comments that she found no way to explain.

Taking the bus downtown, she reached the bakery as soon as it opened. She knew how quickly the place got busy in the morning; the French loved their freshly baked bread. In the evening, it was the same; people stopped by the bakery and took *baguettes* home for dinner as if, without the baguettes, they would seem incomplete when they reach home. A lot of love given to those *baguettes,* She thought..

Min-Seo did not see the lady when she walked inside. She saw a young man attentively cleaning the counter shelves. He did not look at the door when Min-Seo entered.

"*Excusez moi, Monsieur!*" said Min-Seo gazing in the direction of the man.

"*Bonjour, Madame*! Can I help you?" The man came forward indistinctly smiling.

She asked him about the lady who worked there. He told her that *Madame* would come later.

He looked at her, waiting, in case she had any questions; he looked pleased to talk to her.

Not sure what to say next, Min-Seo showed him the hot box that contained the bread pieces she made for the bakery lady. She gazed at his face wondering if he was related to the lady, possibly her son. He appeared to be close to her age. He had a medium height, dark brown hair and a pale skin color. He appeared like a young man who would relax with a cigarette in his hand. He took the hot box, somewhat confused as to how he should acknowledge a box full of bread. He understood she was offering it as a gesture of kindness.

"Oh! *Mon Dieu!*" Min-Seo heard him utter softly as he stared at the bread pieces inside the box. He looked carefully at the pieces as if admiring quietly their unique appearance. Then he briskly went to the back of the bakery. Shortly after, he returned to tell Min-Seo that he would keep a piece for the lady, and the rest he would display on the bakery shelf in case customers wanted to sample a new kind of bread.

Min-Seo could not believe what she heard. She looked at him stunned. She did not know how to respond. He sensed she was worried about something. He abruptly reacted as he saw her face.

"Don't you want people to taste your bread?" He asked in a friendly tone.

The idea was good, indeed! But, Min-Seo could not imagine her bread being sampled by people who walked into the bakery. She had brought them for the lady.

"It is so kind of you, but I didn't make the bread for the bakery."

"I understand. But your bread pieces are new for the bakery. People may like them."

His way of talking told Min-Seo that he was extending a kind gesture for bringing the bread. He suggested out of politeness; she should not act so anxious right away. Min-Seo stood quietly for a few minutes wondering what to do. She noticed the man had gotten occupied with putting the different types of bread on the shelves.

"But I cannot accept any part of the money if you decide to sell them." Min-Seo said out loud looking at the man. She could tell the power of her own voice, how strongly it resonated. She tried to keep a friendly smile.

The man's facial expression became unresolved; he raised his eyebrows, befuddled, looking at Min-Seo. He couldn't understand why she was worried. He told her to speak to his aunt as he handed back the hotbox with the bread to her.

She shook her head astonished, "*Non! Non*! I cannot take back what I made. I made them for *Madame* and her family. Please give them to her."

"That's a lot of bread pieces for her!" exclaimed the man.

"*Pas de problème*!" Min-Seo gave an agreeable smile.

She felt jubilant for instantly responding with the suitable words at the right moment. She was even insistent. She said good-bye cheerfully and left the bakery.

Min-Seo excitedly narrated to Ji-Hoon what had happened at the bakery. She had never imagined the man in the bakery would suggest such an idea. All this time she thought how difficult it was to break the communication barrier, and now she was being reciprocated with so much thoughtfulness for her simple friendly gesture to share her mother's bread.

Ji Hoon grinned. He did not expect such enthusiasm from his wife.

"You will be famous with the customers if they taste your bread," he said in a joking manner.

"I am not looking to be famous. It is just a gesture of friendship".

Min-Seo knew she could not work in France, but the idea of sharing the bread inside the French bakery certainly took her by surprise. It motivated her that she was sharing her mother's bread with people thousands of miles away. She became absorbed in thinking about everything that had happened in the bakery as she began to prepare dinner, warming the rich soup broth and stirring the shredded chicken with vegetables and noodles. She liked cooking time in the kitchen; it was relaxing and she had time to contemplate quietly about thoughts she wanted to pay attention to. It took her a long time to start talking again.

"I have been speaking in French at the bakery," said Min-Seo as she turned to look at her husband who was engrossed in reading a magazine.

The immediate witty laugh from Ji Hoon startled Min-Seo. She didn't think he was listening to her.

"Really? Did they understand you?" He kept his eyes on the magazine as he spoke.

"Of course! I spoke slowly. I used the words and phrases I have been learning in class."

"I am glad the French class is serving you good purpose."

She told him there was more. She was motivated by a quote the French teacher used in class.

She told him what it meant—'If you don't move forward, you recede.'

Ji Hoon turned his head and stared at his wife in a confused manner. He had no idea what she was trying to say.

"The quote inspired you to speak French at the bakery?" Ji Hoon asked questionably.

"The meaning is deep. It applies to everything in life."

Ji-Hoon did not say anything. He looked at his wife, grinning. For some reason, he thought she sounded unusual.

"A quote inspires you to speak French?" Ji Hoon laughed as if he was amused.

"Sometimes, words inspire. You relate them to your own life," said Min-Seo softly.

Ji-Hoon listened and nodded. Min-Seo knew either his mind was someplace else or he did not find sense in her words.

Min-Seo covered the soup container with a lid and turned off the stove. Ji-Hoon watched his wife as she folded the screen door at one side and then went back to wiping the counter, collecting the vegetable peels to throw away. He wanted to say something, but he hesitated.

Ji-Hoon had never heard Min-Seo talk about herself or how she had been spending her days in the new place. He thought the French homework kept her busy. He could not believe that she had taken up extra activities at the bakery to keep herself occupied. He noticed the extra luster on his wife's face that made her inwardly jubilant and confident.

Min-Seo wasted no time in the morning to get ready and catch the 8:20 a.m. bus to the town center. She was anxious to find out if the bakery lady had liked her bread and whether she had displayed some for the customers to sample.

The last two customers had just exited the bakery when Min-Seo walked up to the counter.

"*Bonjour, Madame! Cava?*" Min-Seo quickly recognized the voice before she noticed the lady putting the baguettes inside a woven basket.

She was thrilled to see the bakery lady again. "I missed you yesterday, *Madame*! Did you like the bread I made for you?"

The lady came closer to the counter smiling at Min-Seo. She told her that she had heard everything from her nephew. She liked the taste of the bread and it instantly gave her an exciting idea—she wanted Min-Seo to bake her mother's bread at the bakery every morning, fifty pieces. She would display them in the bakery shelf even if she was not sure whether the customers would buy them. She was planning to pay her 300 franc every week.

For a brief moment, Min-Seo stood speechless, clearly surprised by her words. She did not know how to react. She felt strange that the lady's plan turned out be exactly what she would have liked; it was as if the lady could read her thoughts.

"I cannot earn money, *Madame*. I am a visitor," said Min-Seo hurriedly.

She told the lady she wished the situation were different. She expressed how much she wanted to help her older sister take care of her aged mother in her country. She thought a single life and work would give her the chance to do what she wanted, but life made a different plan for her. Min-Seo had never spoken openly to anyone about her thoughts.

The lady fell silent; her expression changed. Then she said sympathetically,

"*Ma Chérie*! I am glad you told me. I understand what you are saying."

The lady came out from behind the counter towards Min-Seo. For a few minutes, she stared at Min-Seo quietly, thinking, going over something in her mind. Then, she put her right hand gently on Min-Seo's shoulder and looked pensively at the girl's face—Min-Seo's appearance was sincere and natural, nothing striking, yet the lady felt fortitude and endurance hidden behind the mystical tenderness. The girl had an astonishingly conscionable mind.

The bakery lady recapitulated all the things Min-Seo had said. She was seized with emotion. She instantly recollected the heartbreak when her own mother had been ill; she had been eleven, too young to make decisions on her own. She had to live with her aunt. She had heard the news of her mother's demise two days after it happened; her aunt had needed to be mentally prepared to share the shocking news to her. The lady narrated everything to Min-Seo.

"I could never tell looking at you that your life had a bitter story. You are always smiling," said Min-Seo.

"The mind knows how to reconcile. It calms and consoles, then makes you see things rightfully."

Min-Seo listened to the lady. There was truth to what Celia had said; emotions connect people ultimately.

For the next few weeks, Min-Seo made a commitment to work at the bakery for three hours in the morning. She arrived at the bakery at 7:30 every morning taking the bus. Each day she baked fifty pieces of the bread. The bakery lady kept them warm inside a warmer cabinet made of glass. There were none left by the end of the day. On some days, Min-See took up extra duties and decoratively organized the pastries inside the cabinets. She noticed there were bursts of activity at certain times of the day when the lady introduced new types of baked goods that were appealing to the eyes and scrumptious in taste. Even her own bread looked delightful next to the other types of bread displayed.

She liked being in the company of the bakery lady and her nephew assistant; the customers who walked in and out and said "*Bonjour*" to her. She was amazed to see how the customers converged on news happening in the town or even in other parts of France while briefly stopping by the bakery. She listened admiringly, giving them the impression that she wanted to be part of what they shared. She studied attentively their faces, their gestures, the words and phrases they used. Min-Seo became immersed in everything spontaneously.

People found pleasure in conversation; they were passionate and assertive about the subjects, they were socially and politically conscious. The social engagement took priority over a routine lifestyle.

She returned home every day feeling marvelously rejuvenated, entertained by a place that sold baked food. The truth was that she was also learning about people, their lives, and the kinds of events happening in places in France. She even discerned that the bakery lady's nephew gave her a lot of attention, telling her amusing stories in French about his experiences with people, never once paying attention to the fact that Min-Seo might not have followed everything he said in French. But, Min-Seo took his spontaneous behavior well; she felt blissful that he recognized her as someone who was also a part of the bakery.

Ji Hoon had fixed activities at home; he stayed occupied with the same routine every day. He was not concerned with the life outside of work. He knew that his work was enough to bind him to a focused gratifying engagement In the first few days, when Min-Seo started working, she would return home excited to share her day with Ji Hoon. But gradually she withheld her enthusiasm. Ji Hoon's feelings towards the bakery work made her uncomfortable; he did not carry cheerful dialogues with her.

"If you were living in your country, you would have done a better job," Ji Soon said somberly.

"I am not in my country. I am working around my limitations."

"The bakery benefits more than you."

Min-Seo's face flushed up. She immediately understood the complex feelings behind those words. The bakery experience had been a joy for her and never did she feel the way Ji Hoon expressed it. She recalled the days when she sat with Ji-Hoon listening to him talk about the challenging experiences of work life. During those moments, she threw in words of motivation and praise for him because she felt proud of his persistent hard-working attitude. Yet, since the day, she had begun work at the bakery, he had not displayed the slightest interest in what she was doing. Now, she had completed the four weeks she had committed, and she found no value to his words.

"I learnt a lot too. When you give, you get something in return."

"What did you get?"

"A sense of fulfillment." Min-Seo spoke with brazen modesty.

"That you could get from books too."

"You need all your senses to understand the culture of a place."

Min-Seo was not meaning to teach him anything by how she responded. She thought people have a hard time accepting something that is beyond their familiarity. They really don't want to understand it.

She went back to the kitchen work, arranging the fresh fruits and vegetables inside the refrigerator. She thought about Celia who was visiting her family in Brazil. *Celia is like a free bird; she flies to a different nest when she has had enough of one.* Min-Seo smiled to herself as she thought about Celia; she was the first to motivate her. Everything she had told her then, made sense now.

A week later, Min-Seo opened the door to get the mail. Instead she saw a speed post lying in front of the door. Her facial expression instantly turned pensive, she stiffened. Over the last few months she had instinctively developed a very fine sense of what was happening with her mother. Insook's letters did not arrive as periodically as before; Min-Seo knew her sister was heavily occupied with attending to their mother. Now, as she was looking at the letter, her hands slightly trembled as she kept gazing at the envelope that had her and Ji Hoon's names on it.

Ji Hoon was not home. Even if he was, he would be totally unaware of the overload of emotions impending inside her, having accumulated for days. He was wrapped up in his work and in deadlines. Min-Seo avoided adding more to his thoughts.

It is unfair to burden the thoughts of someone who already has so much on the mind. Everyone carries some emotional load, even if it is different from one's own—Min-Seo consoled herself as she walked to her room and sat down on her bed. She felt her heart pounding as she opened the envelope slowly with her fingers. She took out the handwritten letter on thin white paper along with a printed message of a memorial service.

> *Dear Min-Seo,*
>
> *A gift check arrived in the mail from the owner of Délicieuse Boulangerie. Her name is Madame Marie Richelieu. There was a thoughtful letter attached to the check.. She wrote about you. She said she wanted to ease your tribulations. Whatever you have done, I feel blessed.*
>
> *I am writing to tell you that for the first time, my heart is painfully heavy. I have become alone. Our mother left us peacefully in her sleep. She was gone when I came to her room to wake her up in the morning.*

The night before, she had asked me to take out the family photo from the frame and give it to her. I did not ask her why. I knew she was thinking of us all. She told me to sleep longer the following morning; she thought I was fatigued because of her. I smiled and stroked her hair. There was never a day I felt tired serving her. My mind immediately jumped from image to image of every thing I did with her, every story she had told me through the years, how she felt, and how others acted. Then, I saw her close her eyes, like she wished to drift away towards something else, something different she found. She went off to sleep.

The picture was still on her chest when I came to see her in the morning. The spirit of feelings touch distant hearts. There exists no boundary, they harmonize together. Her soft face pure as a child's lay in eternal sleep, free.

May you stay blessed always with your kind heart.

My love to you both, always.
Insook

Min-Seo felt the dryness increase in her throat. An agonizing pain compressed inside her; a sudden heartbreaking spasm tore through her body. She bent her head low, and wept, faltering.

"Maman", she uttered softly as she listened to herself. "Maman!" she repeated again.

It should not have been like that! She pulled herself up and wiped the tear-soaked eyes with a face towel. She sat quietly staring into space.

Emotionally consumed, she thought of the bakery lady, Madame Richelieu. She had never called her by that name. But, what's in a name anyways? It did not matter, Min-Seo thought. What mattered was what she did for her…her generous, thoughtful act without telling Min-Seo.

She had sent a gift check to Insook for the hours she worked at the bakery. The amount she would have paid Min-So if she could work. No wonder Madame Richelieu had asked for the address of my sister! Min-Seo recalled the day when the bakery lady told her she was going to send her sister a 'best wishes' card with prayers for her mother. Tears like tiny crystal beads flowed from Min-Seo's eyes in an unbroken stream as she thought back on Madame Richelieu's words. It suddenly felt like a stirring experience, the way everything happened, as if someone was listening quietly to her heart. Min-Seo stayed sitting on the bed and kept staring at the letter in her hand.

The same evening, a bouquet of red and white roses arrived in a vase at her door. There was a note attached. It was from Celia. She wanted Min-Seo to know that every friendship had its own uniqueness—French conversation with Korean tea was one of a kind and she had plans to continue from where she had left off.

Glossary of French Words

From the Heart

- Mademoiselle   Miss or a young lady
- Bonjour!   Good Day!
- Monsieur   Mr. or gentleman
- Délicieuse Boulangerie   the name of the bakery; Delicious bakery
- baguette   a long thin loaf of a popular French bread
- Camembert de Normandie   famous French cheese from Normandy region
- Bordeaux   wine produced in Bordeaux region of France
- croissant   a popular flaky French pastry eaten like bread
- Merci beaucoup! Avoir!   Thanks a lot! See you again!
- Qui n'avance pas, reculé   Who does not move forward, recedes
- Voix mélodieuses des soeurs   melodious voices of sisters
- Performance samedi á 19 heures   performance Saturday at 7p.m.
- Cava, aujourd'hui?   okay/fine today?
- Oui, cava   Yes, fine.
- Petite   small (referring to physical size)
- Très peu   very little (describing quantity)
- Quatre croissants et une baguette, sil vous plâit!   four croissants and a baguette, please!
- Bien   good!

- Attendez vous quelqu'un?   Are you waiting for someone?
- C'est merveilleux!   It's marvelous!
- Je comprendre   I understand
- Excusez moi, Monsieur!   Excuse me, Mr!
- Mon Dieu!   Oh, my goodness or Oh My God!
- Pas de problème   No problem!

Conscience

The multi-storied apartment complex was in the northern part of Calcutta, six white clustered buildings standing tall at one side of the main road. Crossing over to the other side through a green park like area with a few metal benches was where the whirlwind of commercial activities took place—everything from sizzling food stalls, sweet shops and contemporary clothing and jewelry shops to medical stores, wholesale academic booksellers and musical instrument repair stores. They cramped together along the long narrow sidewalk congested with pedestrians who ambled leisurely window shopping or succumbed to the calls of hawkers, luring them to a plethora of negotiable displays.

The main road had an unceasing flow of cars, vans and trucks. The sounds of honking elevated at certain times of the day while the clarity of the natural sounds diminished and reverberated when the flocks of *koels* fluttered past the windows on warm summer days before the onset of the rains. On building rooftops, the watchful crows sat perched in a single line, cawing reassuringly while soaking in the warmth of the sun. Together they painted the ubiquitous images of Calcutta, a fusion of natural and man-made life performing in perfect synchrony while an ambience of engagement played to the evocative tunes.

This was the typical view from the fourth floor the Nayantara apartment building where thirty-five-year old Uma lived with her husband, Lalit, thirty-seven years of age, and their ten-year-old son, Anik. After eight years of sharing the house with Lalit's parents, Uma purchased the contemporary two-bedroom apartment unit with the accumulated income of her teaching job. It was a dream to own an independent place with Lalit and her son.

It was nearing five in the evening when the taxi dropped off Uma in front of the building gate. The light cool February breeze fanned the evening air as Uma opened the metal gate and walked up the paved walkway to the building entrance door. She saw Pratik, the long-time resident of the sixth floor, languidly leaning against the column, gleefully chewing on a betel leaf, with his mouth so full that he had to wait to speak. He wore a brown full-sleeved pullover and had one hand in his jeans pocket, looking distinctly more casual than he normally did. A man in his early forties, he appeared older, having a neat haircut for his short black hair. He worked his jaws on the betel leaf pleasurably, staring questioningly at Uma as she walked closer to the building entrance door.

"What happened? No car today?" asked Pratik curiously, with a smile that showed his red tainted teeth against his deeply tanned skin.

"I had a meeting with the principal. I didn't want to hold up the car."

"No wonder your better half found good use of it." He laughed loudly.

Uma did not say anything. Pratik was a person who took a lot of interest in loquacious conversations amongst people and who was curious of things happening in people's lives. He reminded Uma of a secret service agent, silently keeping an eye out without anyone knowing that his eyes and ears were pretty much always open, possibly on them.

"I am assuming everything went well," Pratik said.

"The staff was introduced to a new teacher."

"Oh, what'd you know! You are moving up the ladder as a senior teacher, huh?" said Pratik grinning.

"I think that is how it is supposed to happen," Uma smiled. "What are you up to?"

"Waiting for furniture delivery. The delivery men miss our gate every time."

He described how the last five times, the delivery men went past the gate searching for the address. They left him no choice than to wait outside.

Ever since Pratik and his wife Arpitha returned from their first trip to America to visit Pratik's sister's family in San Antonio, they had been constantly renovating and modernizing their apartment. Arpitha wanted the place to be upgraded to the latest decorative standards before her sister-in-law's next visit.

"Our Calcutta home should not appear inferior to what I saw in America," she had expressed to Uma when she started searching for window coverings for her home. Uma found nothing substantial in her comment then and had not said anything.

"Well, enjoy your new furniture!"

Uma parted with a hand gesture and walked up to the mailboxes in front of the elevator. She opened the wooden box and found three letters lying inside. They were all in white envelopes. She picked them up and glanced at the names. All three were for her husband, Lalit Sen. She recognized the company name stamped on the back of one of the envelopes, the other two were unknown.

The elevator door was open. Uma pulled open the black iron collapsible gate and went inside. She pressed the number 4 button. The door closed with a vibration and squeaking sounds; the single dim light bulb on the elevator ceiling flickered inside the partially cracked white shade. Uma had placed a complaint with the building manager to change the light bulb to a higher wattage for brightness and for the safety of the people using the elevator. That was two months ago. Nothing had changed. Three weeks ago she had spoken to the supervisor on phone requesting the same thing. He said he never received the first complaint and he would send someone immediately to put a new bulb. It was still the same. A week ago she made a call to the supervisor again, and briefly stated the problem on phone in case he had forgotten. He said he would call back in an hour to write up a written complaint. It had been over a week.

Uma placed no further complaints. She bought a bottle of lubricating grease and put it on the door hinges, and when the elevator was not in use, she turned off the light, and changed the bulb to a higher wattage. She left the cracked light shade as it was.

Even with the modernization of living, the basic responsibilities of commitment remained unchanged. She assumed she was the only person placing the complaints; others used the elevator as a transport without giving serious attention to the declining conditions.

A flickering dim bulb with a noisy door did not call for urgent attention—Calcutta had bigger problems. Perhaps, it was how most residents of the building thought, she assumed.

Uma's mother, Ratna was sixty-seven when Uma's father, Barun, passed away at the age of seventy-five. Although devastated, her mother did not mourn the loss distressfully, she had anticipated the darkness to enter her life sooner ever since her husband's first stroke. His health had remained unsteady and he had suffered the second stroke in his sleep after a month and left the world.

In three months, Ratna vacated the first floor of the house and sold most of the furniture except the polished office desk and the Mahogany leather armchair that was passed down to her husband from her father-in-law, and restored the oak wood almirah. Ratna did not have ambitious plans in mind except to establish a place that could serve some purpose. She reflected that when she would be gone, there would not be much significance left to the house built with passion by her father-in-law. The invaluableness of things that were dear to the generations before her, would dilute for the generations after her. Her feelings were confirmed when she saw her daughter Uma practically empty her savings account to purchase the modern apartment and furnish the place with contemporary furniture. Ratna found no reason to bring up the subject of inherited property or vintage furniture to her daughter.

In the years of living with her husband, Ratna never held a job outside the home. Nothing was more important than raising her two daughters with cultivated education. Now, solitary, discharged from the life she had with her husband, she started to think differently. She wanted to reach out to help women in her locality. She felt motivated to do something purposeful, to establish a tutoring center for school going boys and girls. Ratna passed the word on mouth to neighbors living on her street, women friends she interacted with and at the places she shopped. She even printed a few notices and left them on the counters of sweet and grocery shops and tailoring boutiques. Within a few days, she received calls from women who were eager to tutor for extra income to supplement their living. They were women of all backgrounds: married, single and widowed, all with Masters degrees in different subjects. A few were homemakers and others had day time jobs: an owner of a book shop, an accountant in a sweet shop, a vocal music teacher, a retired science teacher, a part-time pharmacist. They had grown-up children who were in colleges or who lived far from home.

She spoke to parents about the needs of their children and created a tutoring schedule for five days from six in the evening to ten at night and from nine in the morning to ten at night on weekends. The tutoring center idea moved faster than Ratna expected. She ordered a few tables, chairs and portable writing boards, painted the rooms and installed ceiling lights and fans for the tutoring rooms while she arranged for upstairs to be her living unit.

At the age of thirty-five, energetic and congenial in spirit, with bright eyes, course black hair reaching below her waist, Uma carried a mixture of sensibility and determination that had attracted Lalit in his late teens, she was then sixteen and Lalit was eighteen.

Lalit and his parents were neighbors on the same street where Uma lived with her parents. For fifteen years, they came across each other when they stepped out for school or college or returned home from someplace. On some days, Lalit stood on the balcony with the hope of catching a glimpse of Uma. When he saw her, he shouted vehemently from the balcony complimenting how gorgeous she looked with her waist-length hair. He would start singing the romantic lines of Bengali movies to stir up a profuse conversation openly in public. Uma was amused by the attention he gave her, but she rarely responded back with words. There were people on streets and Uma did not want to make their cherished feelings for each other more conspicuous. She smiled at him bashfully, waving in a friendly gesture as she briskly walked towards her home.

On random days Lalit stopped by at Uma's home to ask Ratna if she needed assistance with anything, making himself nonchalantly comfortable. Ratna never encouraged his frequent visits, often declining his proposition to help her with household chores. She was doubtful about his acts; she thought, at his age, he occupied himself more with carefree engagements than focusing on his career plans. She sensed he had eyes for Uma, and her daughter showed no less, even though, she was less explicit than many girls her age. Ratna remained indifferent to their relationship.

Uma was aware of how her mother felt about Lalit, despite, she disregarded her mother's feelings towards him. She knew it was how adults conventionally reacted when boys of Lalit's age did not exhibit determination towards constructive career plans. Nevertheless, Uma enamored his outgoing, audacious mannerisms that hid nothing about his personality. She watched longingly from the veranda of her two-storied home to get a glance of Lalit walking down the street, his impulsive demeanor putting a smile on her face every time. In those moments, she remembered the heroes of the movies who lured the women with their mesmerizing words, the dreams they imagined together far from their plain, ordinary life. They inspired her; she thought it was how real love between two people was supposed to be. She was unwavering about feeling any other way.

At the age of twenty-two, when Uma confronted Ratna with the wish to spend the rest of her life with Lalit, Ratna felt she was placed in front of an inevitable barrier that would never restore sensibility in her child. At first, she did not give attention to Uma's words; she knew how much Uma's feelings embodied fantasy, a love exaggerated that would not give her the life she imagined.

One morning, Ratna walked into Uma's bedroom to speak to her exactly about the thought that disturbed her mind; Lalit was not a desirable match.

She saw Uma standing in front of the dressing table mirror, combing her long thick hair. She stood looking at herself as if her silent admirer were standing behind her, watching her every facial expression and how she stylishly combed her hair. It was a face in love. She was so lost in herself that she did not notice or hear her mother walk into the room till she heard Ratna pull out the chair from the study table to sit down.

Ever since Uma started teaching at the local school few blocks from the house, she spent time grooming herself on weekends. She oiled her hair for a few hours before washing with shampoo and massaged her face with the milk fat that she asked the cooking lady to set aside after she boiled the milk. She mixed the creamy fat with a pinch of white flour to smear on the face and leave it to dry for a few minutes, then scrubbed off the dried face scrub, removing the facial dirt that had accumulated in the pores of her skin. Every weekend she repeated the skin care technique that was taught to her by her cousin sister when she was trying to bring on a glowing appearance days before her wedding day.

Ratna kept gazing at her daughter. It was obvious, Uma was no longer the little girl she imagined. She noticed how Uma had started to resemble her younger self, yet she was more self-assured and daring than Ratna ever was at that age. She looked taller in her maxi dress, her slender figure with one long braid made her almost appear like a grown woman from the back.

Uma had not spoken to Ratna from the day she announced her plan to marry Lalit. But Ratna would not allow her daughter's silence to hinder what she wished to tell her. Without hesitation, Ratna straightforwardly asserted her feelings.

"A person needs to reflect on hasty decisions made in the prime of one's education and career."

Uma continued to listen indifferently, doing what she was doing. She thought her mother's words exhibited deterrent factors, and she was convinced that her mother would not understand the emotions of love because of her own arranged marriage to her father.

"There is more to life than education and career," Uma said in a stringent tone.

"But, everything has a time."

"My love for him will not change," Uma spoke out her feelings forcefully.

"Love is important, but there is more that needs to be considered."

"You think I will not be able to take care of my family?" Uma impatiently turned her head asking with a questioning expression.

"It's not you, Uma...."

Ratna stopped what she wanted say. She immediately felt distraught at her own words; she found no choice other than to clearly state what she felt. She had known Lalit longer than most as the carefree son of humble parents living in the neighborhood. She imagined him to be neighborly boy, a friend to someone who needed playful company. But, marriage was a different story.

"Reflect on what I am saying, Uma. That's all I ask from you."

"You have no idea what loves means! You cannot advise me."

Listening to Uma's explicit words, Ratna realized there was nothing more she could tell her; Uma had made up her mind. Ratna did not find it worthwhile to discuss the matter with Lalit's parents either, as they were more than keen to have Uma in their family as their daughter-in-law; Lalit's parents had known Uma for many years. Besides, Ratna knew her own intervention could ruin her relationship with Uma. She recognized the unfavorable position she was already in. Ratna decided not to resist any longer. She allowed Uma to fulfill her own happiness.

In the days after, Ratna sat silently in her room with tear-filled eyes in front of the picture of her late husband and recollected the moments when she had consulted Barun for decision-making or moral support on all affairs. Unmatched with both her daughters' views, she now suddenly felt she was standing alone. Her eldest daughter, Aloka, remained unmarried, lived separately on her own, and worked as a lecturer at a college in Calcutta. In contrast, Uma was keen on marriage at an earlier age, insisted on a partner Ratna did not feel confident about, and desired for both a family and a career.

In their thirteen years of marriage, Uma had a stable full-time teaching job at a school. Lalit changed jobs seven times, from a technician in a sales job, and doing entry-level work at software companies to being an associate in an advertising firm…. five times out of an ambition to move ahead in his career, two times against the wishes of his bosses, who had promised him a promotion and salary increase if he completed two years at those jobs. Lalit quit both the jobs within a year. In his last job, he was asked to take a break for a week to manage his alcohol issues. He was distressed for having his responsibilities reduced and other employees replaced to complete the tasks; he was denied access to meetings.

Confronted with humiliation on all sides, Lalit gave up the last job and began helping Kanak Mishra, a long-time neighborhood acquaintance who ran a food catering service in South Calcutta. Lalit assisted in answering phone calls and taking orders on the phone. Between the calls, he sat leaning back on his chair, sipped mugs of tea, and self-satisfied his infatuation with football by reading the sports page of the newspaper. Nothing mattered to him anymore. He felt it was hopeless to tell Kanak to give him more responsibilities with a higher pay; Kanak was somehow managing to pull through with his own business after a few years of decline. Lalit pushed the thought out of his mind. He started to develop a tainted attitude towards people with stable jobs; at times he despised them. He convinced himself that employers took care of their favorite workers, whereas, men like him got left behind; no one looked after them.

Most days, Lalit returned home late at night and slept late till next morning. On other days, he left the catering job early and hung out at a local sweet shop near his parents' home, sipping mugs of tea or smoking cigarettes while sitting on the front step of the shop. He exchanged words with customers who stopped by to buy sweets, and he made jeering remarks at the familiar faces who passed by the shop. On other nights, he would stop by his parents' home without prior notice to have his dinner and when he did not return by nine, Uma knew he would be home past midnight; she saved the dinner for him if he felt hungry when he returned.

Every morning Uma left for her job at school before Lalit was up from bed.

The elevator stopped at the fourth floor. Uma pulled the metal gate open and stepped out. Her apartment was three steps up from the elevator floor.

Uma unlocked the door and entered the apartment. Whatever condition she had left home in the morning, she always returned to find the place in the same disorderly condition…whiskey bottles lying on the dining table, glasses and dishes piled in the sink, water dripping from the bathroom faucet, clothes scattered over the bed or thrown lying on the bathroom floor. The maid, Kali, could never do house cleaning when Lalit was there; he never opened the door. Uma scheduled the house cleaning when she returned home from work in the evening.

She placed the three letters on the dining table and went to her room to change into comfortable clothes. She took out from the closet the embroidered violet-colored kaftan that her sister had bought her from *New Market* the day after Uma's salary raise last year.

"A little something for you to relax in after your hard day's work," Uma recalled her sister's words when she stopped by to give it to her.

"It's about time you got paid extra! Even the low wage workers get incentives periodically." Lalit had mocked when she saw Uma's sister giving her the gift.

Uma listened, she found no worthiness to the things Lalit uttered. She pitied herself for having to listen to such thoughts budding in his mind. She had developed a fine sense for when such sarcastic utterances were made; she disregarded his words. In those times she neither got annoyed at him nor felt resentful towards him recognizing his constrained jobless situation that burdened and affected his reasonable thinking.

Uma folded Lalit's clothes that were lying scattered on the bed and placed the unwashed laundry in a tub in the bathroom. She removed the empty soft drink bottles, unwashed tea cups and accumulated cigarette buds lying in the corner of the bedroom floor. Every day she managed the untidiness of things in the room. In contrast, her young son's small bedroom was organized; everything was in place where they belonged. Uma never had to clean up after him. Today, suddenly, she felt the urge to reach out to her ten-years old son, hug him, and tell him that he was doing more than what she ever expected of a person his age.

Anik was away for a week on a school field trip.

There is always that one unspoken blessing to be forever grateful.

Uma dusted the TV and put the crocheted cover on top. She bought the new TV a year ago after the salary raise from her job. She had wanted to commemorate her tenth wedding anniversary with something new for the home. She never expected Lalit to add to the household luxuries; she did not hold feelings of resentment, either.

But, what hurt her was Lalit's reaction to the TV; he had blamed her for being materialistic and selfish.

"I thought you liked to watch the football matches." Her voice was low and soft.

Lalit had laughed sarcastically. "Really? You thought about me?"

"I did, Lalit. Then you could watch at home and be near us rather than at the sweet shop."

No matter how often Uma made her feelings for him obvious, in spite of him not contributing to the household in any way, Uma did not show any kind of displeasure in her words. She knew that due to the sensitivity of the subject, she would rather maintain calmness at home; it felt more prudent to her in each passing day.

Three days a week, the school bus dropped Anik off at Ratna's home. Anik was in the advanced level of violin; the commute to the music school was closer from Ratna's home in South Calcutta than from Uma's apartment. Ratna took up the responsibility of taking Anik to the violin class while Uma was at work. It was the only way he could continue the music lessons without interruption. Uma brought home papers to correct, she had her own teaching preparation work and manage the home after her return.

Uma was stacking the cups and saucers in the sink for washing when she heard the door click open. She turned her head and saw Lalit at the door. She was surprised that he had returned much sooner than he normally did. He walked in without giving a glance at Uma and started taking off his shoes. Uma finished washing the last few cups and dishes, wiped her hands on a towel, and went towards the living room.

"I am glad you are back early today," Uma said looking at him with a smile.

Lalit remained silent briefly, then, responded indifferently asking for a glass of water. Uma quickly poured cold water from the bottle inside the fridge and brought it to him.

"What about something to eat? Uma asked.

"No."

Uma looked at Lalit's face. The fact that he had returned home sooner, she did not want to start interrogating him. Lately, she felt inarticulate in his presence; she was not sure how he would react to her questions or comments even if they were meant for a casual conversation. Today, she sensed the rigid formality in the way he spoke.

"You have three letters on the table," she said softly.

"So, how did you get home?" asked Lalit abruptly ignoring what she said as he sat down on the sofa.

"Taxi. I had a meeting."

Lalit gave a wry smile. "That's what celebrities do."

"The bus routes were blocked for political protests. I wouldn't have reached home before nine. Besides, you said you needed the car so I didn't insist."

Lalit made an annoying face at Uma. He never liked her bringing up the subject of the car. It was her father's car that her mother gave for Uma's transport to and back from her school job. Uma took care of the driver's fee and car maintenance from her salary. There was no doubt that he liked taking the car to the catering shop; he felt good when the driver dropped him off and picked him up in the evening. He cared for the image of a successful working man. That's what people noticed, he thought. People rarely enquired what kind of work he did when he came and went in a car with a driver. They understood he had a secure well-paying job. But, he never wanted to hear from Uma anything about him using the car.

Uma went to the chair and sat down across from Lalit. His expression was impersonal as if he did not know her. A sudden quietness befell; she wanted to start a topic away from their life, to talk about other things—if something happened at the catering shop, if he has spoken with friends, if he wanted Uma to buy something for him, but she hesitated; Lalit found fault with anything she said. But, no matter how, unenthusiastic she felt, she also had an inexplicable pity for him, for the state of his mind, and his unwillingness to foresee the opportunities beyond the confined activities he wanted to engage in. She recognized that he was embittered, the catering job was a filler job; he hardly did anything other than read the comic section of the newspapers in between taking phone calls from customers; no one can feel happy without a constructive engaged activity. The human mind reacts adversely when left neglected.

Sometimes, when she was alone at home in the late hours into the night, she had faint apprehensions about his late returns after midnight. She lay silently in bed, wondering if he was at a bar drinking or had gotten into an argument with someone. She would fall asleep waiting, and would suddenly wake up to the click of the front door. When he walked into the bedroom, she would quickly sit up and ask him if he had eaten dinner or if he wanted her to make something for him even though it was past two in the morning. He would answer yes and then no. She would smell the alcohol on his breath, but Uma never asked where he spent his late nights or how much longer the late nights would continue. She was reluctant to ask in case it would lead to unpleasant discourses before going to bed. A person should not deal with anger before sleep. She wished she could embrace him before going off to sleep, accommodating all the wrongs of his behavior because if both took the same road, the slightest hope for something good would instantly get erased. She did not want that. For all sane reasons, she made sure her son was busy with his music lessons for three days and stayed with his grandmother to finish homework before she brought him home.

"When is Anik coming home?" asked Lalit in a cold voice, stretching out his legs on the coffee table in front.

"End of the week."

"I never see my son."

Uma was quiet for a few minutes before she spoke. "You are asleep when Aniq leaves for school. When you return, Anik is in bed."

"Why is it my fault?"

"May be if you got home sooner or got up from bed earlier, you would see Anik. He misses your company too."

"You have planned your life well. Even your son's. Keep it up!"

Nothing could provoke more aggravation in Uma than his words. Still, she refrained from blurting out displeasing comments.

"What has happened to you, Lalit?" She got up, walked towards him and put her hands on his shoulders like a mother comforting a child. "Is that what you think?"

"What else? Leaving for work five days a week, keeping a driver to drop you and bring you back, sending the child to an expensive school. It's a good life. Don't you think?"

"One of us has to work. How else will we live? I am trying to do what I think is best, "

Uma responded in a somber low voice.

"Why do you have to make the decisions?" He asked irritated.

"I don't have to. Will you manage everything for me?" Uma said in a polite firm voice.

Lalit did not say anything. She clearly knew Lalit was not in his normal state of mind.

He angrily got up and walked to the table and picked up the three letters. He stared at each letter intently.

"What are these letters?"

"I don't know. Could be the replies from the jobs you applied," said Uma cautiously.

Lalit tore open the envelopes with his hand and read each one quietly. He had a look of indifference on his face, as if the letters were of least importance, then, a sardonic expression came onto him with a sudden burst of annoyance.

Then, there was silence.

"He betrayed me! How could he!" Lalit suddenly shouted.

Uma hurriedly got up and went to the kitchen. His words created a repulsive feeling inside her. She remained quiet. She stood in front of the kitchen window and stared outside. She saw the traffic below, the hectic pace of life. Still, the view restored lightness of her spirit and made her feel everyone was engaged in doing their part, however their life was. So long people were occupied with work or service, there was consistency maintained, there was less of contemptuous feelings.

Lalit went to the sofa and sat down. He leaned his head back and stared at the ceiling. His silence was like the stillness before a storm. He had deliberately habituated himself not to say anything unless Uma spoke first.

"What was in the letters?" Uma broke the silence speaking to him from the kitchen. She wanted to take her time going back to the living room.

"Santosh ruined everything." Uma heard the blunt disregard for someone who once had been a friend to Lalit and whom Lalit had trusted to write a reference for him.

Uma walked into the living room and noticed the torn envelopes and the letters erratically thrown on the table.

"Mr. Amit Sanyal got the reference letter from Santosh. He quoted the lines Santosh wrote. Guess what? I am not a prospective candidate anymore."

Uma was quiet for a few moments. She was anxious to know the details, though, she had a faint idea what they would be.

"Are they true what Santosh wrote?"

Lalit looked at Uma startled. "That I am not a dedicated worker, I am too ambitious without exhibiting effort, I lacked social skills. What do you think?"

"Santosh knew your work history. You changed jobs many times on your choice. You never completed a year with one job," Uma responded calmly.

Lalit looked at Uma disappointed, thinking, she could read Santosh's mind better than he wanted her to.

"Santosh is my friend. This is betrayal. What would you understand!" Lalit protested loudly.

Uma kept quiet. Lalit sounded steamed up to her. He knew Santosh from school years, and they had interacted in several socializing opportunities together. But, in spite of this, there had been moments when Santosh consciously kept his distance from Lalit. He had moved up the ladder in his professional life sooner than many, accepted the arranged marriage his parents initiated, and lived in a joint generous household with his well-established, affluent parents. Uma knew Santosh to be a decent person, so when she heard the sudden outburst from Lalit, she realized their friendship had taken a different turn, possibly intentional from Santosh's part.

"Just leave it, Lalit. Don't hurt your morale by thinking about it." Uma walked up close and gently stroked his hair and his cheeks.

"It bothers me when you say that!" Lalit said in an annoyed tone.

"I am sorry. It just hurts me to see you so upset."

"No one will give me a job! Don't you understand that?"

"Sometimes it takes time, Lalit. It's not the same for everybody."

Uma instantly became quiet after her words. There was something she wanted to ask him, but waited. She saw him get up, collect the torn envelopes and the letters and thrust them forcefully in the wastebasket.

"And you thought Santosh was a good man. See what he did to me!" Lalit turned his head towards Uma and shouted.

Uma stared at his face, stunned. What was he talking about?

"I didn't ask you to write to Santosh for a reference letter. I wanted you speak to your first employer."

"Who? Mr. Nirmal Sengupta?" Lalit gave a sarcastic laugh.

Ever since Lalit had left Mr. Sengupta's company, he had despised the idea of bringing up his name. Mr Sengupta was Lalit's first employer, and the relationship with him had ended disagreeably the day Lalit announced that he would discontinue the job after eight months because of discontentment with the salary. Despite, Mr. Sengupta had called him the following morning to get him to rethink what he was doing, but nothing changed on Lalit's part. He assured Lalit that promotions are considered after two years of work, but he could help Lalit after a year if he displayed good performance. Uma knew Mr Sengupta followed mannerisms of social grace and ethics. He understood Lalit's momentary irrational attitude and despite, kept the position open for a week incase Lalit changed his mind.

"Every man gets the chance to begin anew. There is always that choice. It is up to the person." Mr. Sengupta had prudently advised Lalit in their last conversation on phone.

But, it was not the kind of advice Lalit was looking for.

So, when Uma hinted about Mr. Sengupta's name, Lalit reacted again.

"Mr. Sengupta never speaks about salary," Lalit asserted annoyingly.

"Money should not be the issue all the time."

"What else is the issue then?"

"If you give him something good to believe."

"Like what?"

"That you are willing to work hard and take responsibilities," said Uma.

"What about the money?"

"It will come. You have to do your part first."

"It's not as straightforward as you make it out to be."

"What is your idea of straightforward?" asked Uma.

There was silence for a short moment. She did not know what he was thinking. In the past, nothing she said could convince Lalit. It was not the first time she had brought up Mr. Sengupta. One time, she was appalled by how Lalit responded. He wanted her to speak to Mr. Sengupta's wife, Pritha, to share with her husband how much Lalit deserved a high-paying salary. Uma never anticipated that Lalit would bring up an idea like that. Mr. Sengupta's wife had never met Lalit, she had no idea who he was. Uma knew Pritha's granddaughter went to the same school she taught at, but she had neither met Pritha nor her granddaughter. When Lalit brought up the same idea again with Uma, she told him she would not do that, it was a senseless request. She did not want a person who did not know Lalit, to paint a colorful image of him when Mr. Sengupta already knew what kind of a persona Lalit had.

"You don't understand anything!" Lalit banged his hand on the table in a rage, forcibly pushing the water jug aside.

"Lalit, calm down! Let's forget about all this!"

Lalit looked at Uma annoyingly. "You know what's better? You keep out of my life!" He went into the bedroom and slammed the door.

The sudden blow of words dumbfounded her. The discomfort grew into agitation in her head. She realized he had lost the sense of rational thinking and it had started to become obvious.

Uma forgot she had soaked two cups of tea and had kept a plate of *shingaras* in the kitchen. Every time she thought of creating a homey situation, even to have tea with Lalit, the situation would abruptly change, she would be back again in the same place, lonelier. There had been moments when she wondered how could this beautiful apartment that she had bought with so much enthusiasm and with her own savings could hold so much indignation and void.

In the stillness of the room, she started to think about Anik. She sat down on the sofa. It was lonely without him in the house. She bent her head low and closed her eyes, she felt the intense longing to hold her son near her chest and cry on his shoulder. Her eyes watered; she knew she could never do that! How unfair would it be for her son, still a young boy, to get pulled into her misery? A mother could never allow that.

Uma wiped the tears from her eyes, got up and went to the kitchen. She poured the tea in a saucepan and covered it with the lid to have it at a later time. She put back the *shingaras* back in the same brown paper bag she had bought them in. Two eggplants, a cabbage head, a few tomatoes and potatoes were still inside the jute bag lying on the counter. Kali had bought them for her on her way to Uma's home. She always helped Uma in any small way she could.

She did not take out the cooked food from the fridge she had prepared the night before. She had no appetite. She knocked on Lalit's door to ask him if he wanted something to eat. At first there was no response, then he annoyedly called out no.

Uma went back into the kitchen and closed the kitchen light. She looked at the family portrait on top of the fridge. It was taken on Anik's sixth birthday in a studio. It was the first one, the only one so far.

She returned back to the living room and sat down on the sofa. She turned on the TV and flipped through the channels to reach the news channel. Ever since she bought the new TV, she had not once sat with Lalit to watch a movie or listen to the news as many people did. There could be so much more to talk about than the home-life. Uma stopped on a channel where they were showing clips from old Bengali and Hindi movies; she leaned back on the sofa to listen. The love songs brought back nostalgic memories and heightened her with gloomy feelings. She turned off the TV and sat quietly by herself staring at books on the bookshelf across.

"At the end, just care for yourself when there is no one next to you. It is all right."

She picked up the phone to call her mother. The telephone rang for a few minutes before she heard her mother's voice. It sounded somber, not how she normally spoke. Uma asked about how things were running with the tutoring center, if she met her women friends, if she went out for a movie with them. Ratna answered casually without elaborating. Uma undoubtedly understood something was not right when her mother quickly asked if Lalit was back home.

Uma was briefly quiet and then said, "Yes, he is."

Uma sensed the unusual pause. Her mother never went silent on phone.

"Everything all right, *Ma*??" Uma asked.

"Do you know when Lalit last visited his parents?" Ratna asked instantly.

Uma was taken aback by the question. "Why? Something happened?"

Ratna instantly spoke about Lalit's mother who had called her in the morning. His mother was emotional because Lalit had not met or talked to his parents in the last six months. She wished Lalit had come himself to hand them the check for the loan he took from his father instead of mailing the check.

There was silence. Uma did not say anything; she knew about the loan, but not from Lalit.

She remembered the day she stopped by to visit Lalit's parents, two months after he had taken the loan. She had walked into their two-storied home. They were both living on the first floor while they rented the second floor out to a couple who had established their leather goods business. Lalit's parents had been thrilled to see Uma. The whole time Uma was there, they spoke with pride and relief that their son was finally settled in a high-ranking job. His mother had mentioned sympathetically how Lalit had taken the loan from his father before he had begun his new job. He told his father he needed some extra money for a car he was planning to buy to commute to his job. Lalit's father had willingly loaned him money from his savings. She had said that his father slept without anxiety knowing his son was on the road to being an accomplished man.

The fact that Lalit's parents trusted his every word and excused his long lapse in visits because they thought Lalit was occupied with job responsibilities had momentarily stunned Uma. In that visit, she had suddenly felt she lost composure; she had felt the perspiration on her neck and the heat rising on her face. She had sat in silence pretending to appreciate her mother-in-law's words. She didn't tell them anything, she listened to what Lalit's mother spoke.

Uma had returned home that evening with the sole thought hovering in her head; the loan needed to be paid back to Lalit's father. She neither spoke to Lalit nor wasted time deferring what she needed to do. Immediately, she wrote a check of fifty thousand rupees from her own savings, adding the extra amount for the interest lost from the bank, and mailed the check in Lalit's father's name. She could not allow one more day to go by thinking that Lalit's father had given money to Lalit believing everything his son said. They were not true. Neither she spoke to Lalit nor she told his parents and her mother what she did.

"Don't worry, *Ma*! The loan has been returned."

She was not going to tell her mother how complicated the situation was. There would be many questions, comments that would elevate the predictable pain.

"It was the right action Lalit took to return the loan. But, he could have come himself and returned the check to his father. Six months is a long time not to see them when he lives in Calcutta." said Ratna in a somber voice.

Uma suppressed her tears. The anxiety of contention escalated inside her. It was not about the loan Lalit had taken from his father; it was about how he mislead his parents with false impressions, an untrue image of his own situation. The thoughts traumatized her. She did not bring up Lalit's name with her mother.

"They have rented the upstairs of their home to a business," said Uma.

Ratna was quiet for a few minutes.

"For financial need, I suppose. I don't think they wish to depend on Lalit. They are grateful that he has a steady job to support his own family."

Uma did not say anything; she was the only one who knew the truth; she was the only one who could guard Lalit from further degrading the reputation he had created with people. Even to her own mother, she would not tell everything.

Why insinuate further the already displeasing impressions about Lalit? How does it help him or anyone else other than create an emotional drama that tears everyone's heart apart.

"I am proud that Lalit's parents made a good arrangement for themselves by renting the upstairs," said

Uma emphatically knowing how she truly felt about the situation.

Trust was like looking inside a well, deep, with no distractions around. If reversed, the view is still the same, deep. She was pierced by an intense discrepancy in her thoughts. She didn't feel like talking further.

"Okay, *Ma*. It's late. I will let you go." She gently said good night and hung up the phone.

Uma put the phone on the table. The memories of the younger years suddenly resurfaced in her mind— how she had thought her mother was being inconsiderate of her feelings; how everything she had said then about Lalit, had annoyed her; how she had wished she could run away from home. Now, it was the same. She wanted to distance herself from the repressed conflict of her present life. Even with a stable job, a sensible child, and a good roof over her head, there was a burden of inadequacy. Her sanity was the only thing she could hold on to, it was in her control. She would not allow anything to hamper.

Uma heard the traffic noises on the road, and the voices of people talking on the the verandas on both sides of the apartment. It did not matter it was a Sunday evening. She liked that there was life around, families socialized with neighbors late into the night; they sat together, recollecting scenes from movies or planning for music concerts together. There was always the choice to go sit on one of the benches inside the building complex if she felt lonesome. She could watch pedestrians walk by the building, groups of young couples socialize near the gate, laughing and chatting loudly. Even in the midst of the unfamiliar faces, she would have felt contented. She could turn to them to talk about things in life; she did not need to share what her own life was like.

The bedroom door unlocked and Lalit stepped out wearing the clean ironed shirt that Uma had hung inside the closet. He had taken a short nap and changed. If he had made plans for the night, Uma did not know. He went to the kitchen, took out a sliced bread piece from the plastic bread bag and filled a glass with water. He stood in the kitchen eating the bread, chewing on it slowly, letting the time pass. His tall slender body did not change much from the years she had known him, he had inherited the slender built of his father. It was his tanned round face that normally came across as untended, uncared for, but now, Uma immediately noticed his well-shaved and groomed appearance. Today, he looked much more attractive than what she had seen him in a long time. She could postulate that he had spent time preening himself.

He chugged the glass full of water in one gulp and left the empty glass in the sink. He did not say anything. Uma stared at his indifferent face.

"How late will you be?" Uma asked.

"I don't know."

Uma was apprehensive about what the night would bring along, but she did not ask.

He put on his shoes without glancing at Uma. She sat like a numb statue on the sofa, trying to keep her emotions under control, accepting that she meant very little to him. Lalit opened the door and stepped outside. Uma heard the door lock click.

It was past eleven thirty when Uma last checked the time on the alarm clock on the nightstand. By the time she last heard the voices of people outside the apartment, it was almost midnight. She wondered if it would be Lalit next, his footsteps approaching the door. It never happened. It surprised her how impetuously Lalit managed to take control of situations; he never bore any guilt returning home in late hours without regard for Uma. It was she who felt negligent turning off the lights, going off to sleep when he had not returned, forgiving his every insensitive action towards her. Sometimes she lay in bed filled with restlessness and guilt that she was not able to help him. He was unmistakably seized by unfulfilling circumstances; he had drifted away from his own self.

Uma kept the floor lamp in the living room on for Lalit. She fell asleep reading the *Desh* magazine, waking up suddenly at 3:10a.m. to find Lalit's side of the bed empty, the *Desh* lying next to her. Uma got up and opened the bedroom door, the lamp was still on in the living room, Lalit had not returned. She didn't hear the phone ring. He never used the cell phone that Uma bought him; he said he had no time to make phone calls.

The clothes were ready on the chair in her bedroom. She barely had time in the morning to pick out what she wanted to wear to school. She was used to getting up by five to finish cooking the two dishes for dinner, a vegetable and a fish, and to prepare breakfast and lunch for Anik when he had school. But lately, she found herself waking up earlier, she realized that's what worries did to a person. She used the extra time to finish correcting her students' papers or to skim through the editorial sections of the newspaper. Sometimes, she used the time to organize her clothes in the almirah while she kept the music playing softly on the radio. She would walk into Anik's room just to have a look. She missed him.

She stored the extra cooked vegetables and rice in a separate box for Kali, the maid had four young children at home. Kali became the sole breadwinner when her husband got into an accident with his rickshaw, injuring his left arm and losing the rickshaw. Uma had given him money to buy a new rickshaw, but he had to wait till his arms gained enough strength to lift the wooden bar handle. When Uma mentioned about Kali's husband to Lalit, he blew up in anger for wasting money on Kali's family. His reactions unleashed a swirl of emotions in Uma.

Why would you feel annoyed at a poor man who earns his living pulling people on his rickshaw and who has injured his arms? What wrong did he do to you?

Uma reached school the next day, an hour before the start of the school day. Tall matured Kadam trees stood on both sides of the school entrance gate; their globe-like orange flowers resembled decorations inserted inside the leafy green trees, permeating the clean morning air with a sweet fragrance.

She sat silently in the classroom gazing out the window. A gardener was watering the planters lined along the corridor to the classrooms; there was another who swept the front of the Principal's office clearing away the visible dirt that had accumulated overnight. The streams of orange morning rays fell on the walls of the buildings and lit up the corridors. A freshly developed life outside was returning— bright and new. The light in her north facing room was never harsh, Uma found it calming to admire the warm glow outside instead of feeling the warmth inside the room. She studied the clustered magenta bougainvillea vines that gracefully climbed up on both sides of the building's exterior walls. She had been watching them grow for years; each day their lustrous blazing blooms mesmerized the eyes.

It was the start of the school day. Teachers entered the classrooms before students were let inside. The main entrance main gate was still locked; it opened an hour before the first bell to let the buses in. Uma looked at her watch. She thought of calling Pinaki, Lalit's school friend for many years, to ask him if he knew where Lalit was. But she resisted, for reasons that went back many years when she first met Pinaki and when he had compulsive feelings for her.

The first time she met him was before her marriage. Pinaki was jovially immersed in conversation with Lalit in front of his house. Uma had sensed a passionate delight in the way he had spoken to her when she came forward with the intention to meet Lalit. The uncomfortable candidness of his feelings was revealing, as if his happiness was instantly compensated for the days he missed knowing her. From the intensity of his indulgent words, Uma understood how he felt for her; he would be capable of carrying on a secret relationship with her, if she let it happen. He knew he was cleverer to win his friend to his side no matter what happened between him and Uma. Since then and for a long time afterwards, Uma kept her distance and avoided his presence when she saw him talking to Lalit. Henceforth, he pulled his attention away from her with remorse, realizing that Uma was a lot more effort than what he had thought.

Uma still had forty minutes. She sat quietly, reflecting, then took out her cell phone and punched in Pinaki's phone number. A voice suddenly came on the phone and spoke, "Uma?"

It was surprising how quickly he recognized her voice. "Hello, Pinaki!"

Uma! How are you?" He said excitedly.

"Good. And you?"

"*Bhalo Bhalo*! But, why this early? Is everything all right?"

Uma told him she was at her school job, it was not early. Then, she briefly paused and told him that Lalit had not come home that night.

There was a sudden uncomfortable silence for a few seconds.

"Bear with him, Uma! He is going through troubled times."

Uma did not know what to make of the comment.

"What did Lalit tell you?"

"Lalit tells me everything. You know how long we have known each other."

"Sure, but what did he tell you?"

"He told me how he was mistreated."

Uma refrained from reacting. It would immediately take the conversation off the track.

"Mistreated? Did he not tell you that he chose to leave all the jobs he worked for?"

"He said there was wrongdoing."

"Then Lalit did not tell you the complete story."

Pinaki had understood clearly what Lalit told him, but he did not wish to give Uma the impression that his friend was wrong. He preferred to keep the conversation focused on other areas.

"Can you not understand how unfair it is that his colleagues got promoted in front of him?"

Pinaki spoke forcefully.

"I know them. They are hard working men of Lalit's age."

"Surely you know what 'fair share' means!" Pinaki stirred up.

"Of course! And it comes with scrupulous thinking."

The conversation abruptly stopped. Uma knew Pinaki did not take her words well.

"Do you know what Lalit plans to do?" Uma continued in a somber tone.

"I thought you know everything about his life." Pinaki said grinning.

"That's what I thought, too."

"I have no clue! But for sure, Lalit is waiting for someone to recognize his stressful situation."

Uma pulled herself up in her chair so she could listen carefully to whatever more Pinaki had to say.

"There are people who could help him, you know." Uma said softly.

"Let him do what he likes, Uma! Why are you bothered?" Pinaki sounded aggravated.

"Wouldn't you if you were in my place?" Uma paused quickly trying to control her emotions. Then she asked him again if he knew where Lalit was.

Pinaki sighed. He briefly debated whether he should avoid answering.

"Don't misunderstand him Uma! You will be better off not focusing on him so much."

Uma was suddenly taken aback. She felt the confusion disclose on her face.

"Where is Lalit?" Uma's voice was firm.

"You want to know, then?" Pinaki laughed in a half-suppressed manner. "He was with Rajani Das last night."

"Who is Rajani Das?" Uma instantly stopped after the question. It was as if all her questions had been answered.

Pinaki told her that Rajani Das was a divorced seamstress with a son. Lalit had met her in a bar. She worked as a waitress.

"In a bar? Where?"

"In *Chowringhee*. I have been there a few times. Nice place!"

Despite the aversion Uma instantly felt, she kept silent. She understood that both friends had been in conversation. In a way she was glad Pinaki was not sitting in front of her; she probably would have ended up asking more questions than necessary. She did not feel comfortable discussing about Lalit with Pinaki.

"He called me from the bar last night. He told me about Rajani. He felt sorry that her husband abandoned her. She is single, living alone with her son."

"Of course! *The generous heart that opens one door and slams the other*," Uma thought.

For a few minutes, she fell silent, suppressing the hurt.

"I wouldn't worry if I were you," said Pinaki.

"Honestly, it does not matter."

"You have the choice to do the same." Pinaki grinned at his own prankish words.

Uma frowned. The words sounded cynical. She could almost imagine his facial expression.

"Choice to do the same? What are you saying!"

"I am saying you could be like Lalit. Do things without him knowing." She could sense his sheepish grin.

There was a cold unsettled silence. Pinaki was trying to make sense of her reactions over the phone.

"I see you have remained the same. You have no shame!" Uma said in an indignant tone.

"Don't dismiss the matter so easily. Give it a thought." He laughed awkwardly.

"It is unfortunate that you still haven't understood me. Besides, I wouldn't depreciate myself to your mediocre standards."

Uma told him that she needed to stop the conversation.

"Not everything is about you!" He spoke out loud, mockingly.

Uma fell silent. *The most preposterous thoughts!* She said good-bye and ended the call.

"Uma!Uma!" Pinaki's high-strung voice called from the other end.

Uma glanced at the wall clock; she still had a half hour before students were let inside the classroom. She sat in silence staring out the window and recollected the conversation with Pinaki that she abruptly ended. Surprisingly, she did not feel anger; she clearly understood where things stood. It wasn't like she had shockingly uncovered the secret life of Lalit, she had feelings of apprehension for some time.

What she hoped for was a decent transformed man in Pinaki. It takes a fair amount of will power to change oneself, to develop a sense of conscientiousness, Uma reflected. Uma had been looking for admissible advice from Pinaki in case he had changed. After all, Pinaki was the one of the few people who remained friends with Lalit.

For a long-time she had resisted calling Pinaki because she did not want anything to do with him. But, there was another reason: she was not ready to discover what Lalit was up to. She did not want to distrust him. However, her senses alerted her not to be oblivious as she was still his wife, even though, there was nothing left of his caring feelings towards her. It was why she had phoned Pinaki.

Today, after many months of turmoil in her heart, blurring the little hopes of accommodating Lalit's irrational behavior, she felt good about the firm distance that had been created between her and the man she had loved.

Lalit did not return the next morning. He was not home when Uma returned after work. Uma walked into the apartment feeling a sense of suffocation trapped inside the concrete walls where she had wanted to live peacefully with Lalit and her son. Briefly, in her mind, she relived the day she and Lalit first entered the new apartment; he had been overjoyed the day she put in the down-payment for their own home. Since that day, Uma paid the monthly installments with her salary, even all the utilities, Lalit had no part in it.

She stood in the middle of the living room, staring blankly at the lifeless physical reality of what was supposed to be a home, unable to grasp the meaning of the senseless situation she was now in. *"Why did you do this to me? What did I do to you?"*

She walked into her bedroom and felt impelled by an instinct to act, to unchain herself from the undeserved situation. She pulled out the two suitcases from under the bed, took out some saris, blouses and petticoats from the almirah, and cardigans and maxi dresses from the closet, and tossed them distractedly into one suitcase. She emptied one of the shelves which had her clothes, the other three were loaded with Lalit's shirts, pants, T-shirts, kurtas and pajamas. She saw small notebooks, pens, cigarettes, match boxes, a comb, shaving cream and razor all clumped together on one shelf. The third one was filled with magazines he had picked up here and there, old newspapers, and loose note slips with names and phone numbers scribbled on them. Dust had settled on all the shelves between the things. No matter how often she organized, there was no sense of graciousness in what he did.

She brought Anik's clothing from the other room and packed them in the second suitcase. How unfair was it their son, who had no part in this insensitive drama, had to join the tension because he was still a child? She pictured the sad expression on his face, and her heart heaved in apprehension.

She unplugged the toaster, and tightened the gas cylinder in the kitchen. There was nothing to be washed or put away since she had been out the whole day and no one was home.

The home phone rang just as she was about to exit the door. She thought it was Lalit, may be Pinaki had spoken to him. Maybe he was calling to apologize, to tell her not to misunderstand him, to beg her to pardon him. She would pardon but she would not express anything to him in her words immediately. She would wait to hear what he had to say.

She sat down on a chair and picked up the receiver. A woman's steady voice saying 'hello' came from the other end. In that instant, a series of rapid thoughts flashed through Uma's mind. All kinds of thoughts. Uma perceived the restrained tone from the other end.

"Hello," she said softly.

"I am Rajani Das. I want to talk to Uma Sen, please."

Uma swallowed through the sudden tightness she felt in her throat. She recognized the name.

"This is she," Uma said cordially.

"I assume you have heard my name."

"Yes, I have." Uma's calm voice was not of comfort, thinking what she might be getting herself into. A sudden silence made it seem Rajani was taking her time to speak. There was nothing Uma wanted to say till she had heard her.

"Please don't misjudge me. I am not what you think."

Uma could clearly tell she wanted to pave the way towards whatever she had to say.

"I am very sorry," the woman continued speaking.

Uma leaned back on the chair waiting to hear more. "Please go on."

She heard the woman take a deep sigh. "Even though I don't know you, I feel I can speak to you without hesitation."

Uma did not say anything. She did not want to. She had to begin listening with a forgiving mind. She didn't know her, she couldn't immediately start forming opinions about her. The woman paused briefly, then she began telling how she had met Lalit at a bar in *Chowringhee*. She said she tailored clothes by profession, and she worked at the bar for extra income.

"My husband left me and my six years old son two years ago for another woman. The owner of the bar is the husband of the woman in whose tailoring shop I work during the day. Her husband gave me the second job when he found out I needed the extra income to support my family. I live with my brother's family. I don't want to be their burden, so I contribute to their household while living under their roof. My brother does not want my financial contribution, but I refuse to listen." The woman paused. "A person's own dignity comes first—isn't that right?"

Uma was quietly listening. Then she softly said, 'yes.'

The woman was quiet for a short moment. Uma wondered if she was waiting for her to say something.

"You can continue. I am listening." Uma said.

"The truth is I never thought I would have to defend myself about the person I am. I never even imagined I would be working as a waitress in a bar. It is out of need that I am doing. All my life I have tailored clothes, my husband had a job at a bank. I never knew he was silently carrying on an affair for a year while he was married to me. I found out from his friend's wife. I was shocked, but I pretended not to know till one day when I asked him one straight question…Why have you been dishonest to me? He understood that I came to know and shouted that I should find a life of my own because he liked someone better. He would not support me, but he would support our son. That day, I packed my things and left the house with my son." The woman went silent. Uma felt she had more to say so she waited. She heard the woman clear her throat and take a deep breath.

"He wanted that I leave my son with him and his girlfriend. He said he would raise our son. I told him that my son did not deserve a father like him. He was better off living with his mother even if she could only provide him a modest life." Rajani stopped suddenly.

"I am sorry to hear your story," said Uma's softly.

"I am not a bad woman, *Didi*. I am not."

"You don't have to tell me that."

"The first day your husband came to the bar, he immediately took interest in me. I told him everything about myself what I told you. He seemed unusually sympathetic to my situation. He would gaze at me and compliment my appearance." She paused.

"I will be honest with you, in that moment, I liked how he was paying attention to me. It's a normal human behavior, isn't it, *Didi*?"

She paused again, thinking if Uma would have something to say, but she didn't. She told Uma that they exchanged each other's phone numbers, but when he called her a few times at home, she did not respond to his calls. She knew that she would see him at the bar. He told her to call him during the day at his home number because he was home alone. But she never called him.

The woman stopped. Uma thought she felt uneasy that Uma had not said anything.

"I am listening. Don't worry about me."

"I am so sorry! This kind of conversation should not be over the phone," Rajani said gently.

"It's all right. We do what is easily possible under the circumstances."

She described how he came to the bar every night for a few hours and spent time drawing her attention. But, within a few days, she noticed his unusual style of talking, like he was patronizing her. She started to become uncomfortable and did not want to pay attention—he was just another customer at the bar, no one special. Then, everything changed when he told her that he had a son few years older to hers, and that his wife enjoyed life on her own, and she never cared for the family.

"I was shocked and I understood he was lonely. But, still, I did not want anything to do with him, I did not know him well enough. Then, one night, everything took a strange turn when he asked me to talk to the bar owner if he could lend him fifty-thousand rupees. He told me to tell the bar owner that it was for an urgent reason. Something made me think it was not true. Since then, I have been disregarding his request. But he keeps insisting."

The woman became quiet.

Uma pressed her lips together and gazed out the window. Tears welled up in the eyes. She wished the traffic noises outside were louder, they could at least distort what she had heard on the phone, making her think she misheard things. Everything sounded dizzying, Uma started to lose concentration.

"It is why I made this phone call with the hope of reaching you. I wanted to tell you my story and what is happening," Rajani said.

"I appreciate that you told me everything." Uma responded softly.

"Tell me honestly, *Didi*! Are you annoyed at me?"

"Why should I be annoyed at you?"

"I don't know. In case you think I had something to do with your husband."

Uma was quiet briefly. "Would you not tell me if you did?"

"Please believe me! I am telling the truth."

Uma pressed her lips, suppressing the tenseness inside her. She was not going to be arrogant. For what reason?

"Don't worry!" Uma said.

"But, what should I do about the money?" Her voice sounded worried.

"You do not need to ask the bar owner anything." Uma answered firmly.

"But, Lalit has been insisting. What should I tell him?"

"Tell him you will not do what he asks." Uma answered in an unyielding voice. "You have a mind of your own just as he has."

Rajani did not say anything. Uma sensed that she had a difficult time handling Lalit's persistence, even Uma's words probably sounded resolute. She asked Rajani the name of the bar and the time Lalit visited the bar so she could be there. She would plan to meet the owner, to get everything under her control about the money that Lalit mentioned to Rajani. She clearly understood the unsettled situation Rajani had been pulled into. It annoyed her. She suddenly felt the responsibility to relieve her from the distressful situation.

"I am glad you called me." Uma said in a comforting voice.

There was a brief pause.

"I suppose you were alone when Lalit was at the bar so often," Rajani asked softly.

Momentarily, Uma felt touched by the way she asked; obviously she knew how such a situation feels like to suffer insensitivity and indifference in silence.

"Yes, many nights." She wiped the moisture in her eyes with her hand.

"Please forgive me!"

Uma smiled. She didn't want Rajani to feel the way she was feeling.

"Don't put the blame on yourself when you know you have done nothing wrong. You need to be strong!"

Then, Uma cordially said good-bye and put down the phone. She sat quietly for a few minutes with her eyes closed, leaning her head back on the chair.

She turned off the lights in all the rooms and locked the entrance door. Uma took both suitcases down to the driveway where the car was parked. Kali was entering the apartment complex when she saw the driver loading the suitcases in the car.

"Uma-*didi*! Where are you going?" She gazed at Uma speechless, astonished.

"I will tell you later."

"What about *Dada-babu*?" asked Kali.

"He will come when he pleases. Please stop by and ask him what he needs."

"Will you sell your home, *Didi*?"

"*Dadababu* needs a place to live. I will decide later."

Kali gazed at Uma's face brokenhearted. Never in her life did she think Uma, the caretaker of her own family of four children, would leave the house suddenly, in the most distraught manner. In all her years of working for Uma, Kali had seen how she took care of the household, even the urgent needs of her family while managing her job outside. She had long sensed that Uma's home-life was under troubling conditions, yet Uma expressed very little to her or to anyone.

Kali went close to the car and touched Uma's shoulder gently. "You go on trying to do good, even those nearest you, don't hear you. You stay well, *Didi*!"

Kali uttered softly as she stood close to the car door and wiped her tear-filled eyes with her hands. Uma stretched her arm out the window and tucked a five hundred rupee note in the palm of Kali's hand. "Why are you crying? Buy some sweets for your husband and children." Kali kept staring at Uma's face, stunned, as the car backed from the driveway.

"To my mother's home," said Uma to the driver as she gestured a hand wave to Kali. She took out the phone from her purse to return the call from Anik's teacher, Mrs. Tandon. She had called earlier to share with Uma the impressive essay Anik had written on the topic, 'How should students be responsible citizens of the country?' It was for the 'Better Citizens Project,' a new program introduced in school for all class levels.

Uma smiled and took a deep breath as she heard Mrs. Tandon praise her son, how well Uma and her husband had raised him, and how thoughtful he was as a young boy. Uma thanked and told her how grateful she was for her guidance. She did not tell her how stressed the home situation was for Anik. Restraining her emotion, she ended the conversation with her son's teacher.

All the years of her working as a teacher, to pay for Anik's expensive school tuition, was finally paying off. 'Grow up and be a good human being first, my son!' She sighed, leaning her head back in the car seat as she closed her eyes.

Uma gazed out the window for a few minutes. Her thoughts suddenly drifted to Mr. Nirmal Sengupta. She recalled the day Lalit started his first job at his company. He had given Lalit fatherly advice and introduced him to the team of co-workers. That evening, Uma had made a special dinner for Lalit and invited a few friends he knew then. Lalit wore the nice navy-blue suit, a shirt and a tie that Uma bought him. She had been thrilled for him. Lalit bought Mr. Sengupta a cigar box knowing how much he enjoyed smoking cigars. No matter how adversely Lalit felt for Mr. Sengupta now, Uma sensed something else; she was not going to give up, not yet.

Uma quickly scrolled down the names in the phone's address book searching for Mr. Nirmal Sengupta's name. She missed seeing it the first time, she instantly felt anxious wondering whether his number got deleted. She calmed herself and the sudden frenzy gripping inside her. She scrolled down the list of names again, slowly. Uma saw the name—Nirmal Sengupta, Lalit's Manager. For a few seconds she stared at the name. Should she or should she leave it? She should. Uma punched the digits. A heavy voice sounded from the other side saying 'hello'. Uma introduced herself and asked if he recognized her name.

"Uma Sen?" There was a brief pause before Mr. Sengupta spoke. "Yes, yes! Of course! You are Lalit's wife! Hello Uma! How are you?"

She was a bit startled that he recognized the name quickly. She smiled, paused, letting his words sink in. She felt nervous. She thanked him and asked if he had a few minutes to speak to her.

"Of course. Please go on!" The voice sounded warm and friendly. "What can I do for you?"

"Well, it is about Lalit, my husband. He worked in your company for eight months. It was his first job. Do you remember him?"

There was silence for a short moment. Uma wondered what he might be thinking. She imagined his facial expression…controlled and insightful. Then, he told her that he remembered Lalit well, he had some issues at work that could not get resolved. He was sorry he could not help him.

"He does not have a job. He has already lost time that has affected his morale," she said.

"Did he never work after?"

"He had six jobs."

The brief uneasy silence made Uma impatient. She knew she had to be honest. Lalit's situation was not something she wanted to hide if she wanted to help him. Mr. Sengupta asked Uma why she was calling him instead of Lalit.

"If Lalit is hesitant for reasons beyond my complete understanding, should I not as a family member try my best to seek help for him?" said Uma as she heard her voice change tone, she clasped the phone tightly overpowered by sentiments for Lalit.

There was a brief pause, then Mr. Sengupta asked why Lalit left the other jobs.

"It was always out of disinterest, disregard. But there could be other reasons. I want you to talk to him to assess for yourself. I would like you to tell me what to do."

Mr. Sengupta cleared his voice. He did not wish to elaborate on what Uma said.

"I will do my best."

"I believe sometimes good comes out of someone else trying. Two hands are better than one," said Uma softly.

"I will give him a week. If he doesn't call, then I will call him." Mr. Sengupta spoke gently in a steady, contented tone.

Uma took a deep breath., she liked the sound of his words, she pressed her lips tightly. She was trying to suppress the sensations stirring inside her.

"Thank You! I appreciate your help, Mr. Sengupta! One more request—please do not mention to Lalit that I called you."

Mr. Sengupta grinned. "You can trust me. I won't tell."

Uma thanked him for listening to her and ended the call.

The car was nearing her mother's house.

Before she got off the car, Uma made a last call to Pinaki. She told him to inform Lalit that Mr. Nirmal Sengupta wanted Lalit to call him. Otherwise, Mr. Sengupta would make an attempt to contact him after a few weeks. He wished to talk to Lalit.

"What are you talking about? How did he suddenly remember Lalit?" Pinaki sounded bewildered.

"Lalit's first job was in his company. He knows Lalit well."

For a brief moment, there was silence between the two.

"And if you care for your friend, then please don't let him know I called you." Uma spoke in an unshaken voice.

"Of course, I care for my friend! How could you even bring that up!" Pinaki said loudly.

"Good. Then do as I told you."

"But…." Pinaki stopped.

"Is there anything you wish to ask me?" Uma asked.

"No, no. There is nothing. But, I know you have always been there for Lalit."

Uma withdrew from the conversation on purpose. She had nothing more to say. She said good-bye and ended the call.

Uma quickly wiped the accumulated tears rolling down her cheeks with a handkerchief. She bent her head low and closed her eyes for a few minutes. The car reached the front of her mother's house. Two houses away was Lalit's home. She looked up and stared at the house. His parents were still living there.

She looked down at the gold bangles on her arm that Lalit's mother had put on her on the wedding day. Instantly, she felt sentimental thinking about his mother. There was not a day in the years of living with her that she had made Uma feel like an outsider to the family. Not a single day.

Uma had contemplated on taking off the bangles and keeping them away, but now her heart ached—Lalit's mother had no part in this. As a matter of fact, she had always considered Uma as the daughter she never had. An overpowering feeling of benevolence gripped Uma, an image of Lalit's mother's gentle face and her fragile body draped in modest clothing flashed in front of her eyes. Why would she pull his mother into the tensions between Lalit and her? Uma kept the bangles on her arms.

"The feelings and sentiments for different people should not be mixed together. Everyone is their own self. Every relationship should remain separate."

Uma put the phone inside the purse and opened the car door.

Glossary of Bengali Words

Conscience

- Nayantara — name of the building (buildings are often given names)
- Kaftan — a long, loose dress
- New Market — a popular shopping area from the British colonial time
- Shingara — popular Bengali snack also known as 'samosa'
- Rickshaw — a hand-pulled cart used as a means of transport
- Bengali and Hindi — Indian languages
- Desh — a popular Bengali literary magazine
- Kadam — Bur-flower tree
- Bhalo! Bhalo! — Bengali phrase meaning 'Very well!'
- Chowringhee — A vibrant neighborhood in central Calcutta for business, shopping and entertainment
- Kurtas(pl) & Pajamas (Pl) — Indian cotton or silk outfit of top and bottom
Traditionally worn by men
- Dada-babu — Bengali word meaning 'older brother'
- Didi — Bengali word for sister or someone like a sister
- Rupee(s) — Indian monetary currency

The Landlady

T anvi watched the grey Volkswagen passenger van pull up at the designated parking spot next to the foreign students' office building exactly at 14:00 hours. The driver was a slenderly built middle-aged Caucasian man with a chiseled oblong face and a side-part haircut for his light brown hair; he was undoubtedly old enough to be someone's uncle. The appearance of the driver affirmed what the lady at the reception desk told the twenty-one-years old university student, Tanvi; a man in his late forties, who had been transporting foreign students to their host families for a number of years. He spoke German, Dutch, and also English; it was a pleasantly stated reassurance that communication with him would not be of concern.

Tanvi waited at the front steps of the building with her two pieces of luggage. Her medium-complexion shoulder-length dark hair, and average height wearing a heavy woolen sweater underneath her coat, a warm scarf around her neck, clearly showed that she was a foreign student from a warmer country, even though, it was the month of May. However, the ease with which she stood and observed the surroundings, without the kind of anxiousness that emerges during the first time in a new place, would make a person wonder if she was already familiar with the university town. She looked at the driver as he got out of the van with a notebook in his hand and walked with precision towards her. He wore navy-blue pants, a white half sleeved shirt and black suede shoes.

"Good afternoon! Are you Miss Tanvi Parekh? asked the man, confidently pronouncing the name exactly the way it was written.

"Yes."

"I am Eckardt Krüger. Nice to meet you!" He extended his hand to give a handshake.

"From India?"

"Ja, *aus Indien*." Tanvi answered in German, a bit surprised that he knew where she was from.

He nodded. "Welcome to Germany! I will drive you to your host family's house."

He glanced at the notebook to confirm the address. "Waldenstrasse 69, Flüssemünd?"

Tanvi quickly glanced one more time at the printed address on the housing accommodation paper inside her sling shoulder bag.

"It is correct," she said politely.

"*Gut!*"

He promptly picked up the brown leather suitcase and the black duffel bag and walked briskly towards the back of the van. Tanvi followed him. She watched him place the two pieces on the rack inside, strapping them with a belt so they stayed firmly in one place. She observed the accuracy of the singular activity, methodical and efficient, it was not about plainly flinging down the luggage on the rack. Then, he opened the van door for Tanvi giving a tight-lipped smile, displaying a restrained cordiality.

There were no passengers inside; the two rows each had three seats. Tanvi took a seat in the second row. The interior was immaculate—unblemished seats, spotless tinted glass windows, mildly fragranced. Tanvi had never seen such flawless passenger vans in her country. Eckhardt took his seat behind the wheel. He turned his head and told Tanvi in English to put on the seatbelt. She hesitantly pulled out the robust strap over her shoulder, feeling self-conscious about whether she was using the belt correctly. He waited till she finished.

"Thank you!" He looked through the rear view-mirror and nodded.

She had not anticipated the request for the seat belt. The drivers in her country did not make safety demands and most always, the vehicles did not have functioning seats belts. Even if they did, casualness with safety was normal.

The van started to move. It felt pretentious to be the only passenger inside, like being in a private chauffeur-driven car. She sensed the coziness of physical space with the absence of people. She imagined the inside of a van in her country with people squeezed tightly in their seats, more in number than the capacity allowed. The consensus accommodated flexibility more than comfort or discipline; she quickly recognized the difference.

She looked out the window at the sparseness outside; a meagre number of people on the streets, shaved lush green lawns stretched wide in front of old stone fountains, rustic cobblestone walking paths leading to the archaic brick structures of the university buildings. It was a Friday, in a quieter, less buoyant surroundings than what she was used to. She gazed outside. The novel scenario unfolded like a bright picture on a clear May afternoon, drained of external sounds or smells inside the van. She imagined a van drive in her country. This was refreshing and unusual.

Ekhardt maneuvered through the narrow streets, driving slowly, keeping his head straight. For a short while, he did not say anything, and then, all at once, he slowed down, pointing towards the direction of the Old Town, the famous Main Street that stretched to the city hall. He gestured to the Church of the Holy Spirit, the most famous church of the university town. He said she would soon have the chance to walk on one of the longest pedestrian zones of Europe, filled with baroques and renaissance facades; sample the pretzels from the stands at the side of the walking path; and relish the German Bratwurst or a hearty German meal in one of the restaurants. He said to be careful on the narrow lanes; there were no sidewalks and it was a free zone for bicyclists. He spoke like he knew the town like the back of his hand.

Tanvi was glad that he volunteered to speak on his own. She was still trying to accustom her mind to the things she absorbed around her.

"Is it your first time in the university town? Eckhardt asked.

"First time in Germany." She answered looking at Eckhardt's partial face in the rear view-mirror.

"I noticed you speak German."

"I do." She wondered if her response changed anything; possibly favored the opportunity to use the native language as well.

There was a brief silence.

Tanvi did not elaborate on the extent of her German education. The intense language study had trained her ears to distinguish the sounds and be thoroughly cognizant of German structures and words. She would have to explain, if he wished to know, how some of the Indian languages and German share a historically linguistic closeness with their Indo-European family roots. But, she knew he was only asking out of curiosity from the little he heard her speak.

"Your host speaks German and English," Eckhardt said.

"That's good to know."

He spoke while looking at her through the rear-view mirror.

"The bus schedule would be provided for you by your host."

"Thank you." She appreciated that he made her aware of the little things she did not know. However, she did not think he would speak more than the brief confined informational statements he imparted to her.

The van came onto a road along the Neckar River. A stunning scenery of green wooded slopes came into view. Amidst the exquisite greenery, a majestic red sandstone structure emerged, perched on the slopes of the mount *Königsstuhl,* first constructed around the1300s. The landmark had been destroyed and rebuilt over time. Ekhardt gestured with his hand towards the structure, the castle, saying that a one-time visit might not be enough; there was plenty to appreciate inside historical monument, its several landscaped terraces and the stunning view from the castle top looking into the Neckar valley and the Rhine Plain. He pointed to the Old Bridge which connected the two banks of the Neckar River; he said everyone should stand on the bridge at night, and breathe in the mesmerizing beauty of the castle's nocturnal illumination, an enchanting experience that would remain in mind forever.

Tanvi listened; the words captured her thoughts. She had not expected the driver to speak with so much fervor. Perhaps, it came with his job as a chauffeur to enlighten foreign students with the long-established scholarly town of his country. He listened attentively when Tanvi asked him questions; he answered befittingly, without amplification, maintaining a low voice. The informational narration diverted her attention temporarily from the spurts of homesickness that raced within her, and the sense of contrast between the two worlds, her home in India and Germany.

After a half hour, Eckhardt said they were in the town of Flüssemünd where she would be staying. He continued describing, how the small town had got its name, it was the location where the Neckar and the Elsenz rivers merged, meaning 'the mouth of the rivers.' He pointed to the villages inside the hills connected through trails where people did their promenade, with a *Biergarten* on the way to rest and relax. His every spoken exposition was imbued with meaning for their significance, explicit and entreating. He passed through the town with narrow cobblestone streets, every so often, she saw churches that stood along the way with their elegant architectural styles, remnants of the past that were treasured, and maintained and that shaped the town's character. For all Tanvi saw and heard, there lingered an inconclusive pondering. It was as if she was listening and absorbing someone else's spoken words rephrased from history books or travel magazines.

But they were not adequate. She did not know what she was looking for. She was still pondering. All she knew was that she was hoping to experience more.

The streets led inside the residential pockets, sparsely populated; houses clung to slopes, with red and pink geraniums blooming inside the window boxes. The car drove uphill for a few minutes, taking a few turns, then, slowly stopped in front of a timeworn house with a low picket fence and a gate. It was the last house on the street before the threshold to the woods and trails.

"We are here, Waldenstrasse 69," Eckhardt' said as he quickly got out and opened the door for Tanvi.

'Waldenstrasse', an appropriate name for the street next to the woods, Tanvi thought, '*Wald*' meant 'wood' in

German and '*Strasse*' was "street." Eckhardt hastily took out the luggage and placed them on the sidewalk, away from the street. Tanvi thanked him.

"*Ich wünsche Ihnen einen guten Aufenthalt in Deutschland!*" Eckhardt said politely as he shook hands with Tanvi, he did not say anything further. He swiftly got in the van, gestured a hand wave, and drove away. Tanvi stood for a few minutes. She instantly felt confounded by the briskness of pace; there was no exchange of extra words, as if a clock were ticking keeping track of time delayed by inessential discourse.

Tanvi stood on the sidewalk and gazed at the house and its surrounding. The low wooden gate opened inside the property, stone steps led to the front entrance door through a meagre patch of grassy area. From the front, the house appeared to be a one-floor structure, but Tanvi noticed the steps going down from the side of the house. She picked up the suitcase, slung the duffel over her shoulder and opened the gate. She was thinking of ringing the doorbell at the front entrance, she thought it was the right thing to do, when she suddenly caught sight of an elderly woman coming out the front door, quickly making her way towards her, a mature German shepherd followed behind the woman. The woman must have heard the noise of the gate. Surely, she was expecting Tanvi. As she came closer, Tanvi noticed that the woman's eyes were focused on her with eager interest, and the anticipation to greet her. She had a rosy white complexion, hazel eyes and neatly coiffured course short ash-blonde hair. Her physical characteristics instantly brought to mind the picture of a well-put-together elderly person. She appeared to be significantly more than middle aged, poised and vigilant. She wore a light-colored floral print flared summer dress that dropped below her knees; it complemented her full-figured tall body. Her thin skin-toned stockings matched her leather strapped sandals. The woman came close, commanded the dog to sit, and then, she stretched her arm to shake hands with Tanvi, with a jubilant expression on her.

"I am *Frau* Carlotta Möller, the landlady. I am delighted to meet you!" She spoke while holding Tanvi's hand tightly, her eyes gazing fixedly on Tanvi's face that made Tanvi momentarily self-conscious. Instantly, she began expressing exuberantly in German how charming Tanvi was, how her dark eyes shone like the stones of onyx and her lovely black hair was different. She was thrilled to have a young Eastern girl in her home as a house guest. Pleasantly surprised at her florid exuded words, Tanvi laughed.

Eyes like the stones of onyx? Who speaks in such poetic language these days? Amazing!

But, still, she found the woman distinct and engaging. Tanvi expressed thanks and introduced herself graciously, realizing that she was probably the first Eastern girl Frau Möller had hosted.

"Did you have a good journey?" Frau Möller asked.

"Everything was fine."

"*Gut!* Delays can be exhausting for the body. You have travelled a long distance. Follow me, please." She spoke in German assuming Tanvi understood the basic phrases, after all, she had come to attend a German university. She told her to leave the luggage at the front door and she would help her take them down later.

Tanvi could not believe such an offer from a woman her age.

"Oh, no! I will bring them myself."

Tanvi walked behind her, treading cautiously on the stone path that lead to the wooden flight of steps going down from the side of the house. She watched how Frau Möller walked down steadily without holding the railing. Floral bushes were clustered on one side of the metal railing, the other side was the side wall of the house. The steps landed on a concrete patio enclosed inside a high lattice fence. Beyond were the woods, green and tranquil, not even the sound of birds could be heard. Briefly, Tanvi soaked in the natural silence, the unusual quietness that drowned out any type of human made noise. Even the bustling humanity that she was used to seemed lost somewhere. She felt the coolness of the air, a kind of pastoral earthy fragrance permeated the surroundings.

Frau Möller opened the entry door. They stepped inside a spacious furnished room. Tanvi was immediately struck by the interior, she had not imagined the place to be so perfectly organized from what she had noticed from the exterior appearance. The room had two neatly made single beds, two night-stands, two medium wooden study tables with chairs, a sizeable antique wooden almirah and a wooden dinette table for four people. They were efficiently placed in appropriate areas of the room. The beds had clean comforters, pillows and lightweight blankets. A rectangular wooden mirror with foliage motifs hung close to the two large windows with pull-down shades and white curtains. The worn-out wooden floor was partially covered with area rugs and there were no pictures on the wall.

"This is where you will stay," Frau Möller said.

Frau Möller led the way inside to the kitchen adjacent to the room. The confined kitchen space had cupboards, a sink, a refrigerator and a window. She opened the drawers and showed Tanvi the cooking utensils inside, the specific use of each utensil and the pots and pans arranged inside the cupboard. There were plates, cups and saucers in another cupboard, coordinating in colors and designs, arranged with four of each on one shelf. She showed how to use the four-burner electric stove, how to use the toaster, and how to turn the water heater on and off. The white refrigerator was narrow in size; it had definitely lived its life in appearance, but still functioned. Frau Möller mentioned that the exhaust fan should be turned on if she cooked Indian food, because the small window above the kitchen sink was never opened, along with the windows in the bedroom area; an alarm would sound if they were opened by mistake.

"We do not want to trap the nature's inhabitants inside," she advised in a somber tone.

It was no surprise that with the onset of summer, there were insects that fluttered in the woods and Tanvi instantly understood her concern about keeping the windows closed. But what amazed Tanvi was that how much she paid attention to the well-being of the natural creatures.

Then, Frau Möller opened another door from the bedroom which led to a toilet room and a separate shower room with a white vintage porcelain clawfoot bathtub. A wooden towel closet was outside the bathrooms, each shelf stacked with a specific size of towels, four neatly folded on each shelf. She said to turn on the hot water heater a half hour before a shower, and to never forget shutting it off after, otherwise an alarm would sound. She spoke with astonishing ease, and was precise, like she was programmed to give instructions to foreign students who in her understanding bore diverse living habits.

"I hope you feel comfortable. If you need anything, anytime, please call me." Frau Möller pointed to a button on the wall, she said that if Tanvi pressed it, she would hear the ring upstairs.

Tanvi tried to digest the different types of calling or alert system in the one apartment. A solitary encumbrance suddenly took hold of her, all at once she felt isolated and wistful inside the systematized place.

"Thank you for showing me everything," Tanvi said politely.

"You are not missing your family, are you?" Frau Möller asked softly disregarding her response.

She must have observed something on her face and was quick to express it, Tanvi thought.

"No, I am fine."

Tanvi had no intention of expressing the complete truth; it was her first time alone in a distant country, and furthermore, she had never stayed in a room alone next to the woods.

Frau Möller smiled and nodded feeling satisfaction to the response. She waited a few minutes reflecting on something. Then as she started going up the stairs, she turned and asked,"Should we both converse in German or English?"

"Whatever you wish."

"Then, both. *Manchmal Deutsch*, sometimes English."

Tanvi smiled. "*Klingt gut!*" She was amused by the way Frau Möller responded. Then, she waited till she saw Frau Möller walk up the stairs.

Tanvi brought down the suitcase and placed it on a luggage stand. She laid out her two notebooks, her two pens, a Duden dictionary and a writing pad on the study table. She had the class schedule, and the professor's name in the envelope mailed by the university. She needed to find the street and the building once she reached the university center. The map that the university provided had the street and building names highlighted, she could reach every place on foot.

She arranged her clothes, outerwear, toiletries bag and a small fabric drawstring bag with earrings and necklaces inside the almirah along with the two Indian saris for special events folded separately in another bag. She did not own any formal Western outfits; the two long printed-skirts, two plain waist-length beige blouses, and two black pants were her formal attire for conventional occasions. She hung the three sweaters, two jackets and she kept her pair of gloves and the woolen scarf inside the drawer. She looked at them and thought they were the types of clothes and accessories she would take along to trips to the Indian hill stations in the winter. She knew eventually the warm clothing would be useful for the initial winter days she would spend in the town.

She put the two Indian spice boxes on the kitchen counter in case she felt like having Indian food. She had brought recipes with her. Normally in her country, it was her mother who did the cooking, but now, looking at the place, she did not think she would do much Indian cooking for herself here either, taking into account the small kitchen and the spice smell that could permeate through the house. She was not sure how much Frau Möller would accommodate exotic smells, especially when Tanvi did not know what her personal taste was like.

The sunlight was bright outside, though it did not reach as far into the inside of the room. The light was shaded by the greenery of the woods. Without the natural screen, the sunlight would have penetrated through the glass window and warmed up the room quickly. Now, she felt the comfort of the shaded room, dusky and cool.

She walked around the room trying to get a feel of the place. It was sufficient for two people, even three. She wondered if the presence of a roommate would have given exuberance to the quietness, Frau Möller had not mentioned about another person sharing with her. She definitely seemed like the person who would clarify every detail and leave no doubts.

Tanvi stood in front of the large window near the bed, gazing at the woods across, astonished by how a dense wooded area was behind the house, tranquil and vigorously alive. The abundance of arboreal surroundings would fascinate her family back home when she writes to them. They would imagine a bungalow inside the *Ranthambore National Park*, the famous tiger sanctuary, concealed from the hustle of the human world standing amidst the flora and fauna, she thought. But, then, they would also wonder how she felt in the night when silence compassed the place and darkness prevailed, listening to the stridulating sounds of crickets and the buzzing of fireflies.

She kept her eyes fixated on the lone trail from the window. It went deep inside. How easy it would be to get disoriented if she went for a walk by herself, she thought. Even if she followed the trail, everything was the same inside. She had never walked inside the woods; she had lived her whole life in a city. She wanted to know what it was like, but not just yet, she had to be confident with her sense of direction.

There was nothing around the house that gave the impression that Frau Möller had a family living with her or that she entertained people. The physical presence of homes on the street was no consolation. She saw no one on the street from the partial view of her kitchen window. Whether they had neighborly connections with Frau Möller, she would not know. All she knew was that the woman hosted foreign students from the university, her home was not offered as a public rental apartment. She was a bold woman living alone with her dog.

A sudden knock on the inside door interrupted her thoughts. Tanvi quickly went and opened the door. Frau Möller stood holding a large tray with food items.

"I have brought some things for you to eat and drink," she said as she carefully walked inside and placed the tray on the dinette table.

Tanvi had not expected her to bring a tray full of prepared food for her, walking down stairs. Tanvi was pleasantly astounded.

"It is so kind of you, but you didn't have to go through so much trouble."

Tanvi stared at the assortment of items; a porcelain platter with ham slices another with onions, tomatoes and pickles, a third one with slices of *Käsekuchen*, a basket full of German rye bread slices, a butter dish, a glass container with whipped cream and a jug of cold milk. There was cutlery, a cloth napkin and a paper napkin. Tanvi could not help reacting to the neatly arranged things on the tray.

"You have prepared so much!"

"Who knows how long ago you had a proper meal," Frau Möller said without giving much importance to Tanvi's words of geniality.

She sat herself down at the table with the tray in front of her and examined carefully all the things making sure she had everything in order to prepare the food with her own hands. Tanvi watched how she carefully took a slice of bread, spread thick layers of butter, and placed two slices of ham on top.

"You must eat well to stay healthy. You are far from your family," Frau Möller said as she kept her eyes on the bread spreading the butter on the second slice.

Tanvi smiled; she told her she would be fine. She pulled out the chair across from her and sat down.

"I can make the sandwich myself."

"You are my guest. Let me welcome you."

Tanvi did not say anything. She was not sure what kind of hosting etiquettes Frau Möller preferred. It was clear she was accustomed to taking control. Moreover, she was the host.

"You look youthful. You must be twenty, right?" Frau Möller suddenly asked diverting the topic, giving a quick glance at Tanvi.

"Twenty-one."

"See, I was close. The Foreign Office mentioned something like that." She glanced at Tanvi again as she placed the sandwich on a plate with a few pickles in front of her.

"I was your age once. It was tough for young girls in my time. If you were attractive, even more so." Then she suddenly stopped.

Tanvi smiled and nodded, unsure of what she was trying to say. She sounded self-assured. At her age, so much could be on her mind, even though, she appeared resilient. She watched Frau Möller carefully put a large slice of cake on a plate and smeared it with cream on top.

"There! Never leave out the cream." She slid the plate gently in front of Tanvi.

She generously kept preparing one item and going to the next. It felt like she found something engaging and fulfilling to do after a long time.

"Are you living alone?" asked Tanvi curiously.

"For the last twenty-three years. How old do you think I am?"

"I don't know," Tanvi said hesitantly. She did not want to make a wrong guess.

"I am seventy-five."

"I would not have guessed. You look younger."

I have always looked younger. *Immer*! I worried less even when things were *schlecht*. It was the only way to keep the mind controlled. I had to do it for myself so I could retain my heedfulness to the surroundings," she said in a decisive tone while taking a deep breath and wiping the cream-covered knife with the paper napkin.

Tanvi gazed at her face, she wanted to know more about the woman, and if she had a family, unsure how Frau Möller would react to enquiries about her personal life.

"You have a quiet home," Tanvi said instead.

"I am used to the quietness."

"The woods are lovely next to the house."

"Nature gives solace. It is why profound feelings emerge when you connect with it."

Tanvi had not thought along those lines, but she thought the woman spoke the right words.

"Do you have your family nearby?",

"You mean my children?" She shook her head to a no answer.

Frau Möller paused and did not say anything for a few minutes. She kept arranging the things on the tray without looking at Tanvi. She was going to need time to get used the new guest, but Tanvi faintly sensed the woman would not have trouble, there was something about her persona.

"Have you read European history?" Frau Möller suddenly asked.

Tanvi told her European history was a major part of her school curriculum.

"Then you must know about the Second World War."

Tanvi nodded and told her that she had read about the eventful years in history books, in literary pieces that depicted real stories dealing with the subject.

"We were living in it," she asserted.

Then, without going off to any other topic, she spoke about someone named Hans and then paused.

"This is a difficult conversation, but I feel no hesitation to speak to you. You and I should not remain strangers in the same house," she said calmly without showing any kind of agitation.

Tanvi nodded and did not say anything for a short moment.

"Hans was your husband?" Tanvi asked softly.

"My first love, the only one. Hans was damaged."

Abruptly, she got distracted from what she was saying. She briefly halted and placed the glass of milk in front of Tanvi.

"Even if you don't eat, never forget a glass of milk. Milk gives you energy. You need energy when you are young to keep the body strong."

The sudden assertive words sounded strange in the midst of the conversation about her husband. What's more, Tanvi barely knew the woman. Her own grandmother would have spoken like her. She understood that elderly people had similar tendencies no matter what part of the world they were from. They did not follow formalities; they spoke out what they believed to be the truth.

"It's not a blurry image," she continued, pointing to her eyes. "Look! These have seen everything." Frau Möller took a deep breath, unfazed. She spoke choosing her words carefully.

"Hans lost his right leg. His left shoulder and hip were dreadfully injured. He was disabled. He was thirty-eight years old when he was removed from service. They segregated him because he was incapable. He would have been killed like the others who could not serve. Lukas, his good comrade had the heart to care. He helped Hans escape. Hans stayed temporarily with Lukas's family, but safety was not guaranteed, not in his condition."

She paused and cleared her voice and giving a quick glance at Tanvi.

"But, one must believe, the good exists… it does! An unknown family gave Hans shelter till he was brought home to me. He lived a year hidden in fear with them. No man should have to live like that!"

Tanvi did not say anything, allowing her to continue what she was saying. It was the first time Tanvi came close to someone's life traumatized by war.

"Now, with my story…" Frau Möller resumed, again.

"Hans was a stranger to me when he was brought home. Every ugliness of hardship was on him. He suffered psychological trauma, physical handicaps crippled his movements. When I looked at him, I thought, he was not the boy I had fallen in love with at eighteen." Frau Möller paused. She pushed the tray aside. Her feelings were heavy. Again, the topic changed. She told Tanvi with an affectionate bossiness to eat more if she was hungry. Tanvi recognized the unusual mannerisms of her personality.

"Lucky are those who get the chance to see light before taking their last breath. The pain could not go on forever. *Naja*," She took a deep breath and quickly stopped.

"Do you wish to listen further?" Frau Möller asked looking at Tanvi incase Tanvi found no meaning to her stories.

The question felt strange. This was the moment Tanvi could have said 'it's too sad to listen' but she didn't. She did not wish to draw back, now that she saw Frau Möller wishing to tell her the details.

"Yes, please continue," Tanvi said sympathetically.

"Hans lived with me in this house for eleven years. His physical presence was remote. He sat in the wooden chair in his room and gaped vacantly out the window every day. I would hold his hand and stroke his face so he felt the warmth of my touch. He sensed nothing. He felt no connection, no emotion. He stared at me. This went on for days but I kept doing my part. So did the doctor who came every week to see him." Frau Möller paused. Again, she looked straight into Tanvi's face.

"You see, I was a sensible woman. I was not focused on myself thinking of how my feelings were being hurt, how much I had to endure, how much responsibility was on me alone. Why would I waste myself on such thoughts? My man was suffering more than me. At least I could express, he couldn't even do that." She paused and dusted the bread crumbs from the table. "Everyone has struggles of their own. The best solution is to sincerely recognize that at heart."

Tanvi had nothing to say, at least not at that moment.

"You are not tired, are you?" Frau Möller asked. Her voice sounded soft and concerned.

"Oh, no! I am fine." Tanvi felt touched by her caring words and how alert she was even about the person listening to her. The woman could go on talking about her life without paying attention to the other person, but she did not.

Frau Möller looked at Tanvi's face and nodded. She waited briefly before speaking again.

"Then one day, something unusual happened, like a miracle. Hans stared at my face with wide open eyes like something had sparked in his brain, like he had to immediately express the urgent feelings to me. He started making audible sounds, pointed to the bottle of cognac and gestured with his trembling right hand for me to sit next to him. He mumbled a few words, I understood exactly what he said. I poured him a little cognac in a glass and sat near him holding the bottle. He watched me like a hawk, a stunned expression on his face. "*Alles night gut!* *Alles night gut!*"

He spoke the words, and tears rolled down his cheeks. It was then I realized his words broke through the chained emotions resting beneath the scars. That's all that mattered."

Frau Möller stopped. She turned her head looking outside, gesturing to the woods, keeping her emotions suppressed.

"The nature is calm, isn't it?"

Tanvi nodded smiling.

Then, she focused on her story, again.

"In those times, I had to be conscientious, even though, my life was disadvantageous in every way." Frau Möller gave a sigh of dejection. "But, the end is what counts. Then it is easier to forgive the past. The day finally arrived when the kind liberators reached our doors. While it may have implied, we could never know what joy meant in the troubled world we had been living in, it certainly was a day to rejoice, a day to reap the blessings." She stopped. Tanvi saw the glistening tears in her eyes.

"Hans was lying on his bed, awake, staring at the ceiling. I came close and whispered in his ears-Hans! Hans! *Alles gut! Alles gut!*" Frau Möller stopped briefly, as if to gather her emotional thoughts.

"Hans must have sensed something because he turned his head towards me. He opened his mouth to say something, but the body had no strength to utter the words. He started to whimper like a child, the news was gradually dawning on him. At that moment, I was over-whelmed, caught between looking at him and at what was happening in the world outside. I told him, 'Let's celebrate Hans, Let's have some champagne!' I bent close and put my head lightly on his chest, I felt his trembling right hand on my head. This time I heard the strong whimpering noise inside his chest, the tussle of joy and pain deliberately making him shudder.

Four days later, it was Sunday morning, I came into his room to open the shades to let light in. I did not hear the heaving sounds of his breathing so I stood by his bed and said, "Hans! Hans!" He lay still with eyes closed. Immediately, I touched his forehead. It was cold. I put my hand on his chest. There was no breathing, so I felt his pulse… he was gone. My Hans was gone. I don't know what time it happened."

Frau Möller wiped her eyes taking out a small handkerchief from her dress pocket.

Tanvi listened, stunned; it was not the kind of story she thought she would listen to on the first day in a new place. She told her how sorry she was to hear about her husband.

"Hans left without troubling me. That's the kind of man he was. He was at peace when he left."

The last rays of afternoon sunlight fell through the kitchen window casting brightness in the kitchen and the dining area, it lightened the dimness of the mood.

"Did you not wish to move from here?" asked Tanvi

"Move? For what? To find happiness?"

"I mean, away, to new surroundings."

"Do you think the memories go away when you physically move?"

She answered with an unconvincing smile. She patted her chest gently. "They are here, all here, inside. You can't get rid of them."

Tanvi kept quiet. She felt relieved that the woman was able to share her thoughts to her.

"Please don't mind me telling you about my life. Images recurred before my eyes. Hans and I were married when we were your age."

Tanvi nodded quietly.

"In those days, many women let go their dreams. That was how it was. However, I never let go, I accepted reluctantly. Young men sent me love notes to meet them, to go to dance clubs or movies. They thought I was lonely. I had my man in combat. Why would I think about them? Of course, I was charming, I dressed elegantly. What they did not know was that I would wait for my man no matter how long it took him to return home."

Tanvi kept looking at her face. At her age she had an enticing appearance, with deep-set eyes and a Romanesque nose that brought out the aura of authority in her. Even after so many years, the woman spoke as if the stories had happened in the recent past. Most often, the reality is unfathomable in dreadful situations, it becomes coherent as years pass, impressions describable, and still alive in the heart.

"Women like me have never really been young. We lost the lustiness early. I realized a part of life got skipped in me. I got older."

Tanvi smiled. "Everyone gets older with time."

Instantaneously, Frau Möller reacted. Her facial expression changed; she smiled reluctantly with raised eyebrows.

"Some are forced to get older against their will."

Then a sudden silence exposed an impatient tense vibe.

"Do you have a boyfriend in your country?" Frau Möller asked abruptly with no connection to what she was saying. The change of topic was so unexpected, uncomfortable, Tanvi shook her head hurriedly.

"It is wise. Nowadays, there is less true love."

Tanvi couldn't think of anything to say. She reached for the glass of milk and took a sip.

"I am not looking for a relationship. I have plans to pursue higher education."

"You have come to the best place. Educated girls are a pride for society." Frau Möller paused and looked at Tanvi's face as if she recalled something.

"Your culture has goddesses. They are embodiments of power. Aren't they?"

Tanvi nodded smiling. The comment was most startling coming from her.

"You know that?" Tanvi asked.

"*Natürlich, ja!* Your culture impressed our famous writers, philosophers and historians through the ages. Such fascinating philosophies! Even my father found inspiration in those thoughts."

She narrated how her father had pictures of Indian Deities on the walls of his office. She was a young girl and she had never understood the pictures. She always thought her father was an unusual, eccentric man because of his high regard for those images.

Tanvi stared at her, a rare affiliation with someone in the distant part of the world who spoke about Indian deities that inspired a family member. The thought felt strange.

Frau Möller wiped the tray handle with a corner of the napkin. She arranged everything back on the tray methodically, separating the porcelain wares from the crockeries, and folding the napkin neatly just as how she had brought them down. There were still bread, meat slices and milk left.

"It's important what you see and hear as a young child. The Good. They stay with you."

She continued speaking out her thoughts "They are like poetry and music—beautiful sounds, rhythms, words. No matter where you are, how long the time lapsed, they reemerge in your mind, all at once, at some time."

She paused, spreading the cloth napkin over the uncovered food.

"Have you heard of Beethoven?"

Tanvi was trying to follow what she was saying, her sudden questions extending to different thoughts threw her off balance. Of course, she had heard of Beethoven! Her family has a whole collection of his music. Her uncle is a pianist living in Vienna. She had been to his concert where he played one of Beethoven's compositions.

"An extraordinary musical genius." Tanvi said.

Frau Möller described how Beethoven's *Moonlight Sonate* plays every night when she sleeps. It was the same when she was a young girl living with her parents. Her father was a historian, her mother worked as a jewelry designer. No matter how occupied their life was with their jobs and family, her father had a house rule that all members of the family had to follow. Every evening he wanted the family together in their living room to listen to Beethoven and Bach. It was his way of honoring the creative geniuses. She said there were many.

Tanvi gazed at the woman. The life she had lived sounded so unusually captivating. Was it because she experienced a challenging historical time filled with uncertainties that urged the inner feelings to be transported to the artistic ideals for a mystical initiation?

Tanvi thought Frau Möller understood it that way.

"Music alters human consciousness. It disentangles from the ordinary. The sound is a divine force mentioned in many ancient philosophies." Frau Möller paused. Then she said how it was the same for bad memories—they also came at a person like a powerful indication not to forget. They impinged on the heart with disturbing emotions.

She got up from the chair, pushed it aside. She walked towards Tanvi slowly and then took her hand and kissed it.

"Soft hand. Never let it harden, never! It has been my pleasure talking to you. I wish you a pleasant stay here. Please lock the door after I leave."

Tanvi stood still, looking at Frau Möller as she turned around to pick up the tray. She found no words to describe the woman; she had never encountered someone like her. She was the kind of person who you could listen to and feel she had something substantial to say, every time, whether about herself, about someone else or about the world she knew. All the things she spoke about didn't always happen with people Tanvi met in her regular life. There was something distinctive and unprecedented about the woman's life.

Frau Möller carried the tray declining the help of Tanvi and walked up the stairs with a steady posture.

The next few weeks passed quickly. Tanvi was occupied with classes, presentations, and exams. She attended closed group seminars on literary topics, presented reports, greeted students in her classes and had coffee and *Kuchen* on Main Street. She learnt about events at the university...the student trips, the dance clubs, and the popular bars where students met at night to hang out. Most students conveniently found the places where they desired to be, but she didn't quite feel the desire to partake in such socializing. She returned home sooner with pastries and bread for Frau Möller. She rarely saw the woman go anywhere other than to the local shop at the bottom of the hilly slope to buy the daily needs.

Theo, the dog, invariably, greeted Tanvi at the door. She would stroke him on the head while he sat in front of her, acknowledging the bond of their friendship. Frau Möller appreciated Tanvi's generous gesture to bring her pastries, she kissed her every time on the forehead and uttered, "Bless you, my child!" When Tanvi asked how she managed without anyone's help, she grinned and told her the story of her husband's sister, Klara, who lived in the next town and helped her with anything she needed. She spoke how Klara had remarried a younger man of twenty-five at the age of fifty-eight when her husband passed away, and how she thought she found a life of renewed energy. Even her two best friends had distanced themselves from her watching her keenness in youthful activities at a later age. But two years into the marriage, the young man told her he was in love with a younger woman, he said sorry and left her without any regrets. He did not lose anything, she had been providing the home and the financial security.

"You think maturity comes with age, not always. Klara was whimsical and she learnt her lesson." Frau Möller uttered feeling sorry for Klara. She continued talking about how she mentored Klara to live her life gracefully and advised her that every situation becomes an opportunity for improvement of one's life. After a few months, Klara took to volunteering in an *Altenheim*. She said she still volunteered, but fewer days of the week.

One time, when Tanvi visited her after her classes, Frau Möller brought out a silver plate, shaped like a grape leaf with grapes vines embossed on it. She said it was a wedding gift from her grandmother. She used to put her bracelets on it, she had a few favorite ones that she wore often. The plate had remained locked up inside a storage box under the bed; she had no use for it.

"I want you to have it."

"Me?" The word blurted out of surprise.

"Do you like it?" Frau Möller asked.

"It has special memory for you. Why would you give it to me?"

"Please do not divert from the question. Do you like it?"

"I do, of course!" Tanvi answered uneasily.

It was then that Tanvi discovered further how unusual the woman was. She told Tanvi how she was like the daughter who had come to live with her in Germany. An intense yearning filled her face. Her voice sounded thrilled.

Tanvi did not know how to react to her benevolent outpouring of feelings. She realized Frau Möller would not have given her grandmother's wedding gift to just anyone.

"I don't know how to thank you enough!" Tanvi said.

"Please! Never go into such formalities! The gate to the heart should be kept open. I will never know what your native land is like, but at least, I will have the pleasure of knowing that I have given a piece of my happy life to you."

Her words, chaste and trusting, struck a chord in Tanvi's heart. She felt sentimental. Then she stopped briefly and gazed at Tanvi's face as if she was preparing to tell her something that she not had not told her before.

She told her that she had never had children, she had lost and distanced from everyone in her family sooner than she was supposed to. It was not the kind of life she had imagined she would have.

"Not everyone gets what they desire. It is why you dream, imagine. The unseen is good for the mind. They take you everywhere…. to places, to people, to the life you don't see with the physical eyes. There is vision inside the mind that brings contentment."

She took out a black and white photo from the pocket of her dress and showed Tanvi—the picture of a young couple. Tanvi immediately guessed it was Frau Möller and Hans. She gazed at the photo, emotionally stirred. Frau Möller's charming appearance was like the beautiful young actress from old movies. Hans was an attractive young man. The picture must have been in their youthful carefree days.

Frau Möller grinned and said they had been teenagers, both nineteen in the picture.

Tanvi restrained her emotions. She told Frau Möller that she admired how she had held herself together in an exemplary manner through the years.

She grinned and then waited for a short time without saying anything.

"There are two sides to everything; the one you see, the other you don't."

She spoke softly and then she got busy making hot chocolate for Tanvi.

Tanvi waited outside the Roten Stiere restaurant to be seated at lunch time. She had walked past the restaurant a few times in the past, seeing students and tourists relaxing together. Today, she noticed the usual mix of young and elderly people, couples who had probably finished classes, and a few men taking a break between classes. She wanted to be inside, amidst the animated ambience and the peals of laughter of young people.

"Do you mind sharing a table with three people?" A waiter came towards Tanvi asking cordially as she stood at the door.

The question was unusual, Tanvi hesitated to say yes; she was uncomfortable with the idea of sharing a table with strangers, a custom she was not aware of.

"There are two men and a woman at the table," said the waiter trying to see if it made Tanvi's decision easier. "Sorry, it is a busy time."

"All right.

"This way, please!"

Tanvi walked behind the waiter and reached a table at the opposite end. He gestured to the empty seat with his hand. Tanvi smiled at the three people already at the table; they said 'hello' and continued talking to each other. They conversed in German and their friendship demonstrated agreeable mannerisms. It was awkward to be at a table with strangers, but she realized it was a common etiquette when there were no empty seats in the restaurant.

Tanvi checked the menu; she picked the asparagus soup, the herring salad and a lemonade to drink when the waiter came to ask. She couldn't help overhearing the German conversation as the group chatted and ate. At one point, she even thought of asking something to start a conversation, like if they came to the restaurant often or how long did the restaurant stayed open. Then, suddenly she heard one of students speak up.

"Are you a student in this town?" one of the men asked courteously.

Tanvi nodded. " I am here for six months."

"My name is Erich. My friend's name is Eugen and his girlfriend is Annika," he introduced promptly. Tanvi shook hands saying hello. Each said what they were studying… international law, mathematics and political science. They introduced themselves in English, Tanvi introduced herself and told them where she was from. Erich asked what her native language was. He was surprised to know she spoke two native languages of one country, Hindi and Bengali.

"My parents are from two states with different languages." Tanvi explained.

"Interesting,"

"*Und Deutsch?*" asked Annika grinning, looking at Tanvi.

"That's the addition I made to my treasury," Tanvi said jokingly.

"Then you understand what we are saying at the table. Very convenient," said Erich.

They all laughed.

The waiter brought the salad and the glass of lemonade for Tanvi. He served beer to the others. The conversation continued in German. They seemed to appreciate that Tanvi understood and spoke German; they spoke at ease in front of her. Whatever they said, Tanvi was spontaneously part of the conversation. They asked what she thought about the university town and they covered topics on events happening in the university, weekend life for students and traveling by train to different parts of Germany.

For the first time, Tanvi learnt about *Mitfahrergelegenheit*, a shared ride with people going to the same destination. It was how university students traveled in Germany. Erich mentioned he was making a trip to Göttingen. He said he had pinned a message on the student notice board with his phone number, but he had not heard back from anyone. Students usually responded quickly if they were certain about their travel plans.

Tanvi told him about her interest to visit a family friend in Göttingen. But she didn't think she would get an enthusiastic invitation from Erich to share the ride with him. He wrote his phone number on a paper and promptly showed his student identification card and license. She was struck by his conscientious attitude. It never occurred to her that she needed to look at the documents. She had not made up her mind.

"The ride is three hours and twenty minutes, at most," said Erich.

"*Vielen Dank*! I will let you know."

The ride-sharing idea was new to Tanvi. It sounded adventurous and unconventional. She could not fathom the idea of traveling with a stranger in her country, but somehow, speaking to the student, she did not feel apprehensive, especially because he had voluntarily shown his student ID and driver's license. It was how many university students shared rides to places. He and his friends appeared to be accomplished university students. He told her the date and time of travel, approximately when he would reach Göttingen, and that he normally did not take a break unless it was necessary. She was amazed at how precise and organized the plans were. She never imagined students could be so organized even planning for a trip three hours away. She quickly jotted down her phone number and gave it to him.

"My landlady answers the phone first before she connects me to the caller." Tanvi told him.

The three students chuckled as they exchanged glances at each other. Tanvi felt a bit awkward. They probably never had to experience living in the home of a landlady.

"It's quite alright." Erich answered making the situation seem normal.

Tanvi had not realized how prevalent ride-sharing was for university students till Erich had told him. It was going to be her first long distance trip in Germany if she decided to take the trip. She would leave with Erich the following Friday afternoon at 13:00 hours after her last class and return by train two days later.

Perhaps, she would learn something more about Göttingen when she mentions to Frau Möller. Knowing the woman, she might even give a good history lesson about the place before the trip.

As usual, Frau Möller looked pleased to see Tanvi coming to meet her as she carried the small pots of flowers from outside to put them on her garden window in the kitchen. She told Tanvi that she followed the same ritual every summer for three months, she had the plants absorb sunlight during the day, and the rest of the year, they received either moderate or no warmth from the sun.

She invited Tanvi to sit for a few minutes as she prepared the *Apfelkuchen*. Tanvi followed her into the kitchen. She inhaled the aroma of apples and noticed things lying on the kitchen counter. Frau Möller pulled out a dining chair for Tanvi and asked her to take a seat while she brought out the already prepared large round baking dish to show her the batter mixture; cinnamon, nutmeg, lemon zest, thinly sliced apple quarters pressed into it, and raw sugar sprinkled on top.

"It looks delicious!" exclaimed Tanvi.

"Hold your patience. You will get to taste a popular German apple dessert."

She placed the baking dish inside the heated oven and quickly became occupied with making hot chocolate for Tanvi. She kept busy without looking anywhere.

"What a coincidence that you stopped by on a Wednesday, when I make the *Apfelkuchen*. Bless you! You will be the first to taste."

Tanvi was about to ask why Wednesday, but she heard her start to speak.

She said there is a tradition of baking in the middle of the week, but she had her own reasons. Hans proposed to her on a Wednesday and *Apfelkuchen* was his favorite. Even the night before he took his last breath, he had a tiny bite from her plate.

The woman carried her past while living her present life. Tanvi wondered whether there was a time when she did not recall what she had or did; it did not seem likely. Sometimes, she drifted off into thoughts talking to herself, may be because she momentarily forgot there was someone in the room with her. She said she would give a few pieces to Frau Kranz who lived across the street. Frau Kranz came often to see Hans. She had knitted mufflers, caps, three sweaters for him. Now, her hands were weak so Frau Möller made things for her.

Tanvi let a few minutes pass after which she prepared to tell Frau Möller about her travel plan. She noticed that Frau Möller had an unusual way of talking to herself as she washed things in the sink and cleared her kitchen counter, putting things in places. She kept murmuring to herself about how every little thing had to be managed, not neglected, and how the value of things is determined by how they are taken care of. She appeared extensively conscious about her things belonging in the right places. Tanvi had perceived her mindset from the first day she met her.

Just as she finished putting the last utensils in the drawer, Tanvi mentioned about her plan to travel to

Göttingen on Friday using the *Mitfahrergelegenheit*. Tanvi thought Frau Möller had barely heard what she said, when she stopped short and quickly turned her head and asked in a stiff voice.

"A boy or a girl?"

"You mean the driver of the car? A boy," answered Tanvi cautiously thinking it is what she wanted to know. "He is studying international law."

"Will there be other passengers?"

"I don't know. Most likely it will be with him alone."

Frau Möller turned around and looked straight into Tanvi's face.

"Do you know him?"

"I met him once."

Frau Möller's expression abruptly turned tense, her face blushed pink. She found the response objectionable.

"I cannot let you make a plan like this! Traveling to Göttingen with a stranger? I will not allow!"

Her assertive response suddenly perturbed Tanvi.

"It's just a three-hours ride," said Tanvi softly trying not to excite her further.

"He is a stranger—you don't know him!"

Tanvi told her that he was a university student and she had seen his student identity card and license. She repeated again, trying to make her understand that he was a genuine person.

"I didn't think this would ever happen!" Frau Möller said firmly.

Tanvi watched the somber expression on the woman's face. She felt her heart racing inside, wondering what her final pronouncement would be or if maybe she had already given her final words. Frau Möller brought the chocolate drinks to the table, pulled out a chair and took a seat across from Tanvi.

"How dare he ask you to come with him? How dare he!" she uttered in anger, her face flustered up.

"He asked out of courtesy. It was fine."

Frau Möller bent towards Tanvi as if she wanted to give her a thorough explanation.

"Listen, my child! I have seen the world more than you. You should not trust someone so quickly into the acquaintance. You don't know how he thinks. Your light tan skin and dark eyes are attractive."

Her words stunned and distressed Tanvi. She thought her reasonings were way out of line.

"He is not how you are imagining. Besides, he left everything up to me to decide." Tanvi felt she had to lengthen the explanations to prove her point. She suddenly felt sorry for Erich and his cordial invitation.

The timer buzzed loud, Frau Möller got up abruptly to shut the oven.

"Did he say he likes you?" Frau Möller immediately asked turning her head.

"Oh, no! Of course not!"

"Some are like that. They don't say, they feel inside," she said confidently.

"Please don't worry. I will be fine."

"I can't let you go with him."

The words sounded like the final verdict, then not a word further about Tanvi's plan.

Frau Möller returned to the table and grasped Tanvi's hand, leaned forward and looked into her eyes.

"There is something I must tell you. You must listen. I have seen horrors that have happened to young girls with my own eyes. I was once pulled into that situation, I escaped, hid, then I ran home. I remember every moment... what I did, what thoughts ran through my mind, how my heart pounded as I ran. You don't want to know." Frau Möller paused, she took a deep breath.

Tanvi recognized the woman was imprisoned in her past.

"I don't want to leave this world taking those memories with me but I have to. Do you want to?" Frau Möller asked firmly. She definitely saw herself as person whose experiences mattered more than what Tanvi had to say.

"It was a different time in history. It's not like that now."

It did not matter how Tanvi explained, Frau Möller remained obstinate about how she felt.

"You should have spared me of this discomfort," she remarked heavy-heartedly suppressing the rising temper in her voice.

I am very sorry."

"Did he have girl with him?"

Tanvi shook her head, she felt disappointed with the interrogation.

"That means he is eligible." Frau Möller concluded. "He found a good opportunity to spend time with a girl."

Tanvi recognized it had been a mistake bringing the subject of the shared ride with her.

"I understand a young girl's mind too. You might have felt something for him. Come with me!"

Frau Möller spoke confidently with whatever assumptions she made with her imagination. She got up quickly and walked towards her bedroom. Her behavior seemed urgent as if she had found more stories to convince Tanvi.

The impression of things created by Frau Möller dispirited Tanvi extensively. Her own liberty to do things was being intervened unduly; the sudden over expansion of protective love made a normal situation complicated.

Frau Möller hurriedly walked towards her bedroom. There was something very efficient about her movements. She went to the wooden cupboard and opened it. Tanvi saw the sweaters and blouses hanging inside. She saw her pull out the middle drawer located below the clothes section on top. What she saw next overwhelmed her in disbelief, she was horrified. Her heart started to thump hard. She immediately gasped in shock.

Frau Möller took out a heavy solid metal pistol from the drawer, she held it in her right hand as she pushed with her left hand to close the drawer.

"I would allow you to go on the trip with one condition...this!" Frau Möller held up the pistol in her hand and showing to Tanvi. "If you carry the pistol with you," she said firmly.

She said it would stay in Tanvi's bag, unloaded; it was for her safety.

"No! No! I would never do that!" Tanvi said out loud before she went further talking about the pistol.

"You have to be prepared for dangerous unforeseen circumstances."

She explained how the pistol had history tied to it. It was kept in her home in those years of war for safety of the people at home. She felt thankful no one used it.

"For safety? That is crazy!" Tanvi blurted out excitedly.

She felt her heart pounding, this was an incident that went far beyond what she had ever imagined or ever encountered in her life.

She hurriedly told Frau Möller that she needed to leave right away, she wanted to think about her travel plans. She refrained from bursting into tears. As she speedily walked down the step to her apartment confused and shaken, Frau Möller called out her name from behind telling her not to worry. She would bring a few pieces of the warm *Apfelkuchen* for her soon.

Tanvi hurriedly went to her room, locked the door and lay face down on the pillow. She found it impossible to comprehend what had just happened…. Frau Möller telling her how a pistol could safeguard her, the meaning behind the gesture was like an intense pounding heartbeat. She clearly understood Frau Möller was trapped in the agonizing memories of the life she had lived even as time moved on. The woman acted thinking of her own bitter memories. But, there was something Tanvi understood clearly; she could not allow herself to feel senselessly aggravated by her behavior. Fearful memories had fossilized in her; she realized she could never comprehend the extent of the fear that still resided in Frau Möller.

For the next two days, Tanvi stayed downstairs without talking to Frau Möller. One day, after returning from the university, she found a covered glass container with pieces of *Obsttorte* and a plate of hazelnut cookies on the table; Frau Möller had left them for her while she was away at the university. Tanvi stared at the desserts with uneasy sympathy. There was no doubt, the woman endearingly cared no matter how the circumstances turned out. She was neither ashamed of what she had told Tanvi nor she had any ill intention; it was Tanvi's safety she had been thinking about.

Distrust happens either from ignorance or from experience. The woman still possessed the images of the unpredictable situations of her younger years. Who knows how the memories were playing in her mind. For her, they were real. For Tanvi, it was what happened in movies, not in real life.

Tanvi evaluated her plan. She decided not to act against Frau Möller's wishes even if they sounded precarious and whimsical. She thought she had no right to judge her.

In the evening, as Tanvi prepared dinner for herself, a phone call interrupted her activity. It was Erich. His voice sounded grim as he told her about a phone call from Frau Möller.

"I understand she feels responsible for you, but it still does not justify how she spoke," he said.

Dumbfounded by his words, Tanvi became quiet. She had no idea Frau Möller had phoned him and now she suddenly regretted accepting Erich's cordial offer.

"I am sorry. I did not know she called you," said Tanvi politely.

Feeling dismayed, she told him how Frau Möller was fearful of strangers; and she had told her daunting stories from her eventful past. But, she still felt uneasy that Frau Möller called Erich without telling her anything.

"I think Frau Möller thinks about her younger years."

"It was many years ago." Erich understood what she meant to say.

"Time does not erase everything," responded Tanvi.

Erich kept quiet.

"Perhaps, she found solace in narrating to me what she lived through. She was my age when exciting things happened in her life, then, as the years progressed, she was plunged into distressing moments. She had to concede to unpleasant situations," Tanvi said politely.

"There were many like her."

"Of course, many 'ones' make a large number. Each has a story to tell, each one matters. I just happened to meet one person."

Tanvi was not sure how Erich perceived her words.

He asked cautiously if Frau Möller would prefer to meet him in person.

As much as Tanvi knew it was an obvious better choice, she sensed the tension that could arise. He could be scrutinized with interrogations.

"Probably not."

"Are you sure?"

"Yes." Tanvi did not mention about the pistol that Frau Möller had wanted her to carry. Who knows what impressions he would have about Frau Möller. Tanvi had heard segments of her life, she respected her for the circumstances she bore. There was trust and affinity that Frau Möller placed in Tanvi. A person's soul stretches towards the spirit that embraces the pain, honors the resilience, and recognizes the worth of sacrifice.

"I am sorry it turned out this way," said Erich.

Tanvi was quiet. For a brief moment, she wished things were different. Somehow, the unusual way she had met Erich at a table in a restaurant, suddenly seemed to matter less than the fact that she found him to be a good person even if she did not know him at all. She felt a little drawn to him. This was just the kind of moment, when she could gripe about Frau Möller's whimsical behavior and get the chance to pour her heart out, about how unprepared she had been for what Frau Möller had told her, and for the pistol she had shown her. But, Tanvi, did not tell him anything. He would not know what she had lived through and what a benevolent heart she had.

"Thank you for offering the ride," said Tanvi.

"It would have been my pleasure to drive with you to Göttingen."

After a brief pause, Erich hesitantly asked. "Are you sure things won't change?"

"I am sure." Then, she became quiet for a short moment.

"It was nice to meet you, Erich! *Tschüss!*"

Erich softly said "*Tschüss*" and hung up.

Tanvi sat still for a few minutes staring at the phone.

No matter how a situation begins, no one knows with certainty how it will eventually end.

Tanvi put the dinner back inside the refrigerator and closed the light in the kitchen.

On Friday, Tanvi took the bus to the train station to catch the 13:15 pm train to Gottingen. It was an overcast afternoon. She felt subdued and anxious, she was traveling alone to an unfamiliar place to meet people for the first time. It was not how she had planned to travel. The train departed close to the time she had planned to share the ride to Göttingen. She sat next to the window gazing outside as the train trundled out of the station, passing the platform and buildings, then, swiftly, picked up speed, fast. It traversed the countryside, old towns and villages. The sky was hazy, fine rain drizzled down the window pane, gloominess prevailed throughout. Without the sunlight, the landscape appeared to have lost its gaiety. Cars drove on the country road across the field in the same direction as the train. The train speeded disregarding what was around. It was simpler for cars and trains; they could disregard anything; they just followed commands. It was complex for people; they struggled with choices, and sometimes opted for paths for the well-being of all, serenity, denouncing what they would have personally wished.

Six months swiftly came to an end.

On her last evening Tanvi sat at the study table in her room. She inscribed the last few paragraphs in her journal, events of the last few days that she had missed jotting down. The six months had sped by more quickly than she thought.

The room door was half open, when she heard the soft knock and the words *"Darf ich hrein?"*

Tanvi walked up to the door.

"Of course! Please come inside!"

Frau Möller entered carrying a magenta woolen scarf and a cap in one hand. She held a gift bag in another. She came close to Tanvi, cheerfully wrapped the woolen scarf around Tanvi's neck and put the cap on her head. She said she had knitted the scarf and cap for herself during one of her the winter vacations from school. Tanvi walked in front of the wall mirror to look at herself. She stared at the intricate woven designs on the scarf.

"These are beautiful! You had skilled hands from an early age."

"Nothing matters now. I am glad I found someone to give to."

The words moved Tanvi, but she felt conscious accepting the gifts.

She looked at the woman wearing a bright green-and-white printed flared midi dress with a white belt. For the first time, she realized Frau Möller had a commendable presence of mind even though at certain moments her strong-willed behavior overshadowed the gentleness she conveyed. She was not the kind of woman who would restrict her relationships to people she knew, her ways of thinking did not allow considerations for where the person was from, to interfere with the love she felt for the person.

"Valuable things should remain with those who know how to revere them. I am afraid I am gradually losing those qualities."

"Seems like I am the fortunate one," Tanvi said choking with emotion.

Frau Möller took out the box from the gift bag and opened it. Inside was was a fine silver bracelet with a red tulip flower embossed on it.

"My father gave me this bracelet for my first dance with Hans."

This was something Tanvi had a difficult time accepting. Instantly, on first impulse, she told her assertively that she could not accept the valuable gift of her father. She told her exactly how she felt.

"I cannot accept the gift."

The words did not convince Frau Möller. What she told her next, stirred her more.

"You must accept it for the love that was given to me and for the love I give you."

She responded assuringly with force of her words. It felt overbearing and determined.

Immediately, she said something even more persuasive.

"When I am gone, the bracelet would have no one. The thought is more painful for me. Would you not care for the hurt that I would feel?"

Without saying anything further, she put the bracelet on Tanvi's arm and kissed her hand.

"Please forgive me if I dismayed you with everything I said and did." She continued talking while looking at Tanvi pleadingly. She was talking about the day she showed Tanvi the pistol.

"I didn't mean to horrify you. I have become immune to shock; I don't realize the intensity of the feeling that I cause on others. A part of me has become like a stone, frozen in arrogance. The other part senses the emotions and feelings. There is a struggle inside me. Amazingly, the softer senses triumph every time, unquestionably. Then I realize I still have the worth, I will not give up and allow the heartless behavior to control me."

"I am sorry that I reacted in a shocked manner. I have never faced a situation like that in my life."

"My intention was to protect you."

"But the pistol was such an extreme!"

Frau Möller hesitated to say anything; she looked at Tanvi in a keen manner.

"Do you think I am an insensible woman? Do you?"

Her words gripped Tanvi intensively.

"Oh no! It would be my misfortune if I did not understand you."

"I despise harming people. I despise anyone who does! But I believe in protecting when circumstances endanger the loved ones near me."

Frau Möller grew quiet. She sat down at the table, tears shimmered in her eyes. For a while, she did not say anything.

"I apologize for being so hard on you. I overreacted thinking that you were drifting away to a stranger whom I could not trust."

"I had to tell you how I was traveling to Göttingen. I didn't mean to overwhelm you."

"There is no pain higher than losing people you love and losing oneself in bearing the pain. Sometimes you lose a large part of yourself."

Whatever Frau Möller said, they were true. But, her feelings were complex which made the sensation unsettling.

"For everything one loses, something else is retained. I have my life, and my good conscientiousness and I still believe in the goodness of people." Frau Möller reassured herself.

Tanvi nodded smiling. She gazed at Frau Möller's face. However difficult it was to understand her, she saw a woman with a firm conscience. She felt compelled to tell her she was a great person in her eyes regardless of the situations that took place.

How difficult it would be to describe her persona to someone who has never met her, Tanvi thought as she stared at her face.

"Will you take back good memories of your stay?"

"Of course!"

"Good!" Please call Erich back. He called you when you were out."

Tanvi became quiet. She looked at Frau Möller's face perplexed, caught off balance by what she said. She never thought a call from Erich would unexpectedly get added to their conversation. Even more, that Frau Möller would ask her to call him.

"He called me?"

"Maybe he cancelled the trip to Göttingen."

Tanvi suddenly felt startled and somewhat exhilarated by new emotions inside her. She could not believe this was happening. She tried to suppress her sensitivity thinking Frau Möller would discover everything about her feelings instantly.

It is just a temporary reaction, it will pass, Tanvi calmed herself as she saw Frau Möller looking at her.

"I was once a young girl like you…." Frau Möller gave an emphatic smile. There was a short silence. "Things happen. It is how life works." She paused. "Will you come back and see me again?"

"I want to."

"Be certain that I am alive before you come. It is a long way for you. *Verstehen Sie?*

"You will be here, I know." Tanvi's tone softened. Such endings made her emotional.

"Sie sind mein liebenswürdiger Vögel. Der Vögel hat den guten Sinn."

Then, Frau Möller sat for a few minutes quietly, contemplating. Accumulated tears glistened inside her eyes. The first drop would break free, anytime. Tanvi gazed at the face soft-heartedly.

Frau Möller slowly got up, walked to Tanvi and took her hand. She kissed it one last time.

She said she had arranged for a taxi to take her to the Frankfurt airport. She said she would serve a full German breakfast the next morning before Tanvi left.

Then, she softly uttered, *"Naja, es gibts nicht mehr zu sagen. Lebwohl !* She wiped her eyes with a handkerchief.

She walked in a steady manner towards the door.

Glossary of German Words

The Landlady

•	Ja, aus Indien	Yes, from India
•	Bratwurst	a type of German sausage
•	Promonade	An adopted French word meaning walk
•	Biergarten	an outdoor area where beer and local food are served
•	Ich wünsche Ihnen einen guten Aufenthalt in Deutschland	I wish you a pleasant stay in Germany
•	Frau	woman; usually used before the last name of a woman
•	Manchmal Deutsch	sometimes German
•	Klingt gut	sounds good
•	Duden	German language dictionary
•	Universitätsplatz	The the main university area
•	Hindi and Bengali -	Indian languages
•	Ranthambore National Park -	A national park situated in northern India in the state of Rajasthan. It used to be a royal hunting ground for tigers and leopards, now preserved as a tiger sanctuary.
•	Käsekuchen	cheese cake
•	Immer	always
•	Schlecht	bad

- Naja -   expression equivalent to how one uses "well"
- Alles nicht gut   all not good
- Alles gut   all good
- Natürlich, ja!   of course
- Moonlight Sonata   Beethoven's popular piano piece
- Altenheim   Home for the elderly people /Senior Home
- Apfelkuchen   apple cake
- Mitfahrergelegenheit   shared-ride opportunity
- Und Deutsch?   And German?
- Göttingen -   An university town located in the central part of Germany
- Obsttorte   Fruit Flan
- Tschuss   an informal way of saying 'good-bye'
- Darf ich hrein?   informal way to ask "May I come in?"
- Verstehen Sie?   Do you understand?
- Mein liebenswürdiger Vögel sind Sie!   You are my adorable bird
- Der Vögel hat den guten Sinn   The bird has the good sense
- Naja, es gibts nicht mehr zu sagen. Lebwohl!   Oh well, there is nothing more to say. Farewell/ Live well

Fourteen Days

For several years, she had assiduously absorbed the images of the city, listening to stories from her parents about the place that was their native home. By the time she was six, she recognized that she was the daughter of immigrant parents, as a consequence of being born and growing up in a culture different from where her parents were born and grew up...Calcutta.

Through the passing of years, she had started to learn the traditions of her parent's culture, their significance, the customs, the stories behind them. She had become fluent in their native language, Bengali, though she sensed early on her accent was not like her parents. Sometimes, she would joke with them about the way they pronounced the English words or how they wrote the arithmetic number seven and added the extra vowels in Spelling English words. She understood their ways stemmed from how they had been educated. But what she did not often comprehend were the perspectives from which they explained the cultural concepts. She thought she needed to wait for a later time to understand them with clarity.

Her parents' journey began in the early seventies, before Anjali was born, when they came to America as a newly married couple from Calcutta, her father pursuing a doctoral degree in engineering at a university in Indiana and her mother hoping to continue her graduate studies in molecular biology in the course of their stay. Progressively, they earned degrees, received internships, and adapted to a lifestyle as married researchers. With the passing of each year, the hope of returning back to Calcutta grew grimmer as they established themselves in careers that provided inspiration and opportunities. They jostled with memories of their families they left behind, the city that was their cultural haven; sensational, diverse, blending traditions and the present day—place that thrived in the unbounded energy of the everyday life.

They now embraced another side to their life; the choice to make America their second home. They moved to a suburban town in the mid-west, bought their first home, adjusted comfortably to their American life and subsequently welcomed their daughter Anjali into the world.

It was not unusual that the name Anjali was quietly discounted as she entered school; the usual shearing of the foreign name evolved to the convenient short form, Julie, and so was her natural acculturation to the place she was born and grew up in …. thinking, speaking, believing what she readily related to, understanding the world around her based on the circumstances in which she lived, a mind-set pertained to the reality around her.

The suburban Midwestern American town was Julie's home, a place with sparse communities that stood in the solitary peaceful landscape. A few miles from her home, the rolling plains stretched out to open corn fields, the humanity occasionally visible when she looked out the window. The events of each day stayed as constant as the days before. Even with the transformation of seasons — from the highly anticipated moment in the summer with the arrival of sweet corn to changing colors of the trees to the snow, sleet and bare branches... there was nothing unanticipated that happened where she lived, as if life followed a definite complacent order, conserving to one kind of routine living.

It was her home-life that occasionally brought out the animated, unusual flavors: the cultural attributes of her parents' native home that she tried to be part of, at times clouded with hesitation because of traditions she little recognized, other times sprightly celebrating occasions with families who had connections to Calcutta like her parents. Occasionally, she would be in the midst of the larger Bengali crowds of Chicago celebrating traditional festivals, standing amongst unfamiliar faces with whom her parents jovially chatted. She saw men immersed in discussions of world politics, about scientific research taking place in the renowned American universities, sharing scores of the cricket matches in England and Australia and animatedly exchanging views about the shops that sold the best types of Bengali fish. She listened to their vivid expressions in Bengali, and attentively watched the women in elegantly dressed saris candidly clamor about their recent visits to Calcutta. By the end of every event, Julie felt she had absorbed a high dose of her parents' native socializing culture, even though she never felt a complete part of everything.

Her short trips to Calcutta as a young girl were meant for initiation to relatives who she thought had coddling mannerisms, speaking forthrightly in Bengali accented English so that Julie felt at home and at the same time, they made sure she remembered their names and how they were related to her. So much of the time in those moments was spent in cheerful ambience of embracing people that the aura of the place lifted her spirits stimulatingly. Calcutta is such a happy place to be, she thought. It was in those moments that she wanted to believe she was part of two cultural sanctuaries: the one she belonged to, comfortable and befitting to her perception, and the other, her parents' native home, endearing but remote.

Now, at the age of twenty-five, completing an internship in social-psychology at an university five and a half hours from her home, Julie was inwardly eager to reconnect to the place that remained distant from the time she experienced as a child. The faded images of her childhood were now mere good feelings, fascinating though inadequate in many respects. Nevertheless, she had the advantage of the language that could bring her closer to the culture to fulfill her curiosities.

The taxi stopped in front of the guest house on a late morning in February. The house was on a street with a long row of two-storied single-family homes in one of Calcutta's newer suburbs. The houses stood close to one another. Each was distinct in design, with a marginal plot of land in front yet their exterior appearance had the similar three features: a front porch bedecked with a few cane chairs, a narrow rectangular veranda on the second floor, and a black metal front gate. Definitely, the homes characterized a fresher offbeat presence compared to the legacy of ornate colonial architectures she saw on her drive from the airport.

Getting out of the car, Julie stared at the sizable two-storied sizable brick structure with matured trees on both sides. A male gatekeeper wearing a khaki uniform came forward to ask for her name, and then he pulled open the gate. Julie was instantly struck by the illustrious surroundings of the guest house: white-and-maroon dahlias blossomed in clay pots at one side of the driveway. There were yellow chrysanthemums that thrived in narrow flower beds along the wall of the house. A line of luscious green *Debdaru* trees in front hid the house from the street's view. At first sight, the property did not appear to be a guest house, it was like the safeguarded single home of an established family.

She smelled the blend of unfamiliar extrinsic aromas…. burning incense, exotic spices, pungent mustard, musky smell of jasmine that permeated the air. She immediately felt transported to a place she had never been. She saw birds flutter past every so often, like they belonged to the trees of the neighborhood and gentle street dogs that wandered around aimlessly. She heard faint vocal music coming from the house next door, but She saw no one from the partial view of the street from the kitchen window. Julie stood staring at the uniqueness of the surroundings; it was unusual. She recollected nothing from the images of the stories she had heard from her parents or from being at a place like this as a young girl. Her last visit to Calcutta had been when she was eleven years old.

The taxi driver took out her suitcase and the backpack from the car trunk. An elderly man in a black sweater and pants, with a woolen scarf wrapped around his neck, hurriedly walked up to the luggage.

"Guests don't carry their own luggage. I am here to help you," said the man just as he noticed Julie pick up her suitcase. He introduced himself as the Girish, the caretaker. He lived with his wife and child at the further end of the driveway in a tin-roofed shack with brick walls. He gestured to the place used as a bedroom, with a minor area for cooking food. Julie noticed the two vintage Indian rope beds inside the garage, and a clothes string with folded saris and white *kurtas* hanging. A woman stood with a broom in her hand staring at Julie as she walked towards the entrance door. Suddenly, everything felt outside her familiarity; Julie never thought a garage could be utilized as a complete home for a family.

The owner of the guest house was a woman named Kalpana Deb, an unmarried sixty-seven year old retired teacher who lived on the first floor and converted the second floor to a furnished contemporary guest apartment.

"Miss Deb is inside," said Girish as he placed the luggage in front of Miss Deb's apartment.

Julie had learnt about the guest house from an advertisement inside a Bengali magazine her mother subscribed to. Her parents had approved of the place on reading the description. Julie arranged everything on the phone speaking to Miss Deb. The woman described the accommodation by reading the list of furniture, and utilities and the number of rooms and the bathrooms. She emphasized on the cleanliness of the place and that there was a gate-keeper on duty twenty-four hours a day. Julie had not seen any pictures. The place had sounded like what she wanted…a clean, safe arrangement to stay in for two weeks.

Girish opened the door. Julie entered the apartment of Miss Deb while the caretaker went upstairs to leave the luggage. The sunlit living room had four windows with curtains drawn on both sides. The basic sitting arrangement with a large sofa, two arm chairs, and a wooden center table with a flower vase gave an image of a formal place. On the walls were souvenirs of places in India, the sole foreign decoration was an embroidered Chinese wall hanging. There was a small TV on a table in the corner of the room; it was covered with a white cutwork fabric. A part of the wall had been transformed into an inbuilt bookshelf lined with old classics and other literature. Julie noticed the works of Rabindranath Tagore, Ralph Waldo Emerson, Walt Whitman, Robert Frost, William Shakespeare, William Wordsworth gathered together on one shelf along with the biographies of Subhas Chandra Bose, Mother Teresa, Florence Nightingale Swami Vivekananda and others on another shelf. There was a black-and-white photograph of an elderly couple and another with two young girls in dresses, possibly a photo of Miss Deb's parents and the other of her and her sibling. The room gave an impression of a comfortable living, but no careless spending. Julie heard the sounds of utensils coming from the kitchen. She recognized the aroma of Indian spices; some of her mother's recipe's had similar smells.

A woman walked into the room keeping a steady gaze on Julie and appearing eager to see how the foreign guest looked like in real life. The woman was Miss Deb.

At first glance, Miss Deb seemed somewhat surprised. Perhaps she had expected a young Caucasian woman; Julie's accent on the phone had sounded completely American to her.

"Welcome to Calcutta. I am very happy to meet you," Kalpana Deb greeted Julie.

"Nice to meet you, Miss Deb! I am Julie." She folded her hands in the *namaskar* gesture, the greeting she had seen her parents do with first-time Indian acquaintances.

"Oh! You know that! I am impressed!" Miss Deb said greeting her back and giving a short spluttering laugh. Obviously, she had not expected a young person born and brought up in America to greet her with an Indian gesture. She looked at Julie with interest. The girl had good height, olive skin and attractive features. Her loose dark-brown hair fell to below her shoulders and her getup of blue jeans, a long-printed shirt and a light denim jacket gave every impression that she was a visitor from abroad.

"Are both your parents of Indian origin?" Miss Deb asked curiously giving a quizzical look at Julie.

"Both are Bengalis, born and grew up in Calcutta."

"I suppose Julie is your Western nickname?"

Julie nodded smiling. "You can say that. Anjali is the Indian full name."

Miss Deb smiled without saying anything. She kept her gaze on Julie. It was Julie's casual modest demeanor that drew Miss. Deb's attention. She had probably expected the foreign guest to demonstrate flaunting mannerisms or have a condescending attitude; instead the young woman appeared to be an amiable, balanced person who could carry on a comfortable conversation with anyone.

Miss Deb led the way towards the sofa and told Julie to make herself comfortable. Julie sensed from the woman's body language that she was solemn, and carried a kind of self-assuring vanity about herself. She was dressed in a crisp ironed dark green cotton sari with a mustard border that matched her blouse. Her shoulder-length course grey-and-black hair suited on her polished light complexion and her stylish fine gold rimmed eyeglasses. She maintained a moderately slim physical built and seemed to have adeptly taken care of herself.

"You have a cozy place here," Julie commented trying to ease the sudden newness she felt in the place.

Miss Deb grinned. "The smaller the place, the less on the mind. Would you like a cup of tea?"

Julie shook her head smiling, she had not expected the offer so soon into their acquaintance. She hesitated to tell her that she preferred coffee rather than tea.

"I heard drinking tea was religiously followed in Calcutta."

"A gratifying tradition of the past that continues," said Miss Deb. "Tell me, would you prefer some warm milk? A glass of Coca-Cola?"

"Oh, no! Please don't worry!"

Julie was conscious of her response. She sat looking at Miss. Deb as she collected a few books from the table and placed them on the bookshelf; she seemed like an organized woman. The tiny stud diamond earrings on her ears and a thin gold chain with a small locket around her neck made her classic attire appear austere. Her fine-tuned facial makeup conveyed a younger appearance than what Julie had imagined while speaking to her on the phone. She appeared cordial limiting the conversation to a fewer words rather than being spontaneous.

Miss Deb asked about the long journey from Iowa, and the international flight Julie boarded from Chicago. She said she had stepped out of India once for a short vacation in Singapore with her mother, most always her holidays had been within the country. But ever since her mother's demise two years ago, she never made any plans for travel. Her younger sister was married with a family so Miss Deb had to take the biggest share of the responsibility of her mother. It also meant unwinding herself occasionally in pristine surroundings away from the metropolis for a change of environment.

Her father, who had been an attorney passed away when she was twenty-six and since then the primary responsibility of her mother and the management of her father's lifetime savings had fallen on her shoulders. She thought she carried more burden than girls of her age, though she was fortunate to have the financial security early on. Her teaching career began in her mid twenties and she continued till she retired two years back.

"You have been a teacher for a long time."

"They were the best years of my life, I must admit."

"What kind of school did you teach at?" asked Julie eagerly.

Miss. Deb paused briefly, and looked at Julie in an enquiring manner, as if she did not understand what the question meant.

"I was a teacher at a private school in Calcutta, well-reputed and well established."

She elaborated further saying that the middle-and upper-class families of Calcutta sent their children to private schools. The schools had proficient teachers and followed competitive educational guidelines.

"Sounds similar to private schools in many parts of the world."

She gazed at Julie abruptly for a few seconds and stopped, as if it was irrelevant to talk further about the subject; she also felt she did not hold enough information about education in other countries. She moved on to talk about the winter weather conditions in Chicago and how people coped with air travel, then she enquired about everyday driving in snowy conditions.

"Winter weather must affect the daily life tremendously."

"People manage. Many states have severe winter weather, and people are accustomed to what it brings."

"Well, Calcutta will certainly be a treat for you! But don't get surprised if you see women wrapped in woolen shawls and men in knitted caps. It is still winter here without the snow and very low temperature."

Julie smiled, she thought the description was amusing. No sooner she completed talking about the weather, she suddenly seemed interested to know more about Julie's personal life.

"I suppose you have a significant other at your age." Julie could not understand why she would want to know so soon into their acquaintance. Besides, she was not her aunt or one of her cousins.

"I do." Julie answered smiling.

"I don't want to sound inquisitive, but is he an Indian-American man?"

"No, he isn't. His family is from Indiana."

Miss Deb nodded like she was not surprised, like she expected Julie to have a non-Indian man.

"It matters. Both partners need to be suitable for one another," she said in a decisive tone.

Julie nodded lightly; she was not sure what exactly she wanted to say.

"I suppose your parents were all right about you choosing yourself."

Julie grinned. "My parents had a love marriage of their own when they lived in Calcutta." Miss Deb gazed at Julie's face listening to what she said.

"Oh, did they? Then I assume your parents were alright with your choice."

"He is like a family member for them. My parents know it is about the feelings for a person more than what country the person is from." Julie said smiling at Miss Deb.

An uncomfortable silence settled in the room. Julie did not feel the need to say anything.

"I suppose whatever is accepted with love, cannot cause hardships. Unfortunately, it doesn't always happen that way," she said and immediately became quiet.

Then she quickly stood up and gestured towards the door to the wooden stairs at the lobby that led to the guest apartment upstairs. She said all meals were delivered to the apartment; she needed to choose from the menu kept in her room. Otherwise, the cook would prepare whatever she wanted.

"I would not recommend that you eat out. You don't want to fall ill in a foreign country," said Miss Deb.

Julie was about to tell her that she did not mind sampling a few popular dishes; she was adventurous and knew her limits. For years, her life had been consumed with studies and work, shuttling back and forth from classes, and then getting up early for work on weekends. Now, for the first time, she felt she had the flexibility to experience the strikingly contrasting place. She wished to make use of the opportunities in front of her.

But she refrained from expressing her personal thoughts to Miss Deb.

"Please don't worry about cleaning and washing, either. Everything will be done for you," Miss Deb said as she walked up the stairs in front of Julie.

Julie did not quite understand what the phrase 'everything will be done for you' implied, but she guessed the caretakers assisted with the daily household work.

The furnished two-bedroom two-bath apartment put Julie in awe. It was commodious even for six people. There was a sizable sitting and a dining area, a small kitchen with a refrigerator, and a gas stove with a cylinder. She could smell the newly painted interior and the shiny polish of the wooden cabinets. At first glance, it would not have occurred to her that guests frequented the place; it was immaculately kept.

"Very nice!" Julie uttered astonished.

"A reasonably new apartment. The location appeals to visitors because of the quietness."

Julie smiled while listening to her.

"We had a few tourists stay here," said Miss Deb.

"I didn't think tourists preferred the suburbs to the city."

"Everyone comes with their own purpose."

She went on to mention about two young women who came to do charity work in Mother Teresa's Home; she said they had visited Calcutta before. "No doubt, they preferred the quieter place to spend the night after an occupied day at the Home."

She said the the women had a dedicated mindset and she liked their calm temperament.

Then she spoke about another unmarried woman who came with an unusual purpose—the wish to search 'the soul of Calcutta.' She said she was eager to understand how a city like Calcutta, with its extraordinary vigor, spirit, compassion and a wealth of cultural enrichment…. survived amidst the visible heartbreaking poverty.

"She was right about what she thought and I wished her success in what she came to search." Miss Deb said assertively.

Then she spoke about another couple who made a stop in Calcutta on their way to *Shantiniketan*.

The couple was well versed in Tagore's life and works, with the woman, being a proficient singer of *Rabindra-sangeet*, which of course, made sense, as she had been singing in choir and performing solo Western vocal music for many years with her husband, a professional pianist.

But, then, Julie noticed a disapproving expression come on her face. Miss Deb mentioned about a group of three men who she said were the strangest of all. They came as city hoppers; Calcutta was their last stop. Every morning they left the guest house after an early breakfast at seven and returned past midnight. Miss Deb said she had instructed the gatekeeper to note the time they returned every night.

"I was glad they did not extend their stay." She said rolling her eyes.

"They must have been enjoying the Calcutta city life," Julie said casually.

Miss Deb shrugged, giving a doubtful smile without saying anything.

"Anything is possible! Obviously, they came to know I would not allow drinking, smoking, girls or loud music at the guest house. Sure enough, they found out about the entertaining places they could go to."

Without saying anything more about her guests, Miss Deb led Julie to the veranda, from where Julie could see the view of the street in front of the house. There were private homes all along on both sides of the street. Julie observed the animated surrounding; hawkers called out loudly the things they were selling: bikers whizzed past making ringing sounds, women in saris chatted loudly as they walked down the street. Julie saw how the hawkers parked their four-wheeled carts piled with fresh vegetables and fruits, in front of the homes as women bargained through their grilled verandas, trying to get the best price for the fresh produce. She saw clothes drying on strings on the terraces; bird cages hanging inside the grilled front porches and cats walking on top of the brick walls between the homes (they trespassed wherever and however they wanted to). She spotted two pigeons perched on the rooftop of the house across; they looked like domesticated companions, sitting quietly next to each other, their head turning from side to side, being watchful, awaiting something.

"Amazing!" Julie uttered softly. She was astonished by the completely different life, the morning packed with so many different scenes on one street. She remembered the time when her mother had told her how much she missed the veranda of her Calcutta home:

Your senses touch every significant, gratifying, stunning, questioning facets of human life happening in front of you watching from the veranda. The time passes ponderously and you find exuberant stories to share.

Miss Deb explained about the types of food offered in the guest house. Julie was surprised at the good variety of Western soups, sandwiches, cakes and pastries along with other ethnic choices on the menu.

"You will find food traditions of many cultures in this city," Miss Deb said proudly.

"Oh, really?"

"Throughout history there were many communities who made their home in Calcutta. You would not know who came from where. They have all blended together. They speak Bengali."

Julie recognized a few of the names of the Bengali dishes as she looked at the menu; they were what her mother cooked at home when she had Bengali guests for dinner. Growing up, Julie did not quite fancy the fish soaked in yellow colored curry sauces or the poppy seed dish made with ridge gourd and potatoes, and cauliflowers floating inside thick yellow lentil soup. She had wondered why her mother would go to lengths making such absurd dishes. But now, she wanted to sample a few, to learn about the cuisine preparations of the culture she was also part of. She realized she no longer had an aversion towards certain types of food which she had openly renounced in her unwilling teenage years.

Julie felt a burst of exhilaration waking up the first morning in the guest house. It took her a few minutes to gather her thoughts, and to decipher the faint sounds that came through the closed windows…radio music, the clinking sounds of cups and saucers, people talking in Bengali.

It was already seven in the morning. The morning light was still overcast from the winter dimness. There was something thrilling about the fact that she had spent her first night alone in a place far from what she knew as home. In fact, it had not been as confounding as she thought it would be; the guest house was as comfortable as any good standard bed-and-breakfast places she had been to providing even more benefits, such as lunch and dinner meals, and services from the caretakers. Miss Deb had asked Girish's wife to put up a mosquito net for the night for Julie just in case one or two randomly appeared even though mosquitoes rarely frequented homes in the winter. Julie had declined the idea of a covering on the bed; a netted tent tied with four strings on each corner of the bed frames on top. She would much rather breathe the open air inside the room.

She had stayed up late looking at the picture postcards of Calcutta she had bought at the airport. She jotted a few lines to her boyfriend of three years, Stuart. They were planning for a trip together after the completion of his doctoral degree in international relations.

She spoke to her parents on phone, they told her to drink filtered water during her stay and to connect with a few cousins on phone. Julie excitedly told them how stunned she was by the undemanding pace of life in her first contact with Calcutta at the airport.

"People found no urgency to clear spaces, they took their time walking and stopping, walking and stopping. I haven't seen anything like this!"

"Aren't you in Calcutta to relax?" Julie's father commented jokingly listening to her, her mother was downrightly amused.

"You are in the right place, Julie!"

Then, she told them about the taxi ride. The driver had steered through crowded parts of the city and she had found herself sharing the road with all kinds of traffic... buses, cars, rickshaws, bicycles, pedestrians, and even dogs. She saw decaying buildings on both sides of the road, their cracked columns, rusted railings and grimy windows; the sad hard-to-ignore remnants of the colonial structures that had been left as trademarks of the British heritage. Julie described the unbelievable scenarios she saw when the driver took the flyover. Men, women, and small children lay asleep under the flyover, like bundles of rags cast randomly upon the ground, a family sat around a bowl of rice, scooping out the white rice with their hands. Traffic drove over the flyover oblivious to the human conditions visible between the pillars of the walls.

"The sight was unthinkable!" said Julie. " I had never given thought to the necessity of staying alive. I guess I took it for granted."

"The agony and joy coexist transparently in Calcutta. You will experience both side by side," Julie's father said.

Julie described how she was overwhelmed by another scenario, a completely contrasting locality of open lush green land on both sides of the road: tall multi-story buildings stood in the midst of shaved green lawns;

palm trees and exotic flowering plants embellished the buildings' enclosures, like a protective wall against the dismal scenarios existing outside.

"Such an immense variety of scenarios that grasp the mind! I am stunned and overwhelmed; so many thoughts that normally mattered, slip past indifferently. Never have I absorbed such images of Calcutta as a young girl. I could vividly perceive that this was not a place that makes a person passive." Julie said to her parents before hanging up the phone.

Julie got up from bed and went to look at herself in the mirror. Her lightly tanned face was slightly weary from the travel and the hair revealed itself like it had been blown around by the wind, disorderly. She quickly brushed her hair to bring some order to her looks, washed her face and brushed her teeth. Surprisingly, her eyes did not appear as exhausted as they normally happened with long hours of insufficient sleep, she still felt energetic and enthusiastic after the first night.

She changed into pants and a long full-sleeved cotton shirt, and a light cardigan and she slipped into the strapped sandals she had brought with her.

These are the most refreshing change of winter clothes I would ever wear, she thought. No boots, no coats, no gloves and no snow to deal with for some days. Julie smiled to herself.

The sudden knock on the door got Julie walking towards it in a hurry. She thought it was Miss Deb or Girish wishing to tell her something. Instead, when she opened the door, there was a young girl standing, and holding a basket of flowers in one hand and, in the other, a small tray with a teapot in a tea cozy, a cup, a saucer, a small milk pitcher, a sugar pot and a plate with four cookies. For a brief moment, Julie stared at the girl immensely surprised. She did not know who the girl was; what's more, the way she skillfully held the tray of things dumbfounded Julie.

"I have made morning tea for you," said the girl softly, smiling.

"Oh…that is so kind of you!" Julie uttered gazing at the girl as she let her inside quickly in order that she could put the tea tray with all the things on the dining table. The girl walked in with bare feet, leaving the rubber sandals outside the door, and placed the tray on the table.

"You can keep keep your sandals on. The floor is cold," said Julie politely.

The girl shook her head. "They stay outside. I walk bare feet inside." Then she handed the basket of small white flowers with orange stems to Julie.

"These are for you, *Didi*." The girl's face had a big smile on it.

"For me?" Julie immediately felt touched when the girl called her "*Didi*", a name for an "older sister." Julie remembered the first time her mother had introduced her to an older cousin sister in Calcutta with the word. "Meet your sweet *Didi*!" At that time, Julie had no idea of the amount of love and respect the word also carried.

"These are beautiful! Thank you so much!" Julie sniffed the perfumed aroma.

"They are *Shiuli* flowers. I picked them from the garden early this morning."

"You got up early to pick for me? You are so kind!"

The girl blushed at the words, and grinned humbly keeping her gaze on Julie. From her facial expressions,

Julie could see she was delighted by how Julie spoke; perhaps she seemed different from the young women the girl normally met.

"*Mashima* has a flower garden in the backyard."

"Oh, really? What other flowers are there?"

"*Jaba* (Hibiscus),) *Bel* (Jasmine), *Kadam* (Bur-flower tree), *Rajanigandha*(Tuberrose), *Champa* (Champak), red, pink and orange roses."

The girl recited the names with enthusiasm and then described the characteristics of each incase Julie did not know.

"*Shiuli* flowers are not plucked from the tree; they are picked off the ground in the morning. The flowers perfume the air in the night, they cast off in the morning carpeting the green grass with orange stemmed flowers. *Shiuli* are offered to the gods in the morning."

She told Julie that every morning she plucked flowers for Miss. Deb's living room. It was one of the jobs she had to do. She also had to also take care of the guests who came to live in the apartment. She cleaned the apartment; washed, ironed and folded clothes for the guests, shopped for whatever they needed. Julie quietly listened, somewhat surprised.

"*Mashima* told me you live in a faraway land. She said you crossed the ocean by plane to come here."

Julie smiled. "That's true."

The girl gazed at Julie's face as if pleased with how she interacted with her.

"How old are you?" Julie asked.

"Fourteen."

"You don't have school?"

The girl shook her head. "I don't anymore. *They* won't let me go to school."

The response sounded strange.

"Who won't let you?"

The girl cast her eyes down subserviently, her face took on a reluctant expression indicating that she would not say anything. There were probably things about her schooling that she would not confide to Julie.

"Do you work for Miss. Deb?" asked Julie.

The girl nodded. "Whatever she needs me to do. All kinds of jobs."

She gave a steady look at Julie, watching her face, observing the clothes she was wearing.

"Are you married, *Didi*?" she asked smiling.

Julie shook her head. "No."

"Do you study?"

"You can say that. And work too."

"I want to study the way I used to learn in school. Will you teach me, *Didi*?"

The girl uttered candidly.

Julie immediately felt perplexed by what she said. She presumed the girl had gone to school, but had to stop for reasons important enough. Perhaps for financial reasons? Julie did not quite know how to answer her question.

"Sure." Julie answered so the girl knew how she felt about it.

She looked at the girl's radiant tanned oval face with a small sharp nose and thin lips. Her deep gleaming dark eyes were distinct in her spirited facial expression; they carried loads of emotions not readily explicable. Her course black hair, oiled and shiny, was tightly braided to two waist length braids with black ribbons tied at the ends. She wore a loose, worn-out printed cotton dress that went below her knee. Her uncared-for, delicate bare feet appeared as if they had never experienced socks.

"Can you read Bengali?" Julie asked.

The girl giggled. "Of course! I can write too! I went to school till age eleven."

"What do you like to read?"

"All kinds of stories; I like romantic stories," the girl chuckled, amused.

"Why did they take you out of school?" Julie had no idea who the *they* she was referring to was.

The girl shrugged her shoulders. Again, she was hesitant to say anything for whatever reason.

"Please have your tea, Didi! It will turn cold." She quickly diverted the attention from herself and walked briskly to the kitchen to take out the straw broom and the metal bucket from the cupboard underneath the sink. She placed the bucket in the sink and turned on the faucet. She stood watching till the bucket was filled up half-way, then took the heavy container out of the sink and placed it on the floor.

"What are you going to do?" asked Julie astonished watching everything she did.

"Clean the floor."

"That's a heavy bucket to carry around the house, isn't it?"

"I know how much to fill. That's how I manage."

The fact that a young girl was going to clean her apartment made Julie uncomfortable all at once. She saw the girl carry the bucket to her bedroom and place it near the door. She started to sweep, bending low to sweep the dust from under the bed, then, moving to every corner of the room to collect the dirt. She said she did four homes during the day and returned back to continue with the work Miss Deb wanted her to do.

"Don't you get exhausted?" asked Julie walking towards the room where she was sweeping.

The girl grinned turning her head. "It's my job. I have to do.".

She told Julie to leave all her laundry clothes in the tub in the bathroom. She would wash and hang them outside to dry and later iron them for her. Julie gazed at her listening, startled by what she said.

"Don't bother about washing and ironing for me. I like to do my own."

The girl looked at Julie apprehensively. "Do you wash your own clothes in your country?"

"Yes."

"Iron, too?"

"Yes."

The girl smiled without saying anything and dipped the thick cleaning cloth inside the water with her bare hands, squeezing out the water so it was not dripping. She kept glancing at Julie every so often.

"What about the village girls in your country?" The girl asked.

The comparison felt strange. Julie did not know how exactly to elaborate on the subject in a simplified manner.

"They go to school. They are young like you."

The girl became quiet thinking about something. Who knew what was going through her mind?

Whatever it was, she certainly did not feel the urgency to talk to Julie about it. Julie watched the way she continued with the cleaning steps, poised and dutiful for the job she needed to do.

"Will you teach me English, math, history, and science, *Didi*?"

Again, her question was most unusual. Julie instantly felt drawn by the way she asked the second time. In all likelihood, it was probably the first time someone had paid attention to the girl, Julie thought.

"Sure, if you have the time."

"Why wouldn't I find time for something I like to do?" Her expressive words sounded confident.

"You must have liked going to school."

"Like or don't like…..it doesn't matter if you are a girl." The girl answered back in a matter-of-fact way.

Julie immediately foresaw where the subject was leading. She had read articles on the social circumstances of young girls from poor families in India.. Having a girl born in the family, meant a burden for parents; they had to get her married as soon as she reached her puberty, most always with a dowry. It was an accepted fact, but Julie did not think a maid girl would be vocal about her own situation.

"It should matter if you are a girl," said Julie with conviction.

"I didn't want to stop school, but no one listened to me."

Her words suddenly came out firmly. She picked up the bucket with the dirty water and walked towards the door to carry it up the stairs to the terrace to pour it out through a drain. She returned and filled up the bucket again. Julie stared at the girl wearingly.

This cleaning job takes up a lot of energy," said Julie.

"I am the maid for this apartment."

"But you are a young. Adult women do cleaning jobs."

The girl glanced at Julie as she carried the bucket to the sitting area of the room. She placed it on the floor and wiped her forehead with the sleeve of her dress. She was quiet for a brief moment as if to catch up on her breath.

"You know how a girl should be, Didi?"

The remark abruptly caught Julie's attention. She could not imagine what the girl was going to say.

"How?"

"Bold. Real bold."

Julie was somewhat startled by her candid, honest utterance.

"So bold that the girl makes people inconsolably conscious of the rumors they spread about her."

So bold that no one dares to offend her in the fear that they would never see her again."

The words immediately overwhelmed Julie. Her words released a sense of alleviation from whatever she felt, a kind of desperateness that had instantaneously pushed the words out of the mouth of the fourteen-year old.

"Do you know why I didn't say a girl should be 'loving' and 'kind'?"

"Why?"

"Girls already have those goodness in them. Most people don't see them because girls suppress their spirited self in fear, in pain, in loneliness, in heartache and sometimes just plain humility."

Julie was speechless. Her words astonished her, she did not speak like a fourteen-year-old.

"I am touched by what you are saying." Julie said softly gazing at her face.

"It's just that some girls are not so lucky as others. It has nothing to do with goodness," she uttered.

Julie watched her lift the bucket and go to the second bedroom to wipe the floor.

By mid-morning, the next day, grey clouds drifted in and filled the sky, making even the smallest streak of sunlight disappear. Girish hurriedly came to Julie's apartment to make sure the windows were shut.

"Calcutta has clouds for every season, even in seasons least expected," Girish told Julie as he gazed at the gloomy sky through the window pane. Within minutes came the sudden extraordinary downpour like the clouds could not withstand the burden of weight, and then an explosive boom of thunder disrupted every subtle sound around.

To someone who had never experienced this kind of rain, it would have felt like a tropical adventure, Julie thought. She stood at the window watching the rain. It revealed an unseasonal shine to the green foliage outside, the air refreshed, washing away the flecks of dirt settled in nature.

The downpour lasted a short while followed by soft rain for the next two hours.

Meanwhile, Miss Deb arranged the first lunch with Julie in her apartment. The lunch table was already set when Julie came into her apartment; the plates were laid out on table mats, with forks and knives, small bowls, and covered glasses filled with water. Julie gave Miss Deb a box of chocolates she had brought for her. The woman excitedly took it in her hand studying the pictures on box.

"Foreign chocolates are my favorite." Miss Deb thanked her with a wide smile on her face.

Then, realizing how child-like she sounded, she quickly asked Julie if she was ready for a home-cooked lunch and lead the way towards the dining table.

Miss. Deb took a seat at the head of the table telling Julie that it was the same place she always sat. Julie sat close to her; she could now see the well-done make-up on her face that concealed the lines making her skin appear well toned and luminous.

The maid brought out the Bengali dishes; she was the lady who served the food while another woman cooked in the kitchen. Each dish was served in a certain sequence, in small bowls, following the precise order the dishes were to be eaten. Julie noticed that Miss Deb ate with the fork instead of the fingers which was the traditional way of eating. Her eyes were quietly focused on her plate as she mixed each dish with the white steamed rice. The lady server kept bringing the warm food from the kitchen and putting each course on the plates or serving them in small bowls—vegetable, Dal, fried whole fish, fish curry, mutton curry, and tomato chutney.

It's a treat to eat lunch like this," Julie was a bit stunned.

"It's normal to have four items along with rice. A few more when guests come."

"Also the helpers to assist you in cooking and serving," Julie said glancing at the woman server who kept going back and forth from the dining room to the kitchen.

"That is how it has always been. It is a normal part of home life here."

They talked for a long time about Miss Deb's retired life at home, the caretakers who had specific jobs to perform, and how lucky she was to have old-timers like Girish and his wife to serve her needs. She said she became luckier when the maid girl began living with Girish instead of her own parents; she assigned her all the jobs for taking care of the guests along with her own things she needed done. At times, her stories startled Julie, wondering whether

Miss Deb ever thought about the burdensome jobs she had assigned to the fourteen-year old girl. She wondered whether the woman had a life outside home after her retirement, if she engaged in any type of social work other than taking care of herself. She did not mention anything like that. Miss Deb gave off the impression that, for all the challenges that came with her living a single life, she would not consider surrendering to discomfort or giving time to someone who could benefit from her help.

"You have grown up in another culture. I imagine your impressions of our customs and values are unlike how we understand them." Miss Deb suddenly made the point without looking at Julie keeping her eyes on her food.

Julie listened without saying anything at first even though she understood her thoughts stemmed from certain fixated ideas.

"I respect the values that are part of different cultures. The fact that I am more accustomed to one does not make me disregard the other."

"But living far from a place changes some things."

"It does. However, the distance does not make a person ignorant of cultural knowledge of other places."

"Of course. But there could be misunderstandings if the cultural aspects are not explained to you. You are not living in the place. Not everything is black and white."

Julie glanced at her face as she heard Miss Deb speak with a tone of airy confidence.

"The problem is there are varying interpretations in those explanations."

Miss Deb did not say anything.

Julie immediately understood that whatever response she gave, it might not be worthy of consideration from

Miss. Deb. She perceived Julie as a foreign visitor. Julie's parents would be closer to her thinking as they were born and raised in Calcutta.

"I would not be surprised if you had culture shock. You are not accustomed to things that are openly visible here, a part of life." Miss Deb pronounced her thoughts in way she felt she was in control.

"There are always the desirable and the undesirable aspects. Normally, the desirable ones are readily appreciated. Maybe the undesirable ones need to be better understood," said Julie.

Miss Deb lifted her eyes off the plate and looked at Julie's face briefly. She could almost perceive with her eyes what exactly Julie was trying to imply. She felt impressed by the way Julie presented her thoughts.

"You have a good point, but cultural values are deep rooted. What might seem undesirable to your eyes, could be significant to the culture." Miss Deb said in a conceited tone.

Julie kept quiet briefly and then told her how she felt about extraneous ideas and the undesirable aspects.

"Well, when some undesirable ideas become deeply rooted, change becomes an impenetrable challenge."

"But, of course, most of those ideas have meaningful premises. In order for a society to function in a stable manner, the ideas must be retained in place. You cannot possibly change thousands of years of values in a culture."

Julie became quiet again. She had no intention of immersing herself in an opinionated argument on the merits and demerits of cultural ideas. But she nevertheless wanted to hear what Miss Deb had to say about certain thoughts that Julie needed a rationale convincing on.

"What about the lives of people that get negatively affected by the ideas that have been there for years?" asked Julie.

Miss Deb looked at her in a doubtful manner; she definitely felt she needed to clarify.

"What do you mean? Everyone is accustomed to the values set in place. They know that is how it is supposed to be," answered Miss Deb.

"But people are not mechanical objects. People think, reflect and develop awareness about what is good and not so good," Julie said with assurance.

Miss Deb became quiet. She took a piece of fish from the bowl of curry on her dish and instantly called out to the cooking lady to ask if the fish was bought from the market in the morning. Julie found her abrupt behavior absurd, especially that she never excused herself from their conversation and suddenly started calling out to the cooking lady. The cooking lady hurriedly came out from the kitchen and told her in a subservient tone that the fish had been bought fresh in the morning while the vendors had still been setting up the stalls.

"*Khoob taja machh!*" Miss Deb acknowledged with pleased contentment.

She did not seem concerned that the conversation abruptly got interrupted; she immediately continued from where it had briefly ended.

"Any kind of change shatters the stability of the established ideas," she said.

"But, unless you try to change, how would you know what is good or not so good? Change is worth trying."

Miss Deb looked at Julie in a wondering manner, almost as if she wanted to confront her about what she said, but she left it.

Julie, however, did not want to continue, she sensed a disparity in their wavelengths. She liked that their conversation remained in the periphery of the subject and did not delve into details. She thanked her for inviting her to lunch.

"Well, I certainly hope you have a pleasant stay. By the way, did the maid girl finish all your work?"

Julie nodded with some uneasiness. "Yes, everything."

The conversation with Miss Deb did not leave Julie inspired or excited about a further social time with her. She understood that the woman was driven by some controlled thinking.

But what troubled Julie was the idea of a fourteen-years-old girl working as her private maid; a girl of that age should have been in school instead of doing cumbersome physical jobs. It distressed her that the girl had the desire to learn yet she was made to disregard the thought, perhaps owing to what her family wanted. It was how Julie understood the situation from the brief interactions with the girl. Moreover, after conversing with Miss Deb, she sensed the woman would not entertain the feelings of empathy on the subject. To some extent, she conveyed the impression that the service from the caretakers was a normal part of living; they did not deserve special sympathy by the virtue of the work they did for her or for others like her.

The cooking lady came and took the plates and cleared the table. Julie watched as Miss Deb told the lady to bring out the desserts. She did not get up from her seat.

"Would it be alright if I choose to make my meals in the kitchen upstairs?" Julie asked.

The statement came as a sudden surprise to Miss Deb.

"We have Girish to prepare the meals. It is how we do things here."

"There are vegetable and fruit sellers that walk by the house. Indeed, it will be a pleasing experience to use the kitchen in my apartment."

Miss Deb had a serious expression on her face and did not say anything. Julie understood how she felt about the suggestion, she did not bring up the topic again.

The market center was five blocks away from the guest house. The building with its small shops on two floors, some hidden behind walls and stairs, others lined along both sides of the building...was the central shopping place for the neighborhoods nearby. Vegetable and the fish vendors sat outside the building on jute mats, they sold the fresh produce and catch from the rivers. Women vendors had their babies wrapped in thin blankets lying next to them. They tucked the earned cash underneath their mats, they had no bags. Empty packets, rotten fruits and cigarette buds lay cluttered next to an overfilled garbage can close to where the vendors sat. The inescapable odor of fish remnants filled the drains. Julie saw the black crows on the garbage pile hop once, twice, pick up the pieces and take off. The foul odor had spread close by the building where Julie crossed over to enter. She covered her nose, taking out a tissue from her pants pocket.

Inside the building was cleaner, comparatively, although the dirt stained stairs certainly needed a power wash. She saw the different shops for groceries, medical supplies, shoes, purses, tailoring, and beauty items, along with cafes that catered homestyle food. Even the small tea-shop was doing brisk business selling hot tea, spiced chickpeas, cigarettes and hand-wrapped betel leaves with condiments. Julie saw the sign for the bakery on the second floor and took the stairs up. Entering the bakery, she instantly smelled the intense pleasing aroma inside, the place was different from how she imagined a bakery. It was a no-frills take out place with a glass cabinet, a small electric stove and an oven. She noticed a wide variety of Indian snacks; rows of appetizing cakes and pastries decorated inside of a sliding glass cupboard. A man was frying snacks and placing them on a tray inside a warm portable oven. Julie asked him if she could sample a few pieces before deciding. The man willingly welcomed the idea, Julie chose the *kochuri*, a salty snack with lentil filling.

"Very tasty!" she uttered smiling.

"I make fresh ones again at four o'clock. People buy for teatime. Should I keep some for you?"

Julie laughed. "Oh, no! I will come whenever I please."

"I hope you have a good stay in Calcutta."

Julie was surprised that the man could tell she was not a local resident.

"I am back here after many years," she said in a friendly manner.

The man gave an acknowledging smile. "People come to Calcutta once, and they want to return again."

His words instantly made an impression, Julie had been feeling something close to what he expressed. Amidst the demanding challenges the soul of the city seemed passionately alive.

She told him she wanted two cake pieces and two pastries.

The man picked out the best looking pieces and placed them inside a cardboard box. He added four extra pieces.

"These extras are for a pleasant stay in Calcutta," said the man smiling. "Please don't pay for them."

"That is so kind of you!"

"Come again, *Didi!* I will make fresh ones for you! Stay well!"

How gracious it is to call a woman "*didi*"! Julie liked how the word was used so frequently.

Julie ambled through the second floor browsing through the different shops. She gazed at the line of Indian clothes hanging in front of the shops. She saw stacks of block-printed cotton bedcovers in front of a home goods shop; a crowded jewelry store with women looking through earrings and bangles and a group of men who stood in front of a coffee shop, smoking cigarettes and carrying out loud argumentative conversations. She passed by each shop like a tourist who had come to see Calcutta's business life without any commitment to the place. A few times, she heard the shop owners calling out loud, "*Didi,* please come inside the shop. What would you like to see?" A book-shop caught her attention. There were all kinds of English textbooks and workbooks for beginners. Julie picked up a few books and flipped through the pages. She thought about the maid girl. She wondered if she should start a few lessons with her since she was so keen on learning English and other subjects. It would be intellectually motivating, she thought. Julie picked up four books and four workbooks.

"Do you sell notebooks and pencils in your shop?"

The man picked a few notebooks and pencils and put them in front of her.

"How old is your sibling?" The man asked politely.

Julie grinned. "It's for a young girl of fourteen years."

She thanked the man as she paid for the notebooks and the pencils and walked out of the shop.

Julie took the steps down to the street from where she had entered. She managed to get through the crowds of people inside the building. Just as she stepped outside and walked a few steps forward, her eyes immediately caught sight of a young girl, a little distance away close to the roadside, her back towards her, kneeling on the ground near a gutter, and feeding a limp dirt- covered dog. The horrid condition of the dog stunned Julie, the dog was suffering malnutrition; she could see the thin ribs through her skin. Six pups lay clustered together near her. Julie immediately recognized the maid girl near the dog from her two long braids and the dress. A little boy wearing a torn sweater and shorts sat close to her on the bare ground. He picked out puffed rice kernels one by one from a torn newspaper and put them in his mouth while the girl kept scooping out what looked like a mixture of mashed rice and milk from a stainles steel bowl and kept feeding the starved, shrunken dog. Julie stood still and gazed in shock at the sight of the dog and the little boy.

To whom does one surrender the emotions first? The human or the animal?

People walked by, cyclists rode by, buses loaded with people stopped near the gutter to pick up and drop off passengers. No one looked. The world around was going about its normal business. Undeniable emotions gripped Julie as she walked closer to the maid girl. The girl took no notice of Julie, and neither did the little boy; they kept busy with what they were doing.

Julie waited briefly before turning towards the direction of the guest house. The whole time, she thought about the maid girl… how the girl had resisted talking about herself, how she had stopped school, how she wanted to learn….. Julie felt a strange uneasiness, and a certain urgency to ask Miss Deb about her.

Julie sensed the stillness as she entered her apartment. The place had been flawlessly cleaned. A bouquet of tuberoses were in a vase on the dining table, her bedroom furniture had been dusted spotless and things organized in place, even her clothes were hung inside the wall closet even though she had left her things lying on the bed. Julie knew everything was the work of the maid girl. But, somehow, the organized, tidy place did not lift her spirits. She thought about the little boy she saw, the maid girl, and the dog. It is incomprehensible how a place could be completely screened off from the reality outside, Julie thought.

She stood gazing outside through the crystal-clear glass door that opened to the veranda. The sunlight streamed into the room like it was meant to stir up buoyant feelings inside the four walls, Julie felt just the opposite. She heard faint voice of a man singing soulful songs in the distance. She realized it was the same beggar who sang songs while walking down the street every morning to earn a few paisas. She stared at the sparrows chirping away on the veranda of the house across. The sounds provoked incoherent feelings just as how one feels restless for some vague reasons.

A note from Miss Deb was lying on the table asking her to place her order for dinner. She wrote Girish would pick up the order form at five in the evening. Julie looked at the wall clock; it was nearing five. She quickly jotted soup, western styled vegetables and fish chops on the form. She took the form with her to give it to Girish herself and she spontaneously made plans to talk to Miss Deb after.

Girish was overwhelmingly grateful that Julie had brought down the form to him. He told her she should not go through that kind of trouble, it was his job to bring the form from her apartment.

Julie was a bit amused by what he said and responded politely, "I know."

Miss Deb opened the apartment promptly as soon as she heard the knock. She greeted Julie with a show of cordiality even though she was pleasantly surprised by her presence. She had a navy blue shawl wrapped over her beige printed cotton sari, her hair and face were spruced up neatly as if she was expecting guests. Julie told her she wanted to speak to her about something. Miss Deb made a concerned face in the anticipation that something was wrong; she invited Julie to step inside, and gestured her to the sofa to make herself comfortable and enquired if Julie was all right.

"It's not me. It's the maid girl."

Miss Deb stared at Julie's face with a look of apprehension.

"Did she do something wrong? Please tell me!"

"Oh, no! Nothing like that! She is truly a pleasant girl!"

The response perplexed her all the more. Miss Deb paused briefly, fixed the pleats of her sari, and then asked with a displeased tone.

"Is it anything to do with her family?"

Julie shook her head and then she went straight to the subject.

"The maid girl told me she went to school till age eleven."

Miss Deb cleared her throat. She never imagined there could be interest about the maid girl from a visitor.

'Why are you interested in her?"

"She strikes me unusual. I thought I would ask you about her."

Miss Deb looked at Julie's face wonderingly, at first hesitating whether she should say anything.

"Saras's story is the usual one," Miss Deb began, "Her parents took her out of the village school three months before her marriage. They told Saras about the man with whom her marriage was fixed, a thirty years old man who worked in a liquor shop. The following day, Saras was

nowhere to be seen. She had run away. No one knew where she went. They searched for a week and could not find her. Then, after two weeks she returned to her uncle Girish, the caretaker who works in my house."

Julie stared at Miss Deb stunned. For the first time, she learnt the maid girl's name, Saras...and her uncle was Girish. Somehow, in all her everyday conversations with the girl, Julie did not know those details.

"How is she even allowed to marry so young?"

Miss Deb grinned. "Do you think those people care? A girl needs to be married."

"What do you mean "those people"?

"The villagers. They do menial jobs. Not cultivated.

"Where do they live?" Julie asked somberly, disturbed by how Miss Deb described the people.

She gave a smirk and told her that the village people lived far from the city. But, some created pockets of establishments closer to the city to get to their jobs. She said they did whatever they liked and never followed rules.

Julie examined Miss Deb's irritated facial expression. She did not wish to continue on the subject to further aggravate her mood instead she got back to the topic of Saras which had got sidetracked temporarily.

"So, did Saras's marriage get canceled?"

Miss Deb glanced at Julie. It surprised her that Julie took interest in Saras's story of all people.

"I am telling you because you asked. I find little benefit in speaking about Saras or her family." Miss Deb paused briefly. Julie could conclude from her facial expression that it wasn't the most deserving subject she wished to talk about.

She told how the man's family demanded a large amount of money from Saras's parents. They did not have that kind of wealth and became anxious. In the meanwhile, Saras did not return home so the situation turned grave. The marriage was canceled by the boy's family with a lot of exasperation.

The words evoked emotion in Julie. "Saras must have felt desperate in her situation."

"The girl is fragile in appearance, but she is tough inside." Miss Deb said.

She described how Saras stayed two weeks in the fields without proper meals, She ate fruits plucked from trees, and kept herself hydrated with the village water pump at night when no one was watching. During the day she hid in odd places. That was how she lived.

"She is only fourteen!" Julie was stunned by what she heard.

"Those fields have jackals coming out at night. God knows how they spared her."

Mrs. Deb suddenly stopped. It was as if she was herself caught up in Saras's story.

"Bless her fearlessness!" Julie confidently asserted. She thought it was a blessing that Saras resisted with such a fearless act from what sounded like a forced marriage.

Miss Deb continued telling that Girish was Saras's maternal uncle and guardian. Till the day she returned to him, Girish had no idea about Saras's disappearance. No one told him. When he had heard what had happened, he offered to have Saras live with him and his wife. He came to know that people were big mouthing Saras's brash behavior of running away. It suffocated him to think about the humiliation caused to the young girl he loved so dearly. His own daughter had died of typhoid at the age of six. It is why he is immensely fond of Saras.

Julie listened quietly.

"But her story does not end there. Saras's relatives put a condition on Girish that he could never interfere in Saras's marriage no matter how affectionately he feels for her. Girish keeps his distance from them, but he often remains melancholy thinking about Saras's future. He said that if ever such a situation arises again, he will take Saras away to Benaras to live with his older sister without telling anyone."

Miss Deb sighed and stood up to ring the call bell to have Girish's wife bring tea and biscuits for her. Then she walked to the coffee table and arranged the long stems of the tuber-roses so they looked symmetrical from all angles. She returned back to the armchair and took her seat like a woman who felt blessed and proud of the life she had. Julie waited till she returned to her chair.

"Saras wanted to learn English, math, science, and history from me. I am thinking of teaching her. I bought a few books," said Julie.

The words immediately alarmed Miss. Deb. She frowned with a doubtful expression, then grinned sarcastically as if Julie's comment was the most absurd thing she had ever heard.

"What an ambitious idea! You will teach the maid school subjects?"

"Girls of her age should be in school."

"She is a maid. It is not the norm for most."

"But, she wants to learn. She was taken out of school. She has been deprived of the chance," Julie said politely.

Miss Deb gave a wry smile.

"Girls like Saras are not like our girls. You can't change them or their situation."

Julie was quiet, the words disturbed her immensely.

Why do you value Saras and girls like her so little? Julie felt emotional at the thought.

Miss Deb understood that her words weren't taken well. She avoided saying anything further.

Julie did not wish to abandon what Miss Deb expressed; she gathered her thoughts calmly.

"Miss Deb, you have many kinds flowers in your garden. Are they all the same? Do they all bloom at the same time? Do they all look alike? Don't you think some thrive better at certain conditions than others?"

Listening to Julie, Miss Deb was at first seized by surprise, and then gave a trenchant laugh "Good comparison, but the maid girls are not flowers."

"I think they are. If they are given the care, they could achieve much more."

Miss Deb shook her head softly. She remained silent for a few minutes, a little startled.

"I will be very honest with you. Saras will lose interest quickly. Teaching her the subjects would not take her anywhere. It's a strange expectation."

"She wishes to learn. Should I not take her feelings into consideration when she asked if I could teach her?"

"Of course, she will ask you! She sees you are a visitor and you have time in your hands."

"There is nothing else intellectually inspiring for her to do, other than cleaning people's homes or wander the streets trying to find things to do. May be she approached me because I pay attention in her. Soon her family would make another attempt to get her married to an unknown older man in such an inconceivable age." Julie spoke straight to the point.

"People like you who are temporary visitors seem to have a sympathetic attitude. You make your emotions a tool to understand the reality. It does not work like that."

Julie forced herself to smile." I am only trying to provide an opportunity for Saras's wish, a simple gesture on my part to help her in a different way."

"What will she gain? She will certainly not change the world."

Julie grinned, paused a little. "How can she change the world unless you provide her with educational opportunities?

"I see your visit to Calcutta has struck a new chord. I have nothing to say. I am sorry I will not be part of this."

The uncomfortable conversation with Miss Deb left Julie abruptly discouraged and tense. She knew her own voice sounded desperate and protective towards the girl. She was looking forward to teach her, but Miss Deb did not take the proposal well. It felt like Miss Deb reduced her slightest hope to dust.

How ironic was it that a person who had taught school children her whole life refused to see the potential in a school-age maid girl or even show concern about the reason she was taken out of school. Julia found the thought disturbing.

Julie did not continue talking further, she politely said good-bye and took leave.

The following day, Julie took a tour of Calcutta city, sitting inside the tram. The conversation with Miss Deb on the previous day left her dispirited about the attitude she held. Her words always sounded one sided which left no space for the listener to add a different perspective. Despite, there were inspiring moments of the everyday life whenever she stepped outside.

The overwhelming crowds of people on streets did not make her feel unsafe, even the informality of the everyday life amazed her. It was much the same inside the tram packed with people. She felt at ease sitting by the window, looking out as the tram passed through different parts of Calcutta. All kinds of people got on and off the tram, men gave up their seats if they saw women passengers standing, and at every stop the ticket conductor called out loud to the driver to take caution if a woman or an elderly man was about to get on or off the tram. There was an honest spirit of conscientiousness that existed for others, Julie thought.

An elderly passenger took a seat next to Julie. She wasn't surprised when he casually initiated a conversation asking if she was new to the city; obviously, he recognized that she was not a local person. When he came to know she was a visitor from America, he enthusiastically asked how much she knew about the history of Calcutta.

"I have read some history, but I am sure I could learn more." Julie had responded politely.

He immediately started to share information about the areas the tram was passing through. It almost seemed, he felt it was his duty as a native to the city to elaborate about the places, pointing to the noteworthy buildings, the legacy behind the street names and the homes of famous people.

"Calcutta was once the capital of the British Empire, a gateway to the educational, cultural, political, social center of India; a city with the most stimulating and controversial soul,". He pointed out to the homes of wealthy landlords, homes of writers, musicians, actors, social activists, political leaders, scientists, educationists whose talents sprouted and flourished in the city's diverse environment, and individuals whose pioneering movements brought social and political changes. In the twenty minutes Julie spent with him, Julie felt his narrative generated inquisitiveness to read more about the places and people he mentioned.

"It amazes me how important it is to share even the slightest educational knowledge even to a stranger sitting inside a tram."

"The city's past has been closely adhered to by individuals, memorialized with sentiments. However, the vicissitudes through the years have also insinuated the impression that the inner and outer appearance of the metropolis has altered. The changing times have moved Calcutta to another direction. Change was inevitable."

The man paused and wished Julie an enjoyable stay in Calcutta and a successful educational career as he politely folded his hands to say *namaskar* and got off the tram..

Julie smiled. Through the window she watched the man slowly step up onto the sidewalk and walk towards a newspaper stall. She did not know his name or who he was.

The taxi dropped off Julie near the main road a few blocks from the guest house. She took the street behind the guest house for the first time. Every plot of land was built with two-storied homes, the balconies prying into each other's privacy. The cars and vans belonging to the homes remained parked on both sides of the street, occupying the sidewalk space meant for pedestrians. She assumed there were no rules, so people did whatever was convenient for them. The narrow alleys between the homes had become established ironing place for men and women who earned their living by ironing clothes for the neighborhood homeowners.

Julie had just reached the neighborhood park, when she recognized the meager-bodied aged man in the distance; he was the same man who came to the guest house to collect trash every morning at mid-day. He was pushing a damaged metal cart with two rickety wheels around the periphery of the park, picking up trash with his bare hands and putting it inside the cart. The cart had no cover; it was overfilled with every kind of garbage making it unsightly even at the quickest glance.

The poor man needs a pair of rubber gloves for his bare hands. He is cleaning the filth of the public streets!

Julie stared at him startled. She wondered why the community living in the neighborhood could not pull together to buy the man a pair of gloves and replace his dysfunctional garbage cart. She could not comprehend the lack of public consciousness.

Should they not be concerned for the man who collects their trash and cleans up the streets they live on? It was the lack of inclusive community living that she found troubling. She thought there was no collective betterment that could contribute to a deserving benchmark even though the neighborhood was filled with sizable single homes with two cars and an embellished garden.

Just as she was nearing the guest house, Julie noticed Saras walking from a distance towards her. She wore the knee-length dress that she had worn a few times and the loose rubber Hawaiian sandals. She had strings of jasmine flowers hanging from her left arm as she waved her right-hand walking briskly towards Julie with an animated demeanor.

"*Didi!Didi!* Please take one! They are fresh flowers." Saras stretched out \her arm to show her as she came close.

"What are you doing with so many flower strings?"

"I am selling them. Two *Rupees* for one. I stringed them all."

"Really?" Julie sniffed the sweet fragrance of jasmine.

Saras nodded. "Haldar-*babu* gives me the flowers. I string them and he pays me money from how many I sell."

She said she made the flower strings between her cleaning jobs everyday.

"I want to buy a fancy sari for my mother," Saras spoke excitedly.

"A fancy sari? Oh, really?"

The girl nodded jubilantly. "I see women on the TV wearing pretty shiny saris."

"Where is the TV?"

"In Haldar-*babu's* shop inside the market. There is large TV. He lets me watch. Haldar-*babu* told me that the more flower strings I sell, the more my wish will come true to buy a shiny fancy sari for my mother."

Julie was struck by Saras's words. Her trusting attitude and confidence could appeal to a lot of people. In the circumstances she had been through, she still sparked enthusiasm in whatever she occupied herself with. She said her mother sold fruits every morning at the market from ten till mid-day, then she accompanied her mother to her next housecleaning job. That was the time she saw her mother.

"What do you do while your mother cleans the house?"

"All kinds of things. Sometimes run errands, sometimes serve food to families who visit, and clean up after them. There are lots of dishes to wash. Some days I take out the peas from the pea pods.....But, I can't ever miss Satin-*babu's* massage. He is strict."

"Satin-*babu?* Massage?" Julie asked astonished.

Saras nodded. "He is the man of the house. I have to massage his legs with the special Chinese oil that his son brought for him."

The more Julie heard about the little things in Saras's life, the more she got consumed into thoughts of how the young girl's life was being molded by other people's expectations. No one thought to ask her how she spent her day or whether she went to school. No one guided her towards educating herself and helping her build a future for herself.

"Please give me ten strings," said Julie.

Saras quickly squatted on the ground and carefully laid out the flower strings on her legs.

"These are from me to you, *Didi*." Saras pulled out four extra flower strings.

"Oh, you don't need to give me extra strings."

"I do. You are my guest. You have come from far away."

She had a smile on her face, as if to say how privileged and happy she felt to give back. It was not every day she met someone like Julie.

"Here is some extra for the fancy sari for your mother." Julie handed her the cash.

Saras hesitantly took the notes giving a tight-lipped smile; Julie's gesture was beyond her expectation.

"I will put them in my cash box."

"Your cash box?"

Saras nodded giggling. She said she made a cash box like the one Haldar-*babu* has in his shop. Her uncle Girish kept it safe under his bed.

Julie found her words amusing. "That's a good idea!"

"I will make a flower decoration for your hair just like the one I made for Miss Deb."

The girl was always looking forward to keep busy.

As usual Saras came the next morning to clean the apartment. She brought with her a beautifully stitched flower decoration of jasmine and red roses for Julie.

Julie looked at the intricately hand-stitched piece made with fine threads and flowers by the hands of a fourteen-year old. Saras had wrapped the decoration inside a large banana leaf and tied it with a string.

"This looks perfect!"

"Do you like it?"

Julie smiled. "I do! I very much do! Too bad I cannot keep it fresh eternally."

Saras continued to be cheerful, she told Julie about a time when Miss Deb wanted her to make a flower decoration for her hair. It happened to be her birthday and she wanted to wear it on a hair bun for the dinner at the club with her friend. Saras described the friend to be a man who visited Miss Deb often. On the birthday, she watched how Miss Deb's friend had complimented her on how beautiful she looked with the hair decoration when he had come to take her out for dinner.

"He wore a suit and a tie and brought a gift bag for her. I knew she had feelings for him, I could tell. He was a gracious man."

Saras giggled as if some excitement had seized her and then she felt conscious. She quickly turned towards the kitchen to get the broom to clean the floor.

"When a man is good to the woman he loves, she feels a lot of love for him."

Saras spoke from the kitchen as she turned on the faucet to fill up the bucket.

Julie was pleasantly entertained.

I wonder how Miss Deb would feel if she heard the doting images expressed by the vigilant teenage girl. Julie smiled to herself thinking about Saras's words.

Julie wanted to give Saras break from the tedious physical job. She told her to clean only her bedroom. She watched Saras dip the mopping cloth in the phenol disinfectant water, squeeze the water out and then rub each area of the bare floors inside the bedroom. She kept cleaning while squatted on the ground, pushing the bucket behind her.

"What does you name Saras mean?" Julie asked trying to keep a conversation going so not to feel remorseful about the young girl working as a maid for her.

"My full name is Saraswati."

"Oh, really? The Goddess of wisdom, knowledge, music and arts. That's special."

"You know that?"

"Of course! Every name has a meaning." Julie answered.

Saras paused briefly.

"But, I am no Saraswati. Neither am I a learned person nor do I play an instrument or paint."

"You have hidden talents. How about I start teaching you as you had wished?"

Saras immediately paused and put the wet cloth on the bucket and looked at Julie as if she had heard something out of the ordinary. Then, she told Julie that she had meant to ask her again about tutoring her, but she was hesitant incase Julie got annoyed at her repetitive requests. In the many days she had known Miss Deb, she could never ask her; she feared Miss Deb would get annoyed at her for being too aspiring.

"Don't worry about that. You have enough time with me. We will begin tomorrow."

Saras nodded, the over exuberant expressions on her face could make anyone see how much the girl looked forward to learning again.

"I never wanted to leave school. I never wanted to get married. But, no one listened except my mother. She told me she would take me to her sister's home in *Benaras* so I go to school there. I would have relief from the pressure of marriage. I didn't want to go far from her. I didn't want to get married. So, I ran away."

"Weren't you afraid to run away on your own?"

"You can fight fear to save your life. I didn't want others deciding for my life."

"There is a good reason why you felt that way. Your name is Saraswati."

"That's what I mean! For what was I given the name Saraswati? So they feel blessed to call the goddess's name? Was that the reason?"

Julie was instantly astonished by the way Saras vocalized her feelings. Her words sounded forceful.

Julie walked up to the bag with the books and notebooks lying on the table and took them out to show Saras to ease her feelings.

"See these? Our lessons begin tomorrow."

"You got books to teach me, *Didi*? You really did?" She asked in a tender voice.

Saras quickly stood up from the floor and hurriedly went to touch Julie's feet. Julie was confounded by the humble gesture that seemed noticeably unconvincing, as if Saras needed to be grateful for wishing to learn.

"You should never bow down to anyone for wishing to learn." Julie said giving an affectionate pat on her back, not allowing the young girl to touch her feet.

"You talk differently." Saras looked at Julie's face surprised.

In the days that followed, every morning, looking cheerful and enthusiastic, Saras finished the daily chores, changed into a clean cotton dress that Julie bought for her and promptly went to the dining table. Every day she brought her writing notebook, pencils, and the reading book in a jute bag. Her hair was neatly tied in two tight braids; she wore two silver studs on her ears and had two silver bangles on her arms. For the first few minutes, Julie admired her enthusiasm to finish the housework quickly, complimented on her punctuality and how nicely dressed up she was.

Every day, Saras returned with the completed assignments that Julie had given her the previous day. For the first few minutes, Julie stared at the handwritten pages of the assignments done in pencil. It was clear the girl had gone to school and cultivated a student-like handwriting.

On some nights Julie heard her voice from the window of her room, reading loudly the short English paragraphs in a sing-song manner. She stayed up late writing inside the workbooks, sitting on the cot with the kerosene light on. She learnt forty new words every day, remembered them without effort and was ready for the next set of words the following morning. She even asked Julie to add more work because she said she wanted to learn fast. By the end of the second lesson, Saras had advanced in her pace of reading and understanding the contents of short paragraphs of essays and stories. She could ask simple questions in English and voluntarily used the new vocabulary when responding to questions. She was even faster with math problems. The workbooks that Julie bought were completed in two days without Julie's help and she had to buy a few advanced level workbooks.

"Who will teach me after you leave, *Didi*?" Saras asked after the lesson one day.

Julie did not know. "We will see. Don't worry about that."

Saras nodded. Something on her face showed that she wished to trust Julie's words but she was not sure.

In the early afternoon, Julie stood at the back window of her bedroom and watched Saras pick the *Neem* twigs from the grass. She swept the dry leaves to the corner and made a large pile for the gardener to fill up the cart, and to burn them someplace away from the guest house. She saw Girish's wife sitting on a mat on the grass picking out the damaged rice kernels from a stainles steel platter.

Julie opened the window to let some air in the room, she wanted to cherish the last four days of pleasant weather that she would have to let go of. The next two months after her return back would be cold; sometimes spring blended with winter and the warmth of the sun took its time to be felt.

"*Didi*, do you have *Neem* trees in your country?" Saras called out when she noticed Julie at the window.

"I have never seen *Neem* trees where I live." Julie looked at the stout matured tree with small bright-green leaves.

"The breeze of the *Neem* is a natural mosquito and insects repellent," said Saras looking up at her.

"So, I suppose you don't have mosquito problems here."

"Rarely."

Saras described how *Neem* twigs are used in brushing teeth that keep the gums healthy and how the face cream made from *Neem* made a woman's face glow. In the few minutes, Saras had a lot to share about the benefits of that one *Neem* tree.

"Should I make some *Neem* paste for you, Didi?"

"For my face?" Julie shook her head grinning.

"Every day I make *Neem* paste for Miss Deb. She must have the fresh paste for her face to look young."

A sudden knock on the door interrupted the conversation. Julie went and opened the door hastily. A young woman in a sari stood at the door and gestured a polite *namaskar.* Julie had never seen the woman before. She was average height, had a deep tanned complexion with her hair tied hair in one long braid at the back. She was slender built, wore a cotton sari and had a red dot on her forehead.

"My name is Bharati. I am Saraswati's mother."

All of a sudden Julie was taken aback. She had been curious about how Saras's mother was like listening to Saras speak about her a few times and now she thought she saw some resemblance to Saras.

"Saras has mentioned you a few times," said Julie.

"I call her Saraswati. You understand, right?"

There was something self-effacing and resolute in the way she spoke to Julie almost as if Saras was not the name she recognized. Julie thought she understood what the woman meant by the question. Saraswati was the name of a Goddess; the name represented a deeper meaning.

"Your daughter is a spirited girl. I see her every day."

The woman did not take advantage of the praise; she did not smile, she nodded slowly. Then she started to tell Julie why she named her daughter Saraswati. She said she had prayed for a girl, a wish unlike women her age. There were some who mocked her for being crazy. She said she had wanted a daughter to show others that girls are as precious as boys; they are capable of standing on their own feet and they hold courageous traits. She said that if she had a girl she would not allow her to suffer the indignity that other girls faced. She will educate her daughter just as people educated their boys.

Julie listened to her words. Somehow, when she spoke to Saras, she had sensed her mother to be different, possibly having the similar bold qualities of Saras.

"I know what Saras is like." Julie responded softly.

"I don't call her Saras, *they* do. *They* do not think she is worthy of respect so they changed the name."

Julie was startled. "*They*" meant the relatives, people in her village. Julie had come to know something new about the maid girl's family and the community she lived in.

"The teacher was angry at me for taking her out of school." Bharati paused. "I have come to tell you something. You have to help my Saraswati."

The woman's face was flustered, she looked desperate.

"I am afraid if Saraswati stops learning, they will forcefully get her married. They have heard that Saraswati has a teacher; they are hesitant to approach you. As soon as you leave, they will force her again."

The woman wiped the accumulated tears in her eyes as she continued to speak.

"*They* have fixed a man for Saraswati. He is older. He needs someone to look after him. He is suffering from ailments." She fell silent as she kept wiping her eyes.

Julie stood shocked.

"What you are telling me sounds horrible!" Julie could not keep her emotions under control.

"Once Saraswati is married, I cannot do anything! Saraswati would have to accept everything. She is my girl! I cannot allow that."

The woman spoke with a trembling voice shaking her head. She said her husband has a job far from home. He feels heartbroken and did not know what to do.

"Are you the only one taking responsibility for Saras's situation?"

"What choice do I have, *Didi*? I am Saraswati's mother."

The words distressingly stunned Julie.

"Does Saraswati know?"

The woman nodded. "My fear is she will run away again and she may not return home."

Everything she said dismayed Julie immensely. She hardly had any days left before her return trip, she had no idea how she could help Saras in her situation. Immediately, Saras's animated face, and her affectionate mannerisms pulled at her heart, a kind of painful feeling that happens during a separation from a child one loves. Julie's eyes watered.

"Please, *didi*...I beg that you keep Saraswati engaged with tutoring or speak to the school. The school does not want to take her back anymore."

The woman paused and wiped her eyes with the ends of her sari.

"If you cannot help her, I will be forced to leave her in Benares with my sister. A mother's heart does not give up!" The woman folded her hands and did *namaskar,* then turned around to walk down the stairs.

Julie stood gazing at her. In spite how unbelievable the story sounded, Julie believed her words for the reason that Saras had also conveyed the similar feelings. Anyone would find such a story appalling! Julie thought.

She closed the door, went back to the window and stared out in the backyard. A strained feeling took hold of her. Distracted, she stared at Girish's wife hanging wet saris and blouses on the laundry string that hung from the branches of two trees; Girish was now occupied with wiping the dust off the window ledges. Saras lay on her stomach on a mat on the garage floor, her arms folded and her hands underneath the chin absorbed in reading a book. Her mother had come and left without her knowing.

Julie stood immobile, her gaze fixated on the harmonious life of the three living together. Her heart ached at the agonizing thought of Saras's life after she leaves. It was unbearable; she was appalled at how a girl's life was geared towards deplorable dissolution. So few took notice, so many persisted.

Miss Deb had adopted a lifestyle that provided comfort and service to her living; as long as her own needs were taken care of, nothing else mattered to her. Perhaps, she had her own reasoning; she no longer wished to worry about anyone after years of serving as a teacher and taking the responsibilities of her mother. She must have also lived through some anxious days managing her mother alone. Yet, what surprised Julie was that her attitude towards educating a maid girl; her words appeared so unjustifiable and demure. Julie had expected her to be the first to show encouragement because she was once a teacher.

She instantly wondered whether Miss Deb would reconsider Saras situation to keep a regular tutor for Saras or even speak to the principal of the school to take Saras back. She felt desperate to restart the conversation, one more time. How could she stay quiet after what she had heard from Saras's mother! After she leaves, she would have no control over the young girl's life. The thoughts distressed Julie.

She shut the windows and went to the dresser to look at herself in the mirror. She noticed the light tan that had emerged on her face, a visible mark that she had been on a holiday someplace far from the cold. Holiday indeed!

Certainly, it had not been the kind of holiday she indulged into personal pleasures. It was not what she cared to have, not after knowing the life of the fourteen-year old girl. How could she!

She brushed her wavy dark brown hair and dabbed a little chap-stick on her lips.

Julie picked up Saras's notebooks and went downstairs to meet Miss Deb; she knew the woman was usually home at tea time. She had fixed hours in the mornings and in the afternoons when she normally caught up with the world through the printed sources. Girish's wife opened the door and led her to the front porch where Julie noticed Miss Deb was sitting with a younger looking woman in western clothes of pants, a full sleeve silk blouse and a blazer on top, and having tea. The woman wore pin heeled shoes and wore platinum hooped earrings that matched her choker necklace. The woman stared at Julie as she came and greeted Miss Deb.

"What brings you here, Julie?" Miss Deb greeted Julie as she introduced her to the young woman. "Miss Johri is a successful business woman promoting her brand of cosmetics and exquisite jewelry.

The woman giggled. "Oh, Miss Deb, you inspire me always."

Miss Deb introduced Julie as the guest from abroad.

"A winter vacation in Calcutta, is it?" The woman said looking at Julie as she gave a grin.

Julie smiled without saying anything. She stood looking at both the women for a few minutes. It seemed like Miss Deb was occupied with selecting the lipstick shades and Miss Johri was recommending the colors that suited her skin color.

Julie definitely felt it was not a good time to talk to Miss Deb, but she had to. Time was not on her side.

"Would you have a few minutes for me, Miss Deb?" Julie asked politely.

"Please take a seat!" Miss Deb gestured to the chair. "What's on your mind?"

"I wish I had more time with Saras," Julie said without wasting time.

Miss Deb grinned at the statement. "Not many days left before your return."

Her comment sounded like she eager to see Julie leave. She poured tea into her cup from the porcelain teapot. She asked Julie if she cared for anything to drink to which she said no.

"So far you have done well. Be happy. There are many like her. Learning is not their priority."

Julie was glad that Miss Deb brought up the subject of Saras though it bothered Julie that she did not say out the maid girl's name—Saras.

"Saras is different." Julie said in an earnest tone.

Julie handed Miss Deb the notebooks of Saras so she could look at the girl's written work.

"These are done by Saras."

Miss Deb did not expect Julie to show her the notebooks of a maid girl. It even felt embarrassing in front of Miss Johri. A despairing look came on her face as she flipped a few pages in an indifferent manner. Julie thought if she looked at the girl's written work, there could be a change in her attitude, a little hope to fall back on.

Instead, she returned the notebooks without saying anything. Miss Johri kept her eyes on Julie, carefully watching the conversation between them.

"I would hate to see her stop learning after I leave." Julie continued speaking.

"What do you propose?" asked Miss Deb.

"Would you know anyone who could continue tutoring Saras?"

Miss Deb's face immediately displayed constraint at the question. She hurriedly shook her head. "I am sorry I cannot help you with that."

"You were a teacher. That was why I asked." Julie kept her voice low.

"The teachers I interact with would not reach out to domestic helpers. I would be embarrassed to even ask anyone."

Miss Johri giggled as she looked at Julie. "You have high ideas I must say!"

The comment sounded distrustful, but Julie avoided responding. She kept her eyes on Miss Deb to continue the conversation.

"What about talking to the Principal of the school Saras went to?"

"Oh, you don't give up, do you?" Miss Deb remarked. "I cannot do that."

"Why?"

"You want me to request the village school concerning a maid girl? I see you don't know how the society runs here!" Miss Deb sounded astounded.

"Oh, I know how the societal thinking is! It's just that I don't agree to it."

"What is it that you don't agree?" Miss Deb asked in a firm voice.

"Not giving a chance to a young girl who wants to learn."

"She is a maid!"

"Saras has been learning diligently. She wants to learn like how she did in school till age eleven. She was taken out of school." Julie said in a pleading tone.

"I see no point debating in this matter. Teachers like myself are committed to our students and their families. Why should we in heaven's name take interest in a maid who wishes to learn? We have not become insane!"

"You wouldn't understand. You don't live here." Miss Johri interrupted confidently as if she had also become a part of the conversation.

The words instantly elevated Julie's emotions. She neither liked what Miss Deb expressed nor the way Miss Johri added her own comments taking Miss Deb's side. Clearly, Miss Deb sounded rigid and Miss Johri… why would she even take interest in Saras's life when she was focused on promoting cosmetics and jewelry for her business?

Julie looked at Miss Deb earnestly.

"Saras is a girl just like the girl students you have taught. The difference is she grew up in a village. She never had the opportunity to learn because of societal beliefs, in particular, the pressure for girls to get married. You cannot blame her for the background she was born into. It is not her doing. She will not have the cultural etiquettes or the sophistication of our thoughts. However, she is intelligent with common sense. Even if a teacher showed a little inclination to know her, I would not call the teacher insane, but rather sensible and big hearted," Julie responded with impatience with her forceful words.

Miss Deb did not take her eyes off Julie's face, not knowing what to say to what she expressed.

"Do you realize that there are many like Saras. They find small jobs, earn money and life is good for them," she said convincingly.

"What other choices do those girls have? They have no one motivating them to go to school. They cannot get inspiration from their own families. Education is not even on their mind."

Would you say it will be a good life for those girls as they get older?"

"Questioning our societal system will not change anything."

"It is one child I am talking about." Julie said forcefully.

"One or many…all the same."

Julie abruptly became quiet. She felt she needed to calm down before proceeding again. She gazed at Miss Deb's face as she kept her eyes on the newspaper. She did not look at Julie.

Julie felt the time had come to tell Miss Deb straightforwardly that the woman had no idea about the special qualities buried in Saras because she always saw the young girl in the role of a maid.

"I feel helpless that you as a woman and a teacher do not see below the surface of things," said Julie.

"You will be disheartened at the end. Enjoy your Calcutta stay and forget about her!" Miss Johri added grinning.

"I am sorry we don't think alike," responded Julie in a disappointed tone as she stood up to make her way towards the door when instantly Miss Deb interrupted.

"By the way, why don't you let the maid girl practice Bengali reading and writing."

"Saras reads Bengali novels and writes essays."

Mrs. Deb listened without showing any emotion or curiosity. Clearly, she did not feel comfortable listening to what Julie said, even recognizing the idea that Saras could be at the same level as the fourteen-year old students she had one time taught.

"There is a burden you carry when you allow them to indulge in activities not meant for them. They are better off as they are." Miss Deb uttered with a somber tone of voice.

Julie stared at her dismayed, unable to comprehend the way she analyzed learning for underprivileged children. Miss Deb was not ashamed of what she expressed; it did not matter to her if Saras or anyone like her wished to learn.

Julie did not continue the conversation. She said goodbye to her and Miss Johri and went back to her apartment.

She checked the refrigerator for the left-over food she still had. She could barely finish what Girish made for her lunches. She had told him to skip cooking meals for her. She took out a bag of bread slices and made a cucumber-and-tomato sandwich for herself. It was early for dinner, but she did not mind.

She sat quietly on the sofa with the plate of sandwich staring at the two abstract paintings on the wall across from her, their bold lines and bright colors trying to make connections to her thoughts, creating a type of cognizance of the surroundings she was in. The brightest pictures captivated the most attention whereas the rest of the things appeared mellow, and repelled curiosity. The medley of impressions she gathered in the days of her stay would remain in her just like the pictures on the wall....a few conspicuous, others insignificant. The city she had known in her younger years while visiting with her parents now seemed like an unrefined part of her life. Relatives, family, friends—they sparked joy and hopefulness, the experiences that made her family return, to relive a part of life they understood as Calcutta.

Perhaps, a distinct sense of awareness emerges with age and attitude... a sense of consciousness, a questioning mind rather than staying hopelessly content for a life that was veiled from the other side, completely contrasting and a distressful one. An inner conviction that strengthens the belief that 'love' and 'responsibility' stand together; a realization that even touching the life of one is like lighting another candle to kindle the road with a little more hope to walk forward. Julie was convinced that no matter how many contradictions diluted the essence of the subject, the challenging circumstances required dialogues, repeatedly staying nailed on the subject.

Saras's last tutoring lesson was two days before Julie's departure. After the last lesson, Julie told Saras that she would see her the following day when she came to clean the apartment. But there was more in Julie's heart. She felt pained by the thought that she could not convince Miss Deb to arrange for a tutor for Saras. Moreover, she was tense because of what she heard from Sara's mother. Julie could not get her mind off the thought.

"We will hope for the best for you," she softly said to Saras.

Saras smiled; she did not respond back and walked down the stairs. Julie wondered if she had lost the faith that had started to give her some hope.

I cannot rest my mind after listening to the circumstances under which a fourteen-year old girl has to live.

Julie pondered on the thought as she again went downstairs to speak to Miss Deb.

Miss Deb was in the living room, gazing out the window when Julie walked inside led by Girish's wife. Miss Deb was dressed in an elegant silk sari and had decorated herself with pearl earrings and a necklace. Her perfectly coiffured hair with light make up on face looked dignified. At the first glimpse, Julie thought Miss Deb looked attractive, even younger than she appeared normally. She was definitely dressed up for an occasion and Julie wondered if she had plans for the evening.

"I hope I have not come at an inconvenient time."

Miss Deb quickly turned and looked at her standing near the door.

"I am expecting a long-time college friend," Miss Deb answered.

Julie wondered if he was the same friend that Saras spoke to her about. Before Julie could say anything further, Miss Deb began telling how they occasionally met to have dinner. She said there had been a time in their lives when they both thought about spending their lives together. But, that did not happen. What was strange was that they both felt marriage could ruin the relationship they wanted to maintain; neither of them had the courage to fight the thought. They had stayed as friends since then.

In all the days Julie had spent talking to Miss Deb, she had never spoken about the man in her life, though Saras's words had made Julie wonder what kind of a man she was dating. So, when Miss Deb spoke about her college friend, Julie instantly thought—*A person's life story has unsaid parts. They get revealed when the time is right.*

"It's about Saras, again. Please hear me, Miss Deb!" Julie said without wasting time. Julie could tell that Miss Deb was weary of the subject that Julie kept bringing up.

"Please go on!" She gestured to the chair to have Julie take a seat.

"If Saras does not have a tutor after I leave, there could be grave consequences for her. She will be forced to get married to an aged man suffering from ailments. What could be even worse is, Saras may run away again and never return."

Miss Deb was suddenly stupefied as if it was the first piece of ludicrous news she had heard after a long time.

"Where did you hear all that?" Miss Deb grinned sneeringly.

"Saras's mother. She came to see me."

"Of course she would tell you all that. Gossip makes the drama worthwhile."

"But you know Saras's story. I am certain her mother is not making up stories."

"Don't be too sure of that!"

The denial about what Julie said assured Julie how little Miss Deb had faith in Saras's mother's words.

"Surely, Saras's mother is not asking for money. Her daughter's life could change if no one cared."

"Saras's life is not my concern. She is her parent's responsibility."

"But her mother needs help. She is troubled. Saras works for you. Don't you feel concerned for her well-being?"

Julie's emotions rose suddenly. She could feel her tone changing.

"I cannot carry the burden of the people who work for me."

"I am simply asking to have someone tutor her. You have been a teacher. Surely, you know someone."

"It's absurd that you are asking my help for a maid. Besides, how would a tutor change anything?" Miss Deb spoke with an unpleasing force to the words.

"Saras was taken out of school for marriage. But she ran away. If Saras's relatives knew she was engaged in learning with someone, they would not have the courage to insist because they would know the tutor would be watchful. Do you understand?"

"You should have never gotten involved in her life. You don't live here, you have no reason to meddle in her affairs. I say you stay out of it." Mrs. Deb gave a firm look at Julie. "I am sorry I cannot help you in any way."

Julie was overwhelmed by her conclusive words——close to tears and speechless. Julie imagined herself being Miss Deb, even if Julie differed in views with someone, she could never belittle someone who respected her; who worked for her; whose modest home was the garage of her guest house.

Time passed as both waited for the other to speak. Then, Julie stood up from the chair and softly uttered looking at Miss Deb. "I have two more days left before I leave."

Miss Deb did not say anything. Julie walked out of the room.

Girish brought down the suitcase and the back pack to the taxi waiting in front of the guest house. She saw Girish's wife standing near the gate; Julie went forward and handed her an envelope with some cash for Girish and her for helping her during the stay.

Immediately she noticed Bharati standing alone outside the gate near the taxi.

"Where is Saras?" Julie asked walking near the taxi.

Bharati told her that Saras had been up from early morning feeding the calves. Her family owned two cows, Saras saw the birth of the calves and ever since that day, she has been looking after them. Every day she came for an hour from her uncle's home to check on them. Then, from a plastic bag, Bharati took out a flower arrangement made with white jasmine and pink roses and gave it to Julie.

"This is for your hair, *Didi*! Saras told me to give you. She said you looked beautiful in pink color."

"I wanted to see her." Julie restrained her feelings.

Bharati looked away from Julie's face. She did not say anything trying to control her own heart-wrenching feelings.

"Saras is brokenhearted that you are leaving. She spent the night with me. I heard her weeping in the night.'

Julie's throat tensed up. Bharati's facial expression ached her so much that she could not say anything.

"Thank you for everything, *Didi*! We will be forever grateful."

Bharati wiped her eyes with the ends of her sari. Julie could not conceive the sorrow Bharati lived through for her daughter from the little she heard of her story. What would even a consolation mean for her? Bharati was not looking for solace of words from someone. She wanted someone to do something to help her daughter.

Miss Deb stood silently on her front porch and watched with a grave expression as Julie finished speaking to Bharati. She did not come forward. Instead, Julie went up to her and handed her a white envelope.

"Please read it after I leave." Julie cordially did the *namaskar* just as she had done the first day.

The smiling aspect of Miss Deb's facial expression seemed to quickly return at that moment as she gave an acknowledging nod and wished Julie a safe trip back to her home. She watched Julie walk to the taxi and get inside; it was difficult to tell what she was feeling. She fixedly stared at the taxi as it headed down the road.

Bharati walked away just as the taxi disappeared from sight.

Miss Deb glanced at the envelope in her hand. She sat down on a cane chair and opened the sealed envelope. She took out the white folded letter and gazed preoccupied at the long hand written page in black cursive scripts, the date and place written on top right corner.

> *Dear Miss Deb,*
>
> *There will be many days in the years ahead that I will revisit the memories I formed in my stay at your guest house. Thank you for everything.*
>
> *Never in my life did I imagine my solo trip to Calcutta will bring me close to*

the story of a girl, and open my eyes to a world that went beyond my conceivable imagination. I never thought I would lose my heart to her, certainly not during my stay at your guest house for fourteen days.

I was not prepared for this.

The first day I met her, the girl welcomed me with a basket of flowers. She did it on her own. I did not know her name then. She came every day to clean my apartment. I looked at her fragile feet and hands and thought how could such a young girl do cleaning- jobs every day? She worked like an adult and spoke like someone close to my age. She had knowledge of things I did not know. It was hard to believe she was fourteen years old carrying the sensibility as well as the burden of an adult.

I learnt her name was Saraswati, and later I learnt why the name was given to her, a wishful hope every parent has for their daughter. I also came to know why she was called Saras. It was not out of the convenience of a shorter name, as I would have guessed, but to degrade her from the revered goddess's name that she did not deserve.

Saraswati drew my attention from the beginning…a spirited girl whose unrelenting energy was being wasted with laborious physical work when she could have achieved more with her intelligence and natural talents. I learnt about her personality each day, perhaps because I took notice of her as a blossoming girl rather than as a maid. I was overwhelmed when I noticed the compassion she exhibited for a stray dog on the street; it struck me immediately that she was more than an ordinary girl. When I saw her selling flower strings to earn money, so she could buy a fancy sari for her mother, I already knew she was more mindful than an average girl her age. But, above all, what earned my admiration was her will to learn; she repeatedly asked me if I could teach her the school subjects. Why wouldn't I for a child who wanted to learn?

Saraswati learnt from me every day for two hours after finishing the housework. She stayed up late nights so she had the lessons prepared for the next day. She completed all the work I gave her even with the jobs she did during the day. She learnt multiple subjects without difficulty and never missed a single day. Would you not say she had more in her than we gave her credit for?

As the days passed, I came to learn about her life… the fear, the burden that weighed on the young mind. I was shocked that such a life was being planned for the young girl without any kind of feelings for her. Her consent was not even part of the picture! What could such a child do? I was exhilarated that she had the boldness to run away from something she was forced into—marriage. The freedom to live her life was more important than adhering to the narrow societal customs. There are many who follow what is pushed on to them. but we do not know how their life continues to *be—they are like the sand that gets washed into the sea.*

I do not know how Saraswati's life will be like after I leave. If she runs away from home, again, it will be to free herself from the agony she feels; she is not to be blamed. The onus will be on those who pushed her to this neglectful, situation and on those who did nothing to help her.

I had two days left of my stay from the last conversation I had with you. I did not have time to place an advertisement in the newspaper for a tutor, to receive responses, meet the tutors and make a decision. It would have taken me a long time. Instead, I walked down a few streets in the neighborhood, knocked on doors and spoke to people about a tutor for Saras. Some grinned and closed the door on me, some thought my idea was good, but not feasible, some shook their heads and said no annoyingly, some thought visitors should not waste their time on such problems.

I teared up, but I continued the same the following day......walking the streets and knocking on doors. As I believe, there are people who follow their own mind rather than follow what others say or do. They don't hesitate to be different. I met three women and two men who willingly offered to help in ways that were inconceivable for me. They lifted my spirits instantly and I knew I had found the Calcutta I was searching for.

My choice of the tutor was based on two basic requirements; someone who could undertake the task with insightful and compassionate recognition of Saraswati's background, and who has the knowledge and practical experience to comprehend the extent of diversity and challenges that exist in the society. They are important to keep in mind. Having a high-level degree stamped on a certificate without the willful feelings for a girl's wish and for her prospective future, there would not be much benefit for a girl like Saras

I will take care of the tutoring fee and the cost of education and materials needed for Saraswati, including her clothing, shoes, socks and sandals.

Saraswati has me thet three tutors. The tutors have willingly offered their homes to teach Saraswati.

I would appreciate your thoughtful cooperation as Saraswati begins the tutoring sessions. She will need three hours of relief from domestic work every day. Please be on her side.

With sincere regards and good wishes for you
Julie

Miss Deb sat quietly on her chair with the letter in her hand.

Glossary of Bengali Words

Fourteen Days

- Debdaru — a pyramidal evergreen tree, Polyalthia longifolia
- Kurta — an Indian upper garment for men and women
- Namaskar — a traditional Indian greeting
- Shantiniketan — an university town established by the Indian Nobel Laureate Rabindranath Tagore
- Rabindra-sangeet — the songs written and composed by Rabindranath Tagore
- Mashima — the name for someone who is like a maternal aunt
- Jaba — hibiscus
- Bel — jasmine
- Kadam — bur-flower tree
- Rajanigandha — tuberrose
- Champa — Champak
- Khoob taja machh — Really good fresh fish!
- Kochuri — stuffed pastry filled with vegetable or lentil filling
- Didi — the name for older sister or someone like an older sister
- Rupees — Indian monetary note

- Babu   gentleman, the word is used after the first or the last name out of respect
- Neem   Azadirachta indica; tree used for Ayurvedic medicine

Then and Now

F orty-one years had passed since Reba had met Arati Dutta, a close friend of Reba's maternal aunt, Elaine, with whom she visited Arati a few times at her mansion in a distant part of Calcutta. Reba had been then a young girl growing up in the metropolis in the late 1950's.

Reba's mother Iris had been born to Anglo-Indian parents, and so were the roots of her family's preceding generations who passed down their mixed anglicized culture to the generations after. The culturally mixed families established themselves in the metropolis as a result of the business, education, and cultural engagements.

Iris was educated in a Catholic school in Calcutta, and lived a gregarious life with her parents amongst socially well-placed families. Other than her Western physical appearance of fair skin, and light-colored eyes and hair, along with the way she meticulously dressed up in flared skirts that fell to below her knees and laced button-down blouses, it would have been impossible to believe that Iris did not hold the influences of her Indian roots; she spoke Bengali and Hindi fluently. She was well versed in Indian history and culture and showed no apprehension interacting with people from traditional Indian communities.

The skills of her fine fingers led her to choose the career of a piano teacher at the music school established by her family three generations ago. The school that had begun with two piano students had flourished to become an endorsed music institute of instrumental and vocal Western music. It was in those years of her dedication to the school, in the late 1940's carefully guiding and promoting the gifted individual talents, as well as organizing instrumental Western classical concerts for the connoisseurs of Western music in Calcutta, that she came to know Niloy Mallick, who was a frequent guest at her concerts. She was then in her mid-twenties and Niloy, a few years older. They fell in love and got married. They had two sons and a daughter, Rebecca, also known by her nickname Reba.

Niloy was the Chief administrator of university admissions, a man who had clearly inherited the Indian tanned skin and dark hair, high cheekbones, prominent facial features and a healthy physical built. Niloy's deep affinity with European culture caused him to retain the refined Western traditions in his family, though, he was also an ardent Bengali at heart who believed in following traditional customs such as honoring elders by touching their feet and giving his generous share of financial support for the neighborhood Indian festivities. He participated enthusiastically in Bengali men's choruses for local events and invited the chorus group every year for a Christmas dinner he hosted at his home for his diverse community of friends.

Reba was educated predominantly in an English-peaking environment in an Anglo-Indian school. She spoke English as the primary language at home. Her physical features of good height, and a light complexion, with distinct dark-brown hair and light-brown eyes, aligned her far more with her mother's physical characteristics, although there was something about her fervent fascination for the world of art and culture that reminded people how much more she was like her father.

Niloy saw it to be of utmost educational importance that Reba and her brothers participated in cultural journeys with him, traveling to historical sites in different regions of India to broaden their horizons of unfamiliar terrains. He believed such experiences caused them to develop self- reflection and enlightenment of the mind, lasting a lifetime. But, despite the adventurous journeys to places outside of Calcutta with her father, it was Reba, who insisted him for a private Bengali education at home alongside her formal English school education that she already had. Niloy made sure Reba's wish was fulfilled, and hence every day after her return from school, Reba pursued private Bengali classes at home. By the time Reba was eight years old, she was comprehending Bengali to the level that she had substantially mastered the language enough to read the literary works of Bengali writers.

Unlike the Anglo-Indian community of the time, who preferred mingling amongst families like themselves, Reba's parents associated with the diverse cosmopolitan communities of Calcutta, most often with numerous middle and upper-class families. As a result, Reba developed a resilient personality from interacting with her parents' community of friends. It was in those years, that she met Arati Dutta, a college friend of her aunt Elaine, her mother's older sister, which in turn gave rise to an amiable relationship even with Iris and Reba.

It was no surprise that Niloy wished Reba to pursue her higher education in England as he had done, and Reba also aligned with the idea and took the opportunity to pursue history and anthropology at an established university close to London, though, settling outside of India was not on her mind when she went for her studies.

She was well into the completion of her degree when she received the news of her father's demise in Calcutta which urged her to return to the metropolis briefly. It was then that she started to reflect on her future, whether she should return back to Calcutta or settle in England. For all practical reasons, she did not think restarting her life in Calcutta would serve any purpose after her education in England. She was convinced that being physically present in a place was not a criterion for loving a place by heart; she would always hold the passion for the Calcutta she was born and raised in. Iris did not insist on her return. She thought Reba was better off fulfilling her educational goals in England since it was why she left Calcutta in the first place.

Reba returned back to England, continued her education further, and later, accepted the job of a curator in a museum. She missed Calcutta, but her sentiments for the all-embracing life of London suited to the kind of place she wanted to spend her life in. She began to reflect on making London her second home.

She dated a young man of Indian descent who was born and raised in England. She had thought about taking the relationship further, but when she pictured her life with the man as her partner, she did not feel motivated to continue the relationship. There were cultural and emotional incompatibilities; he lacked cognition and attraction for the culture Reba was born and grew up in. His family had been established in England for a few generations. She recognized the disadvantages of such relationships and did not regret the decision to discontinue.

It's preferable to have a few commonalities in a relationship. I would any day favor rational thinking over blind love. That was what she reflected. Just the same, when she thought about the roots of her parents from two different backgrounds, she found nothing unusual about the way her parents fell in love—meeting at a New Year's Eve concert in one of Calcutta's exquisite hotels. She had romanticized their love-story thinking how enchanting it was. *Sometimes, a person gets lucky,* she had thought. But she recognized that her parents both shared the deep-rooted culture of Calcutta of those years. They both were born and grew up in the same city. Therefore, their sentiments and cultural understanding followed on a similar path.

Reba dismissed the idea of venturing into other relationships temporarily and accepted the single life spending time with a few English young men and women she had come to know.

She offered her mother the choice to spend a year with her so her mother could experience the culture that she was distantly part of. Iris appreciated Reba's thoughtful gesture, but told her that Calcutta had always been her revered home and her heart did not desire any other place even for a short stay. Iris never left Calcutta, but Reba visited her every year during Christmas time.

When Reba left for England, Arati Dutta was already an accomplished woman with education from prestigious colleges in Calcutta and London. Her first career was as part of a teaching faculty. Then, after her retirement, she was an active board member of literacy organizations in

India which caused her to gain her honorable reputation for leadership and generosity.

Reba had no contact with Arati since she was twelve years of age. During her short visits to Calcutta, she had thought of reconnecting with Arati Dutta, but hesitated to visit her, knowing that the gap of many years would have distanced the memories. *I would not know where to begin if Arati didn't remember me at all,* Reba reflected. She recalled the few times when she had met Arati, there were many people in Arati's life then. But, now, it seemed unreasonable to assume that Arati would immediately recall those days with her. She remembered the visits she made with Elaine and her mother to Arati's mansion, years before her aunt Elaine moved to Bombay with her husband. The image of Arati as a beguiling young woman, living with a joint family, in an enormous exquisite house with loyal caretakers, had instantly become a revered picture in her mind. She had found Arati Dutta to be an unique woman, and even the occasional visits had created a deep soulful connection to Reba's thoughts.

The mansion was the inherited property of Umesh, Arati's husband, passed down from his father, grandfather and a few generations before as a pride of the family. Seven years older than Arati, Umesh was the president of a financial company and owner of properties at the time, a dignified man with a sense of ethical values.

The archaic Victorian mansion was a praiseworthy attraction that stood for many years like a star-studded gem on the street. The grandeur of matured trees, floral shrubbery, and an immaculately kept flower garden with plants from around the world, once handpicked by Umesh's grandfather on his travels to foreign lands, created an image of a sensational botanical garden.

In those visits, Reba had felt like an honored visitor surrounded by gracious domestic helpers who took care of the guests. It was a vibrant place with cooks in the kitchen, caretakers polishing the balcony banisters, drivers cleaning the parked cars on the driveway and gardeners busy near the flower beds. What Reba did not know was that it was how the many wealthy *zamindari* families of Calcutta lived, leading an amalgamated lifestyle of anglicized and wealthy Indian culture. She remembered having an impressive buffet lunch sitting on the second-floor veranda with Arati, Umesh and a few other family members, overlooking the magnificent view of the back garden, with fruit trees and domesticated birds that made their insulated shelters nestled amongst the branches of the trees. In those moments, she had felt like she had been transported to a world unlike anything she had ever seen— an exuberant representation of a trans-cultural living amidst serene surroundings and fragrance of the seasonal tropical flowers that permeated the air.

Reba had met Umesh's second brother Utpal, and his wife Debika. They lived in the same mansion on the second floor. Umesh's third brother, Utsav and his wife Chandrima had their living units on the third floor. The three beautiful women of the mansion were close in age, Reba recalled their lively and hospitable personas wearing stylish cotton saris pulled over their shoulders, elegant gold chains around their necks and packs of intricate gold bangles on their arms. The women were the managers of the daily household work; they instructed caretakers to the jobs, but they never entered the kitchen and practically never stepped out of the mansion by themselves.

In her obscured memory, it was Arati's unique personality that she remembered the most. Unlike the women of *zamindari* families, Arati had not limited her married life to the comforts of home. Married to Umesh at the age of sixteen, she came into the family as the first bride, an arranged relationship initiated by Umesh's parents, grandparents and uncles to have a young beautiful bride from a middle-class cultured family in their household. Arati's youthful charm had impressed Umesh's parents enough to pursue talks of marriage soon after they saw her. Arati was married in July 1946.

Soon after settling into her new home, the young sixteen-years old Arati expressed to Umesh her desire to continue education for herself. Arati requested that Umesh speak to his father to have his permission. Umesh, twenty-three years of age, was impressed by Arati's unequivocal wishes, but could not imagine making such a request to his father for his enterprising, spirited sixteen- years old wife. It was outstandingly unheard of coming from a newly married young girl in the *zamindari* household. His timidness to approach his father hurt Arati's feelings, though she understood his situation. She made up her mind to take the bold step herself, and to politely express her wishes to her father-in-law.

"I wish to continue my education which was disrupted because of marriage," she told her father-in-law.

It was the most unanticipated encounter and statement from the new family member. Umesh's mother was considerably alarmed. She told Arati in one firm comment, "Women in our family take care of the home after marriage. Their mind should not wonder about things focused on themselves."

Arati did not show any kind of displeasure towards her words. She knew she could never disgrace her parents and members of her own family by disrespecting the family she was married into; she had to restrain her feelings. However, her father-in-law did not respond to Arati right then. He had nodded somberly to her request; Arati had no idea what she would hear back from him.

After three days, Umesh called Arati to see him in his office. She had to be prepared to listen to what he said no matter how disappointing it was. She could not display any kind of objection to what he decided.

But, what she heard, astonished Arati. He told her that three tutors had been arranged for her education at home. She need not worry about going to school outside of home. Emotionally overtaken, she had bowed down and touched his feet.

Even as Reba sensed Arati to be a broad-minded woman of her time, she could not disregard the fact how Arati continued to follow the attire of conventionalism at home on her everyday embellishments. She maintained the traditional styles of dress up for the family she was married into; it was how she was raised in her own family, to respect and honor the living styles of her husband's family. She always wore elegant wide bordered cotton saris with a matching blouse. Her pastel complexion blended with her bright appealing dark doe eyes. Her long course wavy black hair was parted in the center, and tied behind her in a bun; the red vermillion powder was carefully smeared on the center parting and she had a small deep maroon colored *kumkum* on her forehead. The fullness of her cheerful face with dimples on both cheeks, appeared to fit perfectly with her amiable vitality, a kind of charm Reba found hard to forget.

By the time Reba put her mind to the thought of actually meeting Arati in one of her visits to Calcutta, years had gone by. It was no wonder she felt unusual when she pursued the plan; it was a mixed feeling of ambivalence and nostalgia, considering the many years of no contact with Arati. Reba knew there would be no continuation from when she saw her the last time; memories fade with growing age; some moments get completely erased. Moreover, Arati was no longer living in the mansion Reba fondly remembered, but she had moved to another address which Reba learnt not too long ago.

Reba's family's long-time driver, Shankar, drove quietly through the central part of Calcutta, passing through streets with houses that had black railed balconies and green plantation shutters. He drove through narrow lanes where vendors had their shops packed with people and shoppers squeezed their way through the sidewalks. Reba kept thinking about Arati; she could not believe she had finally decided to meet her. She could still refer to Arati as her aunt, the way Arati appeared to her in those years. Now, those endearing moments hovered in her mind.

Reba stared out the car window, the view outside was no longer graced with aristocracy and grandeur, as she had seen even when she was growing up and what she had heard from her parents when they were school going children. What she now saw were the forgotten grand old architectural structures that stood in the midst of crumbling neighborhoods—the faded legacy of the opulent British past that once was a vibrant part of Calcutta.

She took out a small mirror from her purse and looked at her face. In the lapse of time living in England, her appearance had somewhat altered. Her hair was shorter, with a few strands of grey visible. Her complexion remained lighter, predominantly due to the lack of sun exposure, though, she had always been told she had the visible anglicized appearance which would arouse curiosity of whether she had roots from the northern state of Kashmir. But what had not changed were her sentiments for Calcutta. She used to have multitude of memories with people in various localities and it was because of their insightful thinking and benevolent attitudes that she had grown to love the city.

Shankar turned into a one-way street. The street names on the posts were barely decipherable, the letters erased on discolored boards, dirt and stains covered the street signs. In front of the last lamp post, stood a sizable light-blue building, probably once a noteworthy structure.

"We are here, *Didi*. The Asrita House," Shankar said stopping the car.

From her seat, Reba stared fixedly at the building for few minutes. What she saw and what she had imagined were quite different. She kept quiet. The name of the building sounded like an organization of some sort. A sign on the wall in front read, 'Asrita House - A Home away from Home'. Feeling skeptical, Reba checked the address again. It was the right place.

She got out of the car searching for the main entrance door. She noticed the sign Office with an arrow pointing towards the back of the building. She followed the arrow walking through what looked like a driveway till she came to an open entrance with a few steps. She walked up and landed in a wide open lobby surrounded on three sides by buildings with windows. She did not know what to think; she had never seen anything like that. She stared at the architectural plan of the place. In the center of the entry area was a marble statue fountain of a woman holding a child standing inside an elliptic-shaped water basin. The sculpture brought back images of Italy, the ancient Roman private gardens where the fountains symbolized the classical ideas of beauty, seclusion, serenity and the woman of humility that characterized motherly love and tenderness. The marble surface had stains of dirt; the yellow-and-blue Tuscany porcelain tiles shone bright in the midst of the discolored walls of the basin; the scraggy remnants of once-enticing pieces. There was no water flowing out of the fountain, it had been lying dry for who knows how long. The quaint looking vertical windows of the four-storied building were antiquated, faded curtains hung on them, not replaced or modernized.

Reba walked towards the office room, passing the marble columns aligned on both sides of the ground floor. She had not made an appointment for the visit; she only had the address. Neither she nor Iris knew anything about the place. She noticed an elevator at one side of the entrance and a flight of stairs next to it. Every so often, women in white saris with light-green border walked down the corridors, but it still seemed like a quiet sparse place with infrequent visible activities. Suddenly, Reba noticed a middle-aged woman, wearing a colored printed sari, walking towards the door posted with the sign Office. She stopped and smiled as she saw Reba walking towards in her direction.

"*Namaskar!*" The woman folded her hands and gestured her greeting.

Reba said *namaskar* and gestured back cordially.

"Are you here for someone?" The woman asked.

"Yes."

"Please come in." The woman let Reba enter the office and then she followed her inside. She went to her desk and took a seat. "Please sit down." She gestured to the chair across from her.

She appeared like someone in her mid-sixties with short dark hair till her shoulders, medium- tanned skin on a round shaped face with likable features. She wore a silver rimmed eyeglass which hung in front of her that she put on when she needed to read a message or look through a form.

"Would you like some water?"

"No, Thank you! I am fine." Reba replied softly.

Reba felt slightly unsettled, unsure of what to think about the place though she could clearly guess what the place was—a senior home. It was the first time she was in a place like that in Calcutta.

The office had an appearance of newness. The walls had been painted; the wooden book racks and the two steel cupboards gave the impression of a principal's office room. Pictures of old Calcutta life hung on rustic frames on one side of the wall, and photos of women taking part in activities pinned on a bulletin board on the wall across. The four tall windows poured ample amount of light inside the room, while the two weighty fans hanging from the high ceiling ventilated the air inside the sizable space. The pendulum of the ancient wooden grandfather clock oscillated quietly at its own mundane pace in the corner of the room.

"What's your name?" asked the woman.

"Reba Mallick...full name Rebecca Mallick."

"Are you from Calcutta?"

"I was born and grew up here. I do not live here anymore."

"Where do you live?"

"England."

The woman smiled. "Welcome back! So, who are you here to meet?"

"Mrs. Arati Dutta."

There was a short silence.

"I do not recall an appointment to meet her." The woman looked wonderingly at Reba.

"There was none. I only had the address of this place."

The woman nodded smiling. "How is she related to you?"

Reba smiled hesitantly. "Like an aunt…"

The woman nodded. She said her name was Nibedita Sen. She was the head supervisor of Asrita. She mentioned how Asrita was established twelve years ago as a home for the elderly.

The words instantly stunned Reba. She kept quiet, unable to say anything right then. She had to remind herself that many years had passed from the time she was imagining; it was why her mind felt blurred at the thought of a senior home.

"I never knew Calcutta had homes for the elderly," she said hesitantly.

"We are one of the first ones."

She described how the demand was rising as more young people found jobs outside of Calcutta. Living alone had become an undesirable option for the elderly parents. They were also not willing to permanently live with their children in distant unfamiliar places.

Reba listened absentmindedly trying to absorb the idea that Arati Dutta was living in a senior home. Neither she nor her mother had recognized the address; it had made them wonder whether Arati had purchased another home. But a senior home had never occurred to them.

"I was not expecting to find a place like this for the woman I am visiting," said Reba. She was thinking about Arati Dutta—her loving face, the mansion she lived in.

Ms. Sen smiled. "For many, there is a stigma attached to the idea of the 'old home,' like it is a neglected place for aged people where they feel lonely, away from the normal social activities. But, in Asrita, it is certainly not true," said Ms. Sen softly.

Reba did not know what to say.

Ms. Sen opened the drawer of her desk and handed a piece of printed paper to Reba thinking she was feeling unsettled in her mind.

"You can take a look at our activities."

Reba read the list arranged by time, place, and the person in charge; Yoga and meditation, cultural entertainment (music, dance, drama), lecture discourse on people, history, art, and spiritual thoughts; indoor games, birthday celebrations, strolls in the garden, field trips, tea time at the club house and short movies.

"You are indeed far ahead than I imagined," said Reba.

Ms. Sen smiled. "Socially, Calcutta has always been a few steps ahead of the rest of the country. I consider this work my family. I try to do the best for Asrita."

Reba sat attentively listening to what Ms Sen said. She was not going to tell Ms. Sen about the thoughts coming to her mind about the woman named Arati Dutta.

It takes a lot of adeptness and strength of compliance to make this kind of transition to senior living, Reba reflected.

Arati Dutta did not live an ordinary life. Her life at the mansion was encompassed with numerous types of activities, from the poorest localities to the wealthiest households. She was a dynamic participant of activities in hospitals, schools, and women's organizations. Reba knew Arati's life in Asrita was incomparable to how Arati had lived. Even with the numerous enriching activities, Asrita could not possibly give her the same life she had in the mansion, Reba thought.

Perhaps Asrita became the best option for Arati—it was all Reba could conclude.

Life is about constant readjustment and to expect that change would be just like what it was before, is placing oneself in the puddle of ignorance.

Ms. Sen gestured to the building across; she said the attendants and caregivers lived in that building. Most were unmarried women who had done social work and had a nursing education.

"Amazing! I commend you and your team for the efforts to run this new concept of living."

Again, Reba felt sentimental thinking about Arati; her joint family, the extravagant life, so much of everything. It was dreary to conceive the life she has now. What was supposed to feel like a joyous day, suddenly seemed poignant, and gave an impression of impermanence - what a person has today, could be different tomorrow.

Reba understood from what Ms Sen described that the Asrita building used to be a hotel in the time of colonial rule. Years after India's independence, it was lying abandoned without any management taking control. It reached the worst condition when political changes started happening in the city. Then, later, a reputed women's non-profit organization called *Seva* took control. They had few choices of what the place could be; one of them was 'a home for the elderly' and Ms. Sen took the responsibility. She proceeded to lead the renovation work to bring it to reliable standards fit to accommodate senior citizens.

"Women taking charge of a meaningful social service. Extraordinary!" Reba responded.

"Women can make changes happen when they are given responsibilities." Ms Sen gave an appreciative smile.

There was a brief silence during which Reba watched Ms. Sen pick up the phone and exchange words with someone. The woman appeared composed in her persons, she had a cordial, assuring attitude. Her desk looked an active place with files, stacks of forms, and folders arranged in groups on the table. An old typewriter was on table next to her desk.

"The assistant is escorting Arati to the lounge downstairs. I can take you there," said Ms. Sen as she stood up to escort Reba to the lounge.

Walking down the corridor, Reba noticed the terracotta decorations on walls, flower pots lined along the sides, and well-designed hardy hand railings fixated to the floor as she walked down the mosaic corridor floor. She sensed the peaceful and artistic aura of the surrounding even though subdued feelings kept coming back in her.

Ms Sen opened a large wooden door that led to a long-covered veranda. She gestured to the section where cane chairs and tables were laid out, she said it was where the Asrita members had their afternoon tea at four o'clock.

"Not much different from what I had known in my childhood years," said Reba smiling.

"The elderly members prefer to retain the habits they have always known. Tea time is one of them."

A few marble steps lead down to an elaborate garden with well-trimmed hedges, rose flower beds surrounded by walking paths. Ms. Sen said it was a favorite place to take evening walks since most the older women preferred a quieter, less crowded surrounding.

For a few minutes, Reba stared at the garden thinking how Arati Dutta feels taking walks in the Asrita garden. A feeling of sadness overtook Reba momentarily.

Ms Sen ended the talk and showed Reba the lounge entrance. She wished Reba an enjoyable meeting with her aunt.

Reba stepped inside, walking towards the sofas to take a seat by the glass window. She looked outside…the overgrown greenery provided privacy from property next door, masking the not-so- pleasant looking things lying around. She knew the outside felt gloomier whenever she visited Calcutta; she wished things had changed in the years, but it wasn't so.

There were English newspapers and Bengali magazines lying on the coffee tables. The room looked renovated with modern ceiling lights, fans, Persian rugs laid out in every section of the sitting areas. The vacant walls and the large glass windows made the room appear less crowded. The word *OM* carved on wood hung on the front wall across the main entrance door; it was the first place on which the eyes fell on entering the room.

Reba never imagined she would be visiting a senior home in Calcutta on her visit, let alone one like this.

Two women walked in through the door, the younger woman holding the arms of the older woman. Reba thought she recognized one of the faces, but she was unsure. The older woman's face was frail, with a clean baby-soft complexion, her lush short silver hair had streaks of black, she stopped briefly to look in the direction of Reba, then took careful steps forward to where she was sitting. As they both walked closer, Reba recognized the older woman—Arati Dutta. Reba stood up gazing at her face. For a short moment, Reba felt a little somber looking at her, she quickly hid her feelings. The woman wore a light-green cotton and creme *Dhakai* sari, a matching cotton blouse, a light-green pashmina stole draped over her shoulders. She kept her gaze on Reba with an angelic smile, the dimples still prominent even though her face had lost its round appearance. She looked as if she was making sure of her words before she said anything.

The younger woman, possibly her caretaker, was probably in her early sixties; she had a reserved friendly face.

Reba stepped forward to greet them. Arati pleasantly stretched her arms towards Reba to give her an embrace; she immediately recalled how Arati amiably greeted people when she met them.

"Reba! My sweet Reba!"A delightful smile lit up Arati's face. She hugged Reba passionately and kissed her cheek.

Reba had not anticipated the highly expressive greeting. It was as if she instantly recognized who she was. Reba bent down and touched Arati 's feet, a custom that was ingrained in her from her father.

"Bless you, my child! Bless you! How did you remember me after all these years?" Arati stroked Reba's hair and cheek.

"I cannot forget you," said Reba softly suppressing the emotions as she helped Arati to a sofa across from where she was sitting.

"This is *Hira*. She lives with me. Do you remember her?" Arati said gesturing to the woman to introduce her.

Reba did not remember having seen the woman. It had been many years ago and Arati's mansion life had different kinds of people…. working, visiting, staying… there was no way she would remember the individuals. Besides, when she had visited Arati with her aunt, she had been more fascinated by the decorative appearance of the enormous place than the people.

As Reba sat across from Arati, she perceived the woman in a new light, now that she saw her closely. Her face had lost weight and the features looked prominent. She still looked well principled and possessed the same beauty… her bright eyes and the fine cut of her lips. Her course silver hair showed no part of the scalp; there was no red *kumkum* on the forehead. She was definitely a woman who had lived through changes. She had a thin gold chain around her neck, and two thin, intricately engraved gold bangles on her right arm. On the left arm, she wore the gold *loha*, which immediately surprised Reba as women customarily take off the symbolic part of their marriage jewelry when their husbands pass away. It was then Reba realized there must have been more to the woman's life than what was discernible from outside. Reba saw an expression of both serenity and sorrow on her face.

Arati straightened her sari and leaned back in the chair. She kept looking at Reba, smiling without saying anything for a short while.

"You were a young girl the last I saw you. Your aunt Elaine was one of my best friends."

Reba nodded smiling. She was surprised that Arati had quickly connected her to Elaine.

"I thought you might not remember me."

"I don't forget the faces I meet. I even remember your mother, Iris, a beautiful woman, she had made scones for Umesh and me."

Reba stared at her, feeling the gentle comfort of listening to the details Arati still remembered.

"I am eighty-six years of age and I have come a long way. Life keeps taking me forward and I have to accept that." She paused, self-reflecting on what she said.

"You still look beautiful," Reba said smiling.

"What's the beauty left in me now?" She laughed softly. "Did you ever think I would be in Asrita?"

Reba shook her head, she couldn't find the words to describe. "It seems unreal."

"It's called–reconciling to change," said Arati.

Reba smiled. The fact that Arati said it so simply, amazed her.

"There were many reasons….." Arati paused giving herself time to organize her words.

"After the unexpected death of Umesh's second brother Utpal, his third brother Utsav took his business to another part of India. Umesh was the only one left to manage the mansion. Utpal's in-laws were helping raise his two boys and a daughter while his wife, Debika, started tutoring recitation to young children to keep her mind engaged. The sudden passing of Utpal was a disturbing change for her at a young age, but she realized she could not go on grieving for Utpal, she had to bring inspiration to herself. Umesh arranged a private tutoring room for her so she felt encouraged with her new activity."

"Recitation? That's amazing!"

"Debika had an incredible talent for poetry. We used to have a poetry time in the evening when everyone gathered to hear her recite for us. Utpal came to listen to her every time even though he never recited himself."

Arati paused. She asked Hira to pour her a glass of water from the water jug on the table; she took a few sips. "Events change people's lives."

Reba listened quietly. In the years she came to the mansion, she had seen young girls and boys, but she did not know how they were related to Arati. But she remembered them to be polite, obedient children, at least, that was how they seemed in front of the many adults.

"So, how has your life been?" Arati asked softly.

"I live in London. I am used to the life there now."

"Of course. We knew London as much as we knew Calcutta in our time," said Arati.

"Calcutta has gone through changes from the time I left the city."

"Nothing stays the same." Arati paused. "It is then we learn to appreciate what we had."

"You had an extraordinary life at home."

"Our living displayed all facets of life—extraordinary was one part."

She described how nurturing creativity was a significant part of home life, especially for the children. She told how the family gatherings were meant for sharing the children's talents. It did not matter what the children had passion for; it was a time to share with others.

Utpal's older son created his own magazine of places he traveled with his father and he shared his experiences in those gatherings. Arati's son, Udai played tunes on his spanish guitar and Utpal's daugher, Rakhi, exhibited her albums she created of dried flower decorations made from the flowers in their garden. She used calligraphy to write the names of each flower and the imaginative name she gave to each florid arrangement.

"Rakhi sat for long hours in the back veranda making the decorations while Udai created his own musical tunes in his room. The adults never interfered in how and what they did. Talents develop on their own at a young age. We were there to motivate them."

Arati paused, smiling pleasantly to herself. She carefully chose the next words what to say.

"We thought life was peaceful at home even though strikes, protests, and shut downs had started to emerge in Calcutta. Then, one afternoon our life at home took a shocking turn. Bikash, our dear gardener, fell into the hands of a gang. He was robbed and lay unconscious for two hours on the street. He died before help came. It was the first biggest shock for us. Bikash's father was Umesh's grandfather's gardener. Gardening had been their established practice for generations, Bikash knew about every little bud prospering in our garden. A lot of knowledge had been passed down to him from his father. He took care of the flowers and trees like his own children. The garden lost its charm in his absence. It was never the same."

Arati looked through the window; her mind seemed occupied. Then she told how the caretakers were like family members of her mansion. She spoke about how her husband made rules for them not to socialize with outsiders as they became more vulnerable with social and political changes taking place.

She paused and looked eagerly at Reba, almost as if she was waiting to have her company.

"You look beautiful, Reba. I am sure the life in England has suited to your taste."

"My work keeps me in good spirits."

Arati nodded slowly, keeping her eyes on Reba.

"Is there a man in your life?"

Reba shook her head, feeling a little conscious of the question.

"I feel a sense of contentment settled in me. I don't think about marriage anymore," Reba responded calmly, smiling at Arati.

"You mean to say you have never dated a man in all these years?"

Reba laughed. She liked how Arati made the serious subjects lighthearted.

"I admired a few from a distance. It is not easy for me to fit into a man's life even if he seems suitable. I don't know what it is."

"Of course. You choose who you feel is right for you. But, remember, there is no one in this world perfectly made for you…no one. That is where a woman's sensibility and determination come into the picture. You have to hold onto both, tightly."

"It's what I struggle with. It is easier to handle the sensibility and determination alone, but with another person, it is a whole new set of things."

"There is certainly nothing wrong in living your life alone. As long as you are occupied with good work, living in the company of good people, they bring as much fulfillment as well."

She stopped briefly. Reba could tell from the way she spoke that she didn't delve into too many questions or comments; she had a way of concluding with thoughtful words accepting gracefully whatever the other person felt or decided.

She continued to describe how Umesh had to sell Utpal's businesses after his death. He saved the money in the bank for Utpal's two sons and a daughter. He wanted to make sure his nephews and niece faced no financial difficulties in their father's absence.

"But, money had another side. Our home was surrounded by extremists who took control of Calcutta. They sat and slept outside the home premises for days. We could not step out in the fear of being harassed." Arati stopped. She coughed to clear her throat.

"Why were they outside your house?"

"They demanded money. A lot of money. Umesh believed in peaceful solutions. He knew resisting would be harmful to all."

Reba listened. She had heard of the challenging political situations taking place in Calcutta during her absence, but she could not imagine Arati's family being directly affected in those years.

"We did not believe in distributing money to those groups who demanded to benefit their causes. They were healthy young men who could work and earn. Money was to help those who truly needed it...the poor...who did not have enough to feed their family with young children, take care of their sickness, look after the aged family members with acute health issues, pay the school education fees. There were many such people. But, Umesh knew there would be tension if the wishes of the groups were not fulfilled. He was caught in the dilemma."

She spoke about her children as they got older; they went to colleges and began their own lives. Her son Udai got admission to a well-reputed business school in America. Later, he settled with an American girl he liked; neither she nor Umesh interfered in his decision.

"You have to let everyone live the life they want as long as contentment and harmony are advocated," Arati said softly.

Listening to Arati, Reba could not believe the things she said and the way she expressed them; her idea of conversation embraced profound thoughts. Even at the age of eighty-six she presented the small details of her life with expressions of sensibility and clear memory.

A lady attendant brought three cups of tea and a plate of sliced cake and placed them on the table. Reba instantly knew it was Arati who must have requested the tea and snacks to be brought for Reba.

She continued speaking about her daughter, Urmila, who was a few years younger to Udai, and grew up to be Umesh's right hand. She helped him with financial matters. She became an electrical engineer, got a job in Bombay, and later married her classmate. They had one daughter. It was apparent that the younger members of Arati's family were drifting to their new lives away from the mansion. At one point she expressed heavy-heartedness when she told how her son had wanted her to sell the mansion when he saw Umesh starting to have health troubles. She had hesitated mostly thinking about Umesh because he wanted her to continue living in the mansion with caretakers even after he was gone. He secured more than enough financial wealth for Arati and their children if they wished to live there.

"How could my son ask to relinquish a home that brought joy to my forefathers and to myself? A home is a blessing in life with memories studded inside." Arati quoted Umesh's words to Reba.

"How did you feel about living there?" asked Reba.

"As long as Umesh was alive, I was going to live there. It was my home since I was sixteen years of age." She paused and told Reba to take a sweet from the plate.

Then, Arati described the most shattering experience when Umesh suffered his first stroke a year later, he became bedridden. She could not imagine her life without Umesh by her side. Umesh's youngest brother Utsav and his wife were the only family at home. They had returned from Bombay and they became her greatest support. She hired Bhupen, an experienced and qualified nurse from a well-reputed Calcutta hospital, to help her husband with his daily needs. In a year's time, Umesh went back to activities, but he did not have the same energy as before.

"One day, sitting alone on the veranda, Umesh asked me a strange question: what I would do if he left the world before me. I could not give him a reply. It was like he was saying, "How would you feel if you were alone?" Such a thought had never occurred in my mind. Then as days passed, Umesh started to lose his memory and spoke less…" Arati gave herself a pause to gather her strength and took a deep breath.

"In life you get the strength to come to terms with your worst fear even if it seems the most difficult thing to do. Umesh passed away a year later in his sleep."

She continued narrating about the evening three days before he passed away, when he brought up the most unbelievable topic—their marriage. She said his voice was soft, and he spoke slow. She said when Umesh first saw Arati on their wedding day, he felt she was someone he had known for a long time. He instantly fell in love with her. He could not believe it was an arranged marriage.

Reba started to feel the sentiments stir inside Arati. Listening to her, Reba felt she was sitting right there in the mansion watching their conversation.

"If I ever leave the world before you, please don't take off the *loha* from your left arm and the gold bangles you have worn all these years with me. Keep wearing your nice sarees and dress up as you have always done. It is my wish." Arati quoted Umesh's words and then paused.

"I lost a part of myself with the passing of Umesh," Arati said lowering her eyes.

Reba understood why she had the *loha* on.

"But I had faith that everything would be all right. No situation ever stays the same. With that strength of belief, I rose up and continued again," Arati said softly.

The intense words, however endearing they sounded, were things Reba did not anticipate listening to. It felt like an imaginary world from the pages of a book for the reason that there was so much of profoundness in how she and Umesh had lived. Reba did not know what to say and how to put the right words to her. Anything she would try to express would not come close to what she really felt or meant. She understood that Arati wanted to retell the details of everything that Reba had missed, it was not every day that she met someone who cared to listen to how her life had been.

Arati gestured to her arms. " I still wear the bangles of my marriage."

"And what about you? What did you think when you saw Umesh on marriage day?" Reba asked laughing just to make the conversation lighter.

"I don't remember what went through my mind then. I was sixteen. But what I remember clearly was that I missed my pet parrot "Mukti". She used to talk to me all the time. I loved her. If she didn't see me, she would call out loud,"Aroti! Aroti! *Kothai tumi?* My thoughts were more on Mukti." Arati laughed as she spoke.

There was energy still passionately alive in Arati. Her caretaker, Hira sat quietly close to her, she offered her water every so often. She was a tanned woman, who had subdued, likable facial features; her long hair was tied in one long braid. Her modest attire was limited to a simple printed cotton sari, and multi-stoned earrings that matched her thin necklace. She listened quietly, and smiled every so often when something amusing came up in the conversation. Reba assumed she was not married, even her demeanor seemed like she was there to look after Arati.

Reba understood why Arati decided to live in Asrita. After Umesh passed away and her children dispersed to distance places, she continued to live in the mansion with one of Umesh's brothers and his wife. But she knew she would become depended on them as she got older. It was when she approached Asrita; she knew about the organization through her own work with women in social situations.

"In life you need to live gracefully with a humble mind. Age does not discriminate. Every person faces challenges, the degrees vary. As long as I could walk and think, I did not wish to be a burden on anyone, not even on my own children. I chose to do what was less troublesome for others and for myself. It was why Asrita was my choice. My son did not approve when I made the decision, but in my heart, I knew it was the best decision."

"Quite amazing after the kind of life you had lived."

Arati nodded softly smiling. "Asrita is another kind of living. At my age it is suitable. Why aggravate over looking back and aching in pain? I am not going to have that life back. Now, I am getting used to the life I have."

Reba was quiet for a little while. Then she asked about the mansion. She could not imagine that an inherited estate of such proportion could lie neglected as Arati lived in Asrita. Her family had dispersed to places outside of Calcutta, even her children had settled in foreign lands.

"What's with the mansion now?"

"Locked up and partially empty. Many things were sold to antique stores. Some remain in boxes, others still inside rooms, antiquated. It's good that Umesh's parents and grandparents did not have to see the fate of those remarkable pieces."

Arati said she went back to that life, to those moments in her mind when she wanted to be there, but she had faith that everything would be good even though it would never be what she had in the past.

She spoke how the builders offered her high prices to demolish the mansion and reconstruct modern structures, but she had declined every offer. She said the house would either be donated for a social purpose—to help women of Calcutta or let it remain a Heritage Home.

"A home for the elderly is the first on my mind. No man or woman should have to suffer loneliness and pity, secluded from social activities by living alone in their home. The second choice is a heritage home. Companies could take care and maintain the mansion as a place of attraction for generations to come."

A woman worker of Asrita walked up to Arati and whispered to her that her car was waiting for her. Arati looked at Reba and asked if she wished to visit the mansion.

"Oh, my goodness! I would love to!" She quickly glanced at her watch and said she would inform Shankar. This was a chance she could not miss!

"Who knows what will become of the mansion when you come next time," said Arati.

She stood up, holding Hira's arm and started walking towards the door. She walked slowly with a grace of a gentle dignity. Her physical ability was strong, and she was still mindful of people around her. She waved a friendly greeting to a woman sitting by herself in one of the chairs.

The driver waited at the entrance with the black Ambassador. As soon as he saw Arati and Reba approaching, he opened the back door and waited holding the door.

Arati thanked the driver, and got inside the car. Reba took the seat next to Arati while Hira sat next to driver in the front. Madhav had been Umesh's personal driver for years, now, Madhav's son Mohan, took the responsibility and served Arati.

"Please stop by at the sweet shop at the corner of the next street." Arati told Mohan leaning forward. Reba remembered the shop, it was the same place from where her father used to bring boxes of sweets made with jaggery for her mother.

Mohan drove through the crowded streets and narrow lanes. Reba barely recognized the locality she had frequented years ago. After twenty minutes, the car stopped in an alley in front of a sweet shop with its name posted on an outmoded board. The shop no longer looked like how she had known it, she probably wouldn't have recognized the place if she came alone.

Arati told Mohan to bring the types of sweets she wanted as she handed him the cash. Mohan returned with hard cover boxes of sweets and two large earthen containers of the sweet yogurt covered with decorative paper and tied with a jute string. Arati handed everything to Reba.

"These are for you to take home. Make sure you and your family relish the taste of the sweets."

Reba was instantaneously startled by her gesture of immense generosity. She knew how important this kind of gesture was in the *zamindari* family tradition Arati came from. 'Giving' was a blessing and honor for the family name, it was how Arati had interacted socially all her life. But,what surprised Reba most was that even after many years, when her living style had altered to a new reality, she still held the kind of presence of mind that was prevalent in another time.

Arati took out a small bag from her purse and placed it on her lap. The pleats of her light-green and cream sari had not lost their freshly ironed appearance. Sitting close her in the car, Reba noticed how comfortably she sat and carried the conversation.

"Here is a photo of Umesh. The most recent one." Arati handed the photo of her late husband to Reba.

Reba recalled very little about Umesh's appearance, but now, as she saw his photo, she could fit him quickly in the *zamindar* family lineage…a tall, light skinned man with bold facial features. He brought out a dignified persona.

"I faintly recognize the face now that I see his picture. He was a handsome man."

Arati laughed. "His proud parents expressed the same thoughts to my parents when they came to meet me the first time."

"I am sure they couldn't get their eyes off you either."

"I was young, bubbling with life. Appearance was my last concern," said Arati.

"Honestly, I cannot imagine you in an arranged marriage."

"First came marriage, then came love. My parents brainwashed me with such thoughts," said Arati smiling at Reba. "We were restricted in many ways. Falling in love with a boy or a girl was banned from our thoughts. Can you imagine how painful it was to suppress the feelings of love in a young heart? All the joy and heartache had to be kept in you."

Reba felt an indescribable sensation as Arati narrated the fragments of her life. She continued to describe how, for generations, the men in Umesh's family were the landlords who managed the businesses. Their home life was a contrast to their life outside the home. Their wives came into the family as very young brides, but lived without the freedom and independence that they wanted. They were protected with comfort and luxury, and they rarely stepped out of their opulent, monotonous living style. They were taken care of by domestic caretakers; there was no dearth of pampering.

"Life appeared peaceful, but there was the struggle of feelings in the hearts of the young girls as they grew to be young women. The men enjoyed life to the fullest outside the home, but their wives could never complain, could never express feelings to others. The husbands had to be respected." Arati spoke with a determined yet passionate voice.

She said Umesh brought changes for the first time. He encouraged the women in the household to step out to educate themselves. He was not strict about what the wives wished to do. Sometimes, he differed from his brothers though they they were more broad minded than many men in those years.

"As young women, we conformed to good behavior. We believed in maintaining self-respect in front of others, and in return, we tasted freedom for the first time. It was then we started to recognize the value of independent thinking."

The car stopped in front of the huge wooden gate in the middle of the high walled enclosure.

The gatekeeper walked to the car and greeted Arati bending his head low through the open window at the driver's side. Arati said that six generations of the gatekeeper's family had worked at the mansion. But she already saw changes; the newer generations of the families preferred other kinds of jobs outside of Calcutta that gave them better pay and opportunities.

Mohan drove the car through a long driveway with green lawns on both sides. Two massive marble lion sculptures stood at the center of both the lawns. He stopped the car in front of a long line of front doors. He opened the car door for Arati and Reba to step out.

For a few minutes, Reba stood mesmerized staring at the enormous brick-colored sandstone mansion with a flamboyant terrace of dancing figurines perched on the columns. She could not recall in her memory the details when she came as a young girl. Suddenly, the architecture felt like a renowned structure that she saw pictures of in books.

Arati took out the keys and walked slowly towards the long open corridor with Corinthian pillars. She unlocked one of the large teak entrance doors.

"Here we are! The home I entered at sixteen years of age," she said.

Reba stepped inside staring at the immenseness of the interior, awestruck. She had a difficult time imagining how a newly married young girl could absorb the magnitude of the place coming in for the first time. The walls had the burnt appearance of old architecture, the cut-glass Belgian chandelier hung at the entrance and the fluted Corinthian Pillars surrounded the large courtyard inside the mansion. Colonnaded balconies and stairs surrounded the courtyard leading to the family quarters on different levels. The arches designed on top of the balcony were studded with stained glass and the walls were made of decorative tiles and murals.

Arati walked towards the courtyard at the back. She said it was place where the annual festivities were celebrated with a lot of pomp and show. The women of the family did the *Alpana* on the courtyard floor, and everyone wore their new clothes bought for the occasions, even the servants and caretakers were gifted with new clothes and jewelry. The family tailor came a month before to take the measurements so the clothes were ready on time. The feastly lunch during those days had many types of food and sweets, and everything was managed by the cooks.

Reba stood gazing at the courtyard. She suddenly felt fortunate to see the shadow of Calcutta's illustrious past. In the years she had lived in Calcutta, she never took tours of mansions. They existed as part of the city's legacy; she never marveled at their worth. She knew her parents had acquaintances who resided in mansions, and they visited them when they received invitations for celebrating special occasions. She did not remember attending such occasions with her parents, the adults were the invited guests. But, now, after years of living away from Calcutta, she realized the worth of the estimable structure, though she was saddened by how it stood isolated and inconspicuous.

"How many mansions are there like this one?" asked Reba.

"Calcutta used to be called the City of Palaces in the time of colonial rule. The wealthy businessmen and merchants liked to display their opulent lifestyle in the city, though, they had their *zamindaris* in rural areas of Bengal. Many of these luxurious mansions resembled castles and gardens in Europe. It seems inconceivable now, but they existed with grandeur in this city. Our grandfathers and great-grandfathers were fortunate to have lived a very different lifestyle," said Arati.

"A magical period in Calcutta's history," Reba uttered mesmerized by what she saw.

Arati mentioned how there was a great deal of generosity with wealth. Umesh's great grandfather funded schools and colleges and also built *Dharmsala* in sacred places for people to use. But there were also the *zamindars* who wasted a lot of money on their extravagant lifestyle that they went bankrupt or into heavy debt. There were both sides to the wealth." Arati paused.

She spoke about the stories that happened in the *zamindari* life. Some incidents impacted her and her sister-in-laws when they came to know the bits and pieces of the incidents. They could neither enquire about the details nor were they told what happened. They had to remain silent.

She narrated about Umesh's father's friend, Kantideb, and how he had underground safety vaults in his mansion where he safeguarded the cash. Each vault, the size of a massive room, had hundreds of iron chests filled with fortune that he had accumulated. She said Kantideb had every material wealth a man could wish for and no end to his desire for a rapturous lifestyle outside of home, wasting money on alcohol and young unwed women who sang, danced and entertained him and his friends.

"It was Kantideb's gentle-hearted young wife, Tandra, who silently suffered." Arati softly uttered. "She knew about his life outside the home, but never said anything so as not to dishonor her husband in front of his family."

Arati paused and took a deep breath. Reba understood that even speaking about people connected to her family brought back profound, disturbing memories.

"As I believe, each person is responsible for his or her own happiness and peace," said Arati softly. "Kantideb committed suicide after his return home late one night. He over-drugged himself and lay on the floor in his living room. It was learnt later that Kantideb had a son with a woman entertainer. The family was close-mouthed about the incident. Tandra was warned not to ever talk about the incident or speak about her husband."

Reba could not believe the details that Arati narrated.

"The compulsion to attain the worldly desires without reflecting on the consequences was a kind of life some *zamindars* plunged into. They never thought about their young wives at home," Arati said somberly.

"While the aggravated situation was being suppressed in Kantideb's family, the woman entertainer sought Tandra's help. The woman did not have money to support her infant child. She sent handwritten messages to Tandra secretly through a goldsmith who visited the mansion to repair women's jewelry. It was how Tandra learnt about the desperate situation the woman was in.

"How did Tandra react? She herself was going through unimaginable heartbreak for what happened to her husband," Reba asked curiously.

"Would you believe she was pained at heart to hear about the young woman with the infant. Tandra secretively sold some of her own jewelry to support the woman. She knew financial help could never come from Kantideb's family."

"Tandra must have completely trusted the woman to recognize the situation as honest," Reba said.

"The woman was not a well-educated person. She was also poor, unmarried and earned her living entertaining Kantideb. Tandra recognized how the woman's life abruptly got altered to a situation that was considered shameful in the social circumstances she lived in. Kantideb was gone, but she had her life to live, and had to take care of the child. Tandra understood the woman's situation."

Arati walked towards a marble bench facing the courtyard and sat down. She gestured Reba to sit beside her and stroked Reba's shoulder gently in an affectionate manner.

"But not all women thought alike. There existed rivalrous, intrusive feelings amongst them, they were also young in age. Tandra's covert act was noticed by Tandra's sister-in-law, and she reported to Kantideb's father. Tandra knew how the ordeal would end once her father-in-law came to know about her supporting the illegitimate child of Kantideb. He would take her to court."

Reba sat listening totally stupefied. She had no words at first, but then she reacted.

"To court? But the child was also Kantideb's?"

Arati smiled and shook her head gently.

"It takes more to open the heart. Not all *zamindars* had wealthy hearts. The woman was a mere entertainer, not the same family status. Besides, Kantideb's father could never tolerate the thought that his daughter-in-law extended help to the entertainer woman on her own. A woman in a *zamindari* household was expected to stay behind a drawn line."

"And Tandra?"

"Well, her story is the saddest of all. Tandra left the house on a full moon midnight and never returned."

"You mean she secretly left the house without telling anyone?"

Arati nodded softly.

"But, why full moon? Wouldn't she know people could see movements, shadow…" asked Reba confused but invigorated.

Arati smiled. "Interesting that you asked. But, Tandra thought differently. The light of the moon guided her out of mansion premises. She followed a secret path through the trees and bushes behind the mansion. The moon was her guide."

Reba sat speechless for a few minutes. It was difficult to imagine a young zamindari woman could be so bold.

"And then?" Reba asked impatiently as if she did not want to miss anything to the story.

"A few days later one of the gardeners found a gold anklet lying near the bushes. He thought it must have come off her feet when she was hurriedly running away." Arat paused.

"No one heard about her ever since. No one mentioned Tandra's name. Not all *zamindaris* had happy ending."

"Did Tandra have children?"

"Tandra's two children, a daughter and a son were taken care by her sister-in-law. They were seven and ten years of age when Tandra left the household." Arati said softly.

Reba listened. It was difficult to grasp the extremities of the luxuriant life style. There were no make-believe characters, just real people creating unrecorded incidents.

"It's unbelievable that Tandra left her children," uttered Reba.

"She knew her life would end anyways if she went to the court. Do you think her act would have been forgiven? Never."

Reba wished she knew what happened to Tandra, but it was a sensitive topic to continue talking with Arati. She sensed what the end would be.

Arati walked towards a large room and unlocked the wooden door. Reba stepped in to view the room. The windows had the old embroidered drapery and a long line of oil paintings lined on the wall. She said the room was for all-night music programs. Famous musicians of the time were invited to the mansion to perform. The young wives were not allowed to listen to the musicians sitting in the same room, they listened from a small room across. She elaborated how the Indian classical music was a favorable entertainment for male members of the family accompanied with alcoholic drinks. Young women of *zamindari* culture could never be directly part of such activities.

Arati opened the door to the neighboring room where the invited English guests were entertained. The English couples danced to the Western music tunes. She said such occasions were more frequent before she came into Umesh's family or even before she was born.

"Remember, there were generations who lived in this mansion even before my time. A lot had already changed when I came as a young girl."

Reba devoured the images portrayed through Arati's narration. She remembered how her mother attended social gatherings in Calcutta hotels and clubs where Anglo-Indian couples entertained themselves with dancing and singing. She would stand near the door and watch her mother dress in a long formal western dress with fine jewelry and her father wore a nice suit with bow-tie. They both went to the social gatherings and returned late in the night. It was the kind of life she had seen in her own family and both her parents immensely enjoyed those social occasions.

Arati locked the doors of the two rooms and led the way up the stairs. She took soft steps holding the teak wooden banister as Hira followed behind her. Reba's eyes traced the intricate lattice work on the balconies and railings, she gazed at the smooth beige marble floor and thought how the footsteps of many *zamindari* generations had treaded the bare floors; she was now walking on the same floors.

As they reached the top, Arati pointed to a part of the first floor where there were two types of kitchen arrangements that were part of the household. One was an English kitchen where Anglo-Indian and Muslim food were cooked and the other was a Bengali Kitchen run by Brahmin cooks. She said the cooks were kind hearted, loyal men whose sincerity towards the family was pure.

Reba stared at everything in wonder, it was not a mere brick house, there was a splendor and geniality studded in each wall, a fragrance left in each room of the old-world culture. She understood why Arati did not wish to give up the mansion to real estate developers to erect modern high-rise structures; it would mean the loss of a heritage.

"Calcutta will never have anything like this again," Arati uttered confidently. "Architecture needs to be preserved just like artwork from famous painters. Look at the Western nations...they respect and honor their historical past keeping the old treasures in museums. They set up historical sites so that people can learn about and appreciate them."

Reba suddenly felt emotions seize her words. Calcutta was her city too. But at the time, she had never placed importance to the historical emblems. Back then they had existed as immense homes in the city. Now, she suddenly felt benevolently connected in her spirits to the city that had once embraced the old-world charm.

The back of the second floor had the living quarters of the families, secluded units for each family. They were far from the sections where guests and business visitors came.

Arati turned the lights on to let Reba look at one of guest rooms. The mesmerizing sparkle of the grand crystal chandelier hanging from the high ceiling reminded Reba of the elegantly decorated palaces of Europe casting light to the room as if a grand entrance were about to happen. A large king-size four poster bed occupied the center of the room. In the corner stood two ornate mahogany armchairs and marble side tables. The room looked authentic with exquisite furniture. She saw two floor fans at two sides of the bed. Arati said the room was meant for Umesh's grandfather's second brother who stayed with the family for a few days at the end of every month when he had to discuss business with Umesh's grandfather.

"He was unusually attached to the droning noise of the running fans," Arati laughed as she spoke.

She described how the two floor fans were kept running at full speed on two sides of his bed all through the night because he could not sleep without the sound. What was even more absurd was that, along with the two fans, he had two caretakers who fanned the air during his afternoon naps to keep the mosquitoes away because he refused to sleep inside a mosquito net.

"He was our family member, but sure enough, he was full of strange quirks," said Arati amused.

Reba looked at her watch. It had been two hours of her getting the tour of the mansion.

She walked with Arati to the backend of the floor till they came to an open semi-circular balcony overlooking the back garden. Reba immediately remembered the place when she first came, she had heard the steady chirps of birds, but today she heard no sound. Arati told her that there was something about the new air of Calcutta—it pushed them away. The man-made pond still had some green vegetation growing, the lotus buds and water lilies bloomed with the loose leaves and moss that floated around. The stone benches throughout the garden looked stained with rust, fixed to the ground without any use.

"On many evenings we heard soft movements close by. The deers and their fawns came close to the pond in the back garden, the fawns followed their mother everywhere. This was also their home. In winter, the garden became a birdwatcher's paradise when pelicans frequented the estate and stunned our eyes."

Reba looked at Arati's face and saw the many different emotions in her eyes—gratitude, affection, sorrow, separation—nestled close to her. It was as if she was permitting herself to relieve her inner feelings, apprehending that someone was listening to her.

She recalled the crystal-clear nights, when the family sat together on the terrace and stargazed at the celestial happenings above. Umesh used to tell them the names of the stars, constellations and the myths behind them.

Everything sounded so extraordinary that Reba wished she could have experienced those moments with more perspective living in those historical times. The city changed so much through the passing of years—it was hard to believe.

Arati held onto the banisters as she gently took steps going down. Hira kept behind her without physically assisting her. Perhaps, Arati wished to stay free while moving around in her own home, just as she had done all her life, Reba thought.

They walked outside of the mansion, to the back end with the expanded green landscape.

Arati gestured with her hand to an immense round cemented structure with an iron grill. Reba immediately thought it was a secured well for water storage.

"Oh, no! It was a water reservoir for a pet crocodile," Arati said laughing.

"A crocodile on the property?" Reba gasped.

Arati said Umesh's grandfather had a pet crocodile he brought from *Sundarban*. He named him Bhim. He was taken care like a family member. He would come out from the water and bask in the sun on the cemented patio built for him. He lived a good life till he was returned to *Sundarban*.

"What about managing the crocodile on the property?" Reba could not imagine such a thought.

Arati laughed. "There were a few caretakers solely for Bhim. Umesh's grandfather did not have to do anything.

He visited Bhim once a day and collected Bhim's daily updates from the caretakers."

"Why was he returned?"

"It was Umesh's grandfather's last choice. Bhim was growing in size and strength which started to become an arduous task for the caretakers. Umesh's grandfather hired a few more people just to take care of Bhim. But, they were still not enough."

Reba could not fathom the type of life the *zamindari* families had. Everything sounded like a fantasy story.

"It was an emotional day for Umesh's grandfather and the caretakers. They shed tears for Bhim the morning Bhim was taken back to be released in the salt water of *Sundarban.*

Reba listened enthralled. "This is a story to be shared with children," Reba laughed and said out loud.

Arati walked towards the portico under which carriages and cars were parked; all the vehicles were foreign made. She spoke about the two carriages standing without the horses; they were used by Umesh's parents for their leisurely ride to *Garer Math* when they had the horses. The two polished vintage cars—the Austin Healey 3000 and the vintage English MG…were used for business and for traveling to social engagements; they still functioned, but there was no one to drive them. Arati went close to the cars and touched them.

"Our family used these vehicles for many different occasions. Calcutta had many such cars on the roads. It was a different time."

"Visiting the mansion must bring back so many precious moments for you," Reba said.

"As a woman I lived and saw the material comfort of good life as well received the protection and love of a joint family. However, as a young woman, I had to give up the freedom that girls and women aspired to have. I was expected to be content with the wealth of things I was given. It was when my struggle began."

"What do you mean by struggle?" Reba was taken aback by her words.

"I refused to extinguish the candle burning inside me and to obey what was decided for me. Who are others to know what made me content?"

"What were you looking for?"

"Education to cultivate deeper so I could extend my hand to a larger world around me."

"That's what education is for…." said Reba.

Arat laughed. "But it was not the norm. I disappointed the family elders. They raised their firm voices on me. I certainly would not imply that I was some sort of an arrogant, remorseless woman. I was not. But I had an able mind of my own, a lot of self-dignity ingrained in me from a young age."

Reba was trying to imagine what it would be like to resist expressing disapproving thoughts as if they did not matter coming from a young woman.

"How did you react?"

"I never argued back to the disapproving attitude against me. However, what I did was, I did not let go what I wanted to do. I was firm. I made sure I was able to devote few hours of my day to pursue an education for myself and I would not allow anyone to hinder me."

"It must have been tremendously challenging to do something for yourself with so much disapproval from others."

Arati nodded. "It was the idea that women should stay inside a protected walled home to educate oneself, without mingling with the world outside, was not acceptable for me. Material comforts do not enliven the spirit inside a person, they are temporary fulfillment."

Arati stopped and sat down on a metal bench on the lawn. Her physical stature was fragile, but she found the energy to continue. Her gentleness with grace and dignity inspired reverence for what she spoke.

"We live in a different period in history now. I feel proud that women nowadays are moving ahead with their own willpower. They are strong, willing to pay the price for securing their own place in the world. The society is far more accepting than in our time."

"May be more women should have been like you," Reba said grinning.

"Mind you, there were strong, young women in those years who put their foot forward to bring change. But they paid a much higher price to retain their dignity, sacrificing much more than the society ever gave them credit for."

Reba nodded quietly. She was now aware of the two kinds of conflicting existence enduring together....a world of charm and glamour, and a place with untold heartbreaking stories. She kept remembering Tandra, and how she left home and her children so as not to face shame and humiliation. Reba found everything about the story inconceivable yet it was a real story from Arati's family.

Arati continued to describe how Umesh did not follow or believe in stringent unyielding ideas like many men his age. She narrated their personal story, which went beyond parochial conventionalism. Perhaps, as a result of their receptiveness towards charitable causes and altruistic attitude for the humanity they served, they paid no heed to short-sighted, doctrinal ideas that hindered advancement of the unprivileged lives dissimilar from their own.

"We did not have to look far to see how toilsome the life of a young person could be."

Reba thought there was a sense of displeasure and misfortune in the way Arati spoke the words.

"Umesh helped relieve the burden of a young widowed girl who earned her living as a server to the guests of the *zamindars* in their palatial mansions. Each night she went to different estates from her village home to fulfill her duties. She was dearly favored for her diligent, hospitable service. The dark skinned, bright-eyed, attractive girl drew the attention of *zamindars* because of her independent and dutiful persona. Her name was Suneela. She lived with her mother-in-law in the outskirts of Calcutta in a village. Her husband died of TB leaving her with a newborn girl; Suneela was nearing sixteen. *Zamindar* Jagmohan had spotted Suneela on his village tours one day. She was walking on the roadside carrying a pot full of water on her head. There was something about the girl's confident external persona that attracted Jagmohan. He stopped and asked her name, where she lived, about her family. He came to know she was a young widow. Suneela instantly recognized from the horse-driven carriage that Jagmohan was a *zamindar*. She had to respect the man owing to his status."

Arati stopped briefly and looked at Hira walking towards her; she came to enquire if Arati needed anything, at which she smiled and shook her head. Arati stayed quiet for a few minutes and then continued.

"Jagmohan made a trip to Suneela's village after a few days, asking the local people if they heard about a girl named Suneela. Surprisingly, he found the humble abode where she lived with her mother-in-law. Suneela was feeding a doe and her kid when Jogmohan came close and called her name. She told him that she took care of animals for people and she got paid for the job. Her mother-in-law took care of her infant when she attended to the animals. It was at that moment Jagmohan quickly made the decision to offer her a better-paying work that would support her family. But, her problems did not end. Her mother-in-law was not willing to take care of the infant girl and expected her to manage on her own." Arati stopped again and looked at Reba.

"See, even a girl of sixteen years is forced to look after herself and her child. Life can be unfair."

When Umesh saw Suneela at the mansion of Jogmohan, she used to bring her infant wrapped inside a blanket and leave her lying in the courtyard of the enormous home. The mansion guard sympathized her, told her he would watch the child while she did her duty in the night.

"It was how God worked through people," said Arati.

That night, when Umesh returned home, he went to his office and stayed awake for many hours. Arati knew something had happened. She went to his room and saw him sitting quietly on his armchair. The moment he noticed Arati, he told her to come and sit by his side.

He appeared concerned. He took her hand and held it gently.

Then, he passionately looked her into her eyes and asked if she would be willing to raise an infant girl as her daughter.

Arati paused. She took a deep breath.

"I looked at him perplexed, I did not know what he was talking about, my thoughts immediately wandered into inconceivable questions—Did he have a child with another woman?

I was twenty-five years old. I could not imagine asking him, it was like I was questioning my trust, my faith in him. I was deeply overwhelmed by what he said, yet the idea of an infant girl in my family made me extremely eager, pleased. I asked him to tell me about the child. It was then he narrated about Suneela and her infant."

Arati stopped briefly and smiled at Reba. Then she told how overjoyed she had been about having an infant in the house again; her son Udai was eight years old and her daughter Urmila was six. She made sure Suneela full-heartedly gave her consent to Umesh and her. Arati to raise her infant. Arati personally went with Umesh to meet Suneela in her village.

"When I saw Suneela the first time—her sparkling eyes and soft dark-brown complexion, draped in modest clothes, her waist-length hair in a single braid, walking out from the door of her home—I felt that her presence told me everything I needed to know."

Arati said Suneela visited every week at the mansion to see her child, but as the child grew older, her visits became infrequent. She consciously surrendered her child to Arati and Umesh, she said she did not wish to make her child's life complicated. She knew her child was under the care of the best parents she could ever aspire to have.

"It must not have been an easy decision for Suneela."

"Suneela thought about the child's life, her future more than herself. Our home was open for Suneela if she wanted to see the child. But she never came."

Arati became quiet briefly, Reba did not say anything either. Reba felt she journeyed a whole new dimension of a life lived.....extraordinary, in every sense of the word.

Arati continued narrating how she participated whole-heartedly in the education of Suneela's daughter from school till college. The girl developed a knack for painting and participated in a local paintings' exhibitions to display her work. As she reached twenty-two, Arati and Umesh were keen to see her settled. They spoke to her about marriage. They were even thinking of introducing her to a young man. But she confided to Arati what she wished…. she did not wish to marry. Instead, she wanted to spend the rest of her life living with Arati and Umesh. At first, they felt apprehensive about her decision to stay single; they explained to her the consequences of an unmarried life, when they would be gone. But,nothing changed her mind. Then, Arati guided her to the path that would enable her to study and work outside the home while she lived with them.

"I told her that she needed to do something fulfilling on her own for her own life," Arati paused for a moment and then she surprised me.

"She is our *Hira;* A genuine jewel in our life. She will inherit a part of the wealth just like our other children. She could share with Suneela if she wished to."

Stunned by the story, Reba could say nothing more. She now knew who the woman was with Arati. Reba told Arati how unusual her story was for the family traditions Arati came from. She had never heard a story like the one she narrated.

"Unusual? I would not say that. You don't hear every story considering the fact that people who take the unconventional road, find no reason to broadcast it to the world. They do it because they see a need to help someone, to care for someone, to ease someone's burden. There were individuals and families in those years who exhibited generosity and benevolence of character in different ways.

It was not wealth, it was not fame. It was about having an enlightened attitude towards humanity."

Arati paused her words as she slowly walked towards the car and handed the keys to the gatekeeper. For one last time, Reba took the walking path through the sprawling property, the peaceful and intimate garden nestled behind the yellow clustered flowers of *Radhachura* and the red flowers of the *Krishnachura* trees. She strolled through the tropical garden indulging all her senses with the fragrant flowers, the exotic herbs and the reflecting pond with floating pink water lilies. The Bengal trumpet vine, with its purple flowers, had climbed the walls around the garden giving it the likeness of a purple-and-green carpet pasted on the brick wall. She smelled the damp soil of the flower beds, the display of the natural spectacle of flowering plants—marigold, royal poinciana, cyclamen with their brilliant colors and cheerful appearance. She saw the protected area dedicated to the native plants from various regions of the world, an astonishing selection of invasive greenery that had survived through the years. She sensed the mixed floral fragrance that blended with the clean, refreshing oxygen deprived elsewhere—serene haven untouched by the turmoil of the changing world.

She walked back to the car. Arati was already sitting inside. Hira waited outside till Reba came to the car.

"Hope you liked the visit," Hira said politely. It was first time she spoke to Reba.

"Marvelous! I am glad I came."

"A remarkable place. I feel I just retraced back in time," said Reba as she took the seat next to Arati.

"The Calcutta of yesterday. The last remnants of whatever is left to cherish," said Arati.

Reba nodded softly. "And now you have Asrita."

Arati was quiet for a moment. Reba stayed silent. She felt overwhelmed by the experience of the mansion visit.

"Time is not stationary, so also is our life. It is a journey of changes through varied stations along the way that we will cherish, memorialize and depart from. Contentment, not yearning, is what will make the experience at each station worthwhile. I know I had an extraordinary life at the mansion— I experienced all kinds of taste, it is what the life offers—a variety. I look back to appreciate, but not lament over it. There is no burden felt as long as I cherish and accept the change. I believe Asrita is my last station in this world. What is there to worry about?"

Reba stayed silent. Arati was different from any woman Reba had ever met. Even more so the way she reasoned her thoughts about the truths of life. She made it seem simple, perceptible. She was elated with grace of her profound thoughts; the assuredness and faith in the life she was living and a gratefulness for the life she left behind without longing in sadness. It was no wonder, even after all these years, Reba wanted to meet Arati, to reconnect with the impressions she had left on her mind years ago.

The *chowkidar* was standing at the gate as Mohan slowly drove the car out.

He saluted a *Salaam* to Arati.

"*Shukriya*, Karim.!" Arati gestured a quick wave with her hand and rolled up the window. She waited briefly and said, "To Asrita House."

Glossary of Bengali Words

Then and Now

- Zamindari   the system of landholding
- Zamindar   landowner
- Didi   a name used for 'older sister' or someone like an older sister
- Kumkum -   red vermillion powder for the round dot on forehead for married woman
- Namaskar   Indian greeting
- Seva   the word means 'selfless service for others
- Loha   the wedding bangle worn by a married woman
- Kothai Tumi?   where are you?
- Alpana   sacred paintings of motifs done with rice paste for special occasions
- Brahmin   the Hindu caste allowed to be the cooks for zamindari families
- OM   The sound of the word represents the union of mind, body and spirit. It is a spiritual icon.
- Sundarban   one of the largest forests on the coast of Ganges delta by Bay of Bengal
- Dharmsala   a rest house for pilgrims going for charitable or religious purposes
- Hira   The words means 'diamond'
- Chowkidar   gatekeeper

- Radhachura   yellow flame tree with yellow colored flowers
- Krishnachura   royal poinciana with flaming red flowers
- Salaam   an Arabic salutation means "Peace be with you"
- Shukriya   an Arabic word meaning "Thankful" / "Thank You"

Change

Mia gazed at the photograph of her and Glen leaning against a coconut tree on their first morning in Tahiti. Glen's right arm around her shoulder while she tightly clasped his hand.

She was twenty-three and Glen twenty-six. Both were wearing light-green T-shirts and shorts.

There were radiant smiles and the fondness of adventure written on their faces as they had their first photograph on the French Polynesian island. A tourist walking by had seen them relentlessly taking pictures of the natural surroundings, and he asked if they wanted their photo taken, an indebtedness she now suddenly felt to the stranger. He was the reason she had that first photo with Glen on the island.

Today, after twenty-five years of pleasure and tribulations, she found the photo tucked inside the journal they had created, with her handwritten descriptions and the colored sketches drawn by Glen. Till that moment, the documenting notebook had escaped her memory.

It had been hidden underneath the stacks of photo albums inside Glen's office cabinet which she had opened to dispose of the extraneous papers stored through the years. The blue soft cover notebook had every page filled with written words about the island and sketches Glen had made with colored pencils.... turquoise lagoons, white sandy beaches, volcanic peaks behind the lush greenery of rainforest, tumbling aquarium-blue waterfalls. Expressing through images and colors had been his passion since childhood, in between the routine activities, wherever and whenever he had the yearning. She saw their names and date scribbled at the bottom of each page, the picture quality illuminated like it was freshly illustrated yesterday. The trip happened a year before their marriage.

Now, as she was at the age of fifty-six, the images of the past resurfaced in her mind, moments she wished she could permanently block out and those she would embrace with endearment for as long as she lived.

After twenty-five years of marriage, her life took an agonizing turn when she encountered the sudden harsh moment; her soul mate Glen had met with a devastating car accident at the age of forty-nine and passed away. He had been on his way home from work.

Listening to the voice of Glen's brother, Jeremy, who had rushed to him when it happened, Mia had instantly been forced to confront the other side of life... not as something mythical but something that could happen to anyone, anywhere, unplanned. She was instantly forced to comply with the untimely dismal reality without being offered the time to ask, why.

She was shattered; nothing had ever made her miss anyone so profoundly as the loss of Glen from her life. Mia had been forty-six.

Aggrieved, she took the remorse on herself, irrationally, as if she had failed him. He could not even call her when he suffered pain. She castigated herself for not agreeing to go for a few days trip to Lake Tahoe when he wanted her to; usually he never made abrupt suggestions knowing how occupied she was with her school job. Mia had hugged and told him that she preferred a longer, planned holiday time with him. She had known it was not the response she wanted to give. Her own words were causing her anguish now. She seemed to tell herself—Don't try to plan your life all the time. What's wrong with being spontaneous?

Years passed and memories with Glen remained anchored in her mind.

They first met at a Golden State Warriors basketball game; Mia and Glen were both basketball fans. She was with her older brother and Glen with his father, seated close at the Oracle Arena as if their connection was destined to happen. A long time passed before Glen got the confidence to initiate the first move, gazing constantly at the attractive twenty-two years old girl with light tanned easy-going face, and bright-brown eyes, her light brown hair tied in a ponytail at the back. He asked Mia if she was a fan of the Warriors.

"You bet. Always been and always will be," she said.

Glen laughed, "I see you are loyal."

It was how their first conversation began, laughing and joking, and then it slowly diverged into topics about themselves. In just a few words with her, he was quickly captivated by her way of talking, natural and enticing; he felt eager to know her.

Mia told him she never coveted spontaneous living. She liked planning her life, even her teaching job with school children necessitated her following the same routine. On weekends, she either visited her maternal grandparents twenty minutes away from her suburban home or made a routine stop at Barnes and Noble to browse the latest published children's literature.

Other times, her place was at the kitchen experimenting with recipes she gained from watching the adult women in her family... her grandmother, her mother and her aunts.

"California has been home for my family for many generations," said Mia with a smile.

"What'd you know! Mine too! Probably not as long as yours," Glen had responded with keenness.

He asked if Mia was her short name. Short for Amelia. The long name stayed on her school and college certificates and driver's license. Everyone called her by the short name, she had told him.

Glen told her he was at his first job, creating and maintaining a database at a start-up computer company in San Francisco; it kept him occupied five days a week. On weekends, he visited art museums or jogged through the Golden Gate Park with his friend. Their lunch was usually at a beach restaurant with an ocean view. His favorite was a barbecued beef brisket sandwich, a kale salad and beer. He was not in a relationship, he never liked anyone enough.

At the close of the game, as they said good-bye, he willingly invited her to an informal lunch date. It was obvious from his facial expression that he was abashed at his own boldness to ask. It was his first formal date, Mia felt honored. The thought of meeting him again had crossed her mind. The personable young man with lightly tanned skin, dark brown hair, and a balanced way of talking seemed like someone she could talk to at ease. She was pleased he made the move.

The lunch date was the beginning. Over the next few months, they spent many days together, sometimes staying at the coasts of Santa Cruz, Monterey, Carmel, and Pismo Beach; walking the trails inside Muir Woods;

or visiting the Art Center of Morro Bay in Central Coast. Mia brought bags of cherry tomatoes, apricots, plums and nectarines from her grandmother's garden to keep themselves healthily recharged on those road trips. Sometimes, they would lie on the lawns of local parks, embracing tenderly together, conversing about places that would be on their bucket list, far from home, and imagining themselves living in other countries, being free-spirited and adventurous. Glen appreciated her jubilant and versatile persona and Mia was amused at herself for thinking such far-fetched ideas; in all her growing-up years, the farthest she traveled was to Crater Lake, Oregon when she and her family camped out amongst mountain hemlock and ponderosa pines.

Despite this, the outdoor adventure did not compare to the heavenly experience of camping under the majestic redwoods that soared up like living skyscrapers, she had told Glen.

The Golden State had always been her fond home.

Within a year, Glenn moved from a shared living to an independent apartment for himself in south bay where his company's new office had expanded. He was earning well to take care of the rent, maintenance of the car and all his living expenses. He bought simple functional furniture, two paintings of Picasso, another black and white picture by Ansel Adams for the wall, and an indoor ficus plant to make the apartment homey. He thought about Mia. He wanted her to feel at home; it was as if he had decided to spend the rest of his life with her. When he invited her for dinner, he cooked dishes with concise recipes, keeping in mind what she liked. He was never much of a cook with the stove. He was accustomed to the barbecuing culture in his family's kitchen; his father was the cook, and his mother took care of the bills. It was why the grill was the favorite cooking station for the social gatherings in his family. The male members took control of the kitchen far more frequently than his mother; she made the social hours entertaining, conversing about life's diverse topics, and sometimes voicing firm opinions about social issues. Perhaps, it was why he was familiar with quick meals and never vexed about the broad range of cooking styles.

Mia was already into a year of teaching when Glen asked for her hand in marriage.

For the first time, she suddenly felt the burden of responsibility to manage a job and the married life. Nevertheless, she wholeheartedly embraced the unexplored arena, planning to make the one- time event memorable, and focusing attention on the little details to preserve for the years ahead. They married a year later, she was twenty-four.

"Tuscany, Italy would be the perfect place to cherish our honeymoon," Glen told Mia as they looked through the pictures of museums in Florence and read about the Tuscany culinary culture. He booked the villa nestled in Tuscan rolling hills to stay in with Mia and researched the well-reputed restaurants, Chianti vineyards, and the train connections to Florence, Pisa, Siena and Lucca. Mia made the schedule of their daily plans, and the list of the places they would visit, eat at and shop in. She started taking basic Italian classes for the memorable honeymoon holiday with Glen.

"What do you know? My linguistic boundary is also stretching!" she had told Glen laughing.

What pleased her the most was that she had started to feel confidence in the idea of traversing the boundary to new places. She never really thought about adventures of travel to far places till she met Glen.

After a year, Glenn was offered a senior position as Data Scientist at a Tech company. Mia was expecting their first child, Pierce. She expressed her exuberance to Glen, "Our first baby brought you luck with the new job." Glen stayed in the same company in the years ahead.

With the arrival of their second son, Grant, Mia changed to a part time teaching position. Glen and she bought a home in the suburbs surrounded by greenery and a community of progressive-thinking people. Mia's mother took care of Grant for a few hours a week while Pierce was in preschool. She reminded herself that she needed to set her priorities as a mother, keeping a balance with everyone's circumstances in mind. It was the decision she felt was right.

As days passed, she felt a kind of inner gratification that everything fell in place as best she wanted them to be, she was content being a part-time working mother. Many a day she would brush off comments from people that she 'had a perfectly planned life' or that she was 'fortunate not to have to experience life's difficulties'…. that she should consider herself lucky.

Sitting on the carpet with the journal in her hand, Mia gazed preoccupied, at the drawings created by Glen. Even her own descriptive words were filled with vigor and richness, she remembered it was exactly how she had felt within.

Then, she recalled the initial days after Glen was gone, when she had been plunged into the unusual circumstance with her two boys; Pierce was twenty-one and Grant nineteen and she was forced to take the role of both parents, challenged yet hopeful.

She knew she had to learn along the way, she would not know everything. At times, she sensed Pierce's dispassion towards her, he could not accept the fact that his mother would be his sole caretaker for everything, including the types things he cherished doing with his father. He remained withdrawn. Mia understood her son's silence was a sign of heartbreak; Glen had a tender heart for Pierce, his first child, like that of a father towards his only son. Pierce expressed himself more to his father, he chose the private school in California that Glen had gone to, he wanted to be like his father, even though, he had the choice to attend an equally good school closer to home that Mia had gone to. She tried to remind him that his father would want him to share things with her in his absence; she was ready to listen whatever he had to say. Pierce avoided such conversations. She did not know how long the residue of pain would continue to hurt Pierce, and even her, with the prolonged aloofness of her son.

Two years younger, Grant was open to conversations with Mia and she could reach his mind with ease. He chose a school out of California because independence and adventure took far more precedence over following in the footsteps of his parents. At times Mia wondered how her two children could be so different that she had to adjust herself to two sets of communication rules to follow.

The decision to stay with her teaching job became the most imperative consolation in those days, distancing her from the memories that were magnified in every part of the home. At times, she was a recluse in her home, longing to be with Glen, questioning her future, reflecting on herself, trying to find answers for the fragments of her unsettled life, desiring inner calmness and strength.

She remembered her grandmother's words, "If someone unequivocally searched for something, it emerged in surprising ways. Sometimes, patience was the hope."

Now, at fifty-three, with her sons Pierce and Grant both with jobs in two different places in the country (Pierce in San Diego and Grant in New York City), Mia was surprised at herself for reaching the distance she had gone alone, and for the inner adjustments she had to make, pulling through constrained moments with her sons, forgiving hurtful words, remaining complacent in situations where she normally would have reacted. She realized she no longer had the protective gear that Glen provided, nor did she have the consistent umbrella of support of her parents; they had aged and needed to focus on themselves. Mia accepted the choices she was left with, even the decisions her sons made. She contemplated on their contentment first before what she wished. She kept herself at the back seat when it came to making decisions for other people. She convinced herself that what she now had or how she lived, did not have to be exactly how it was in the past. She had a new chronicle to her life; it should not shake her cognizance and identity.

The transitions did not diminish the charisma in Mia; her willingness to extend herself to social situations stayed unaffected. With her sons living away, she was an empty nester. She continued her job steadily, made herself approachable in social situations and kept up with interests outside of work and home. In the passage of time, she had altered her lifestyle which helped her to stay active in health and physically tuned, exercising three days a week for forty-five minutes. The yoga class at the health club added stimulation; she met women of all ages and exchanged ideas on women's health, meditation, travel, and discovering the creative sides of people. She read books on cultural ideas that connected the world, attended lecture discourses at university campuses and attended newly released book reading events in the local libraries. She watched film festival movies in theaters with two women from the health club, and on weekends took day trips to Napa, Sonoma Wine Valleys and the fishing village in Bodega Bay with women's groups to be in the company of new people. The places she visited in her growing-up years, she now delved into them from another angle for the complacency and uniqueness they offered. Two times a week she volunteered at the senior center. She came into connection with women who looked for companionship, focusing on thoughts that provoked a deeper meaning of life.

Mia began to absorb mentally that it was how her life would be for a long time…independent and purposeful. When she thought deeper, she reflected on loneliness. It was human made, she concluded. The alienated feelings could be subdued if she learnt to take control of herself; external help should not be the first choice. She gave credence to the fact that if everything in life materialized how she wanted them to be, it would be unreal and mundane. It is by living through the challenges that one learns the broader perspectives of life. All the years she spent raising her boys, traveling with family, being socially engaged with Glen and keeping occupied with managing the little things of home-life, a significant part of her own life had escaped her attention. Back then the priorities were different. Now, she was at a new phase; values shifted because of age and circumstances. Now, she was reconstructing her life, carving afresh path where she could breathe a different kind of air and cherish the moments, whether alone or with people.

The farmer's market was the outdoor gathering place of community members of all colors, nations, languages, ages, and professions mingling in one large heterogeneous body of people, an iconic picture of the world we lived in. They came every Sunday to shop the fresh organic produce of California's local farms. Mia used come two times a month when Glen was there, she now frequented the market every week. She indulged in the seasonal hybrid of fruits and vegetables, the new trends of probiotic drinks, savory dips made with fresh ingredients like mint, yogurt, garlic and artichokes and all kinds of bread recipes that catered to every taste and health need possible. Mia opted to have a vegetarian diet two days a week. Glen was a lover of meat and fish. He used to get the fresh fish and crabs to make grilled recipes. She now coveted the diet change in her life, perhaps surrendering to his absence.

She recognized a few familiar faces at the market every time she came. One of them was Glen's tennis partner for some years, Kyle, a married man with two children in college. She met him a few times at the market, he took notice of Mia before she noticed him. He would walk up to her, and enquire about her work, and about her sons. Other times, he would just pass by asking how she was doing. Mia had seen his wife when he and Glen used to play tennis together, but ever since Glen's demise, she had no news of Kyle's family life. That was till one day, as she was speaking to him at the market, he told Mia about his divorce two years back. At first, on hearing the news, she looked at him in obvious bafflement. She could not believe Kyle was going through personal changes; his external appearance and demeanor never reflected anything.

"Great to see you, again! Looks like you are still a regular at the market," said Kyle laughing as he noticed Mia picking out a bottle of Beet Kvaas drink.

"One of the many benefits of living in California, don't you think?"

"Cannot deny that! More so if you are into the trendy healthy food." Kyle laughed.

"A place can spoil you."

"I bet you never thought about moving out of state."

"I have been here all my life. For such a plan, it would have to be something extraordinarily desirable to my heart," said Mia smiling.

He asked if her boys felt the same way and Mia told him they had their own views and interests. Her son Grant was the adventure guy and Pierce preferred more time inside libraries.

Mia resisted prolonging the conversation. Kyle was in high spirits, he took a lot of interest in her current life.

"Well, let's catch up sometime over dinner. I would love to hear about your work with young children," said Kyle as he handed her a name card, smiling at her.

"Sure," Mia responded softly. She had not been expecting a name card from him.

By the time Mia reached home, the day had warmed up. She was on summer break from school, June was the month she had the garden clean-up done; the weeds were taken out from flower beds, and the overgrown bushes and shrubs were trimmed. She still needed to plant the pots of marigolds, pansies, petunias and zinnias to bring color to the flower beds.

Pierce was planning to reach home by late afternoon to stay for a week. Mia saw him in February when she made a trip to San Diego for four days during the one-week school break. The trip was to see her cousin sister, but Mia did not wish to decline the invitation from Pierce to spend a day with him and his fiancée in his two-bedroom condominium before returning back. She probably would have avoided going to see him and made a phone call to talk to him briefly if he did not insist on her visit. Mia thought his fiancée Sofia was keen to have her visit when she spoke to her on phone. Sophia wanted to make the custard fruit tart that she had learnt from Mia.

In the last two visits of Pierce to the house, Mia had been unsure how his stay would turn out, and even if nothing eventful happened, she would feel relieved to be by herself again when he was gone. The dark-blonde haired boy with a quiet facial expression, and a self-assured clarity in his eyes visited home like a duty he needed to fulfill. Most always he came without his fiancée so he could candidly spend time with his mother. In those days, spending time with Pierce, Mia had sensed an unraveling of personality traits in him that she had not perceived in the past. She noticed how Pierce had started to contemplate on serious subjects and avoided casual conversations. Even Mia's situation as a single person, living alone without his dad for the past seven years, gave him unsettled feelings in a strange way. He was anxious how his mother would cope alone as she grew older. Mia held back on what she expressed to Pierce; she avoided disagreements on his short visits. It confused her why such thoughts were suddenly dawning in his mind when she had an active life as a teacher, her extracurricular interests, and her few good friends she had since many years.

From his words, she recognized where his views were taking shape from. The animated togetherness of the past with Glen and the occasions they celebrated together with family and friends were suspended in Pierce's mind, they were the best times of his life, and he seemed to be searching to revive them again.

In the last seven years, Mia rarely entertained at home, except occasionally when her two women friends were over for coffee or dinner on weekends. On those days, she felt inspired to cook or bake something special when they visited. But Pierce didn't give much importance to those infrequent social times at home that his mother enjoyed. When he heard, he asked her how she could think occasional dinners at home with her two friends as anything special—she was not an old woman. He expressed concern about living her life as a single mother. Once he told her openly, "The more I see you, I cannot imagine this kind of solitary life of yours lasting forever." Mia understood what he meant. She responded that there was no reason to think the way he was feeling, she was living the life she wanted, it was not solitary, it was another version he had never seen. She even revealed to him the emotions that crept up inside her. She spoke the truth about how much she had wanted to spend the rest of her life with his father, she had no control over what happened. All things considered, she needed to distance herself from reminiscing about the past every time, and to move forward to harmonize with the new life of her choice. It was what his father would have wanted.

"Do you remember the potpourri of rose petals, pine cones, orange peels, and cinnamon that scented the rooms in our home in the weeks of November and December?" Pierce had asked softly on his last visit.

Mia nodded smiling. "I loved them."

"I miss them." Mia heard something in his tone that made her realize there was more.

Even after many years, Mia was a little in awe to hear him talk about moments that happened years ago. She thought the years would have distanced him from the memories.

She knew even as quiet young boy, Pierce cherished social company at home more than his brother, occasions when guests laughed and chatted till it was time to bring an end to the night. For Thanksgiving, relatives traveled from afar, and they sat around the table recapitulating on things that happened in their lives while relishing the variety of dishes. On Christmas Eve, Glen's parents and Mia accompanied the family to church at midnight, opening the gift boxes and the surprises inside the stockings the next morning with exhilaration. In the morning, Mia and her mother prepared the breakfast of eggnog, pancakes, bacon, leek and tomato quiche, cranberry scones and cinnamon rolls. Every dish was home-made; the kitchen was the liveliest place in the house. Mia lit candles on the dining table and took out the traditional Christmas plates, glasses and cutleries The two grandmothers sat at the heads of the table, the grandpas decided what champagne would be served along with the apple cider. The aunts, uncles, and cousins arrived during the dessert time; Aunt

Lillian brought her home baked pumpkin pie with roasted pecan sparkled on top.

But, the glamour of excitement had ceased ever since Glen's passing, and there was always a sense of dolefulness that consumed Pierce every once in a while.

Grant, on the other hand, spoke about the past as a 'brief memorable time' and he accepted the altered life submissively.

"Moments come and go. A person learns to revere the past, not ache for it." Mia responded eluding to appear not so straightforward with Pierce. She wanted to convey that one had to accept with the altered life; it was what kept the life at peace. On those days of his visit, Mia was sure they were not the kinds of philosophical words Pierce wanted to hear.

Pierce arrived close to the time he was supposed to. He had driven up from Southern California. He had his duffel bag with two pants, two t-shirts and a computer bag. Mia made his favorite dishes—chicken fettuccine alfredo, a big bowl of green salad and chocolate strawberries. He was a happy camper when it came to food; whatever she made, he devoured it thoroughly. He usually spoke when they were at the table sitting together or leisurely relaxing at the back patio. The house seemed quiet even when he visited because he rarely socialized with his friends at home. Mia wished it was different, then she would feel satisfied seeing him enjoy time with his friends at his own home. Today, he seemed especially composed as he pulled out the dinette chair to sit the table while Mia was occupied with baking in the kitchen.

"So, what were you telling me about teaching disadvantaged children?" Pierce asked, pouring a glass of pineapple juice from the glass bottle on the table.

"It's a volunteer work with children who need help with reading and writing."

Pierce nodded without saying anything. He sipped the juice and took a few pieces of the trail mix of almonds and cranberries from the bowl. Mia suddenly got tensed up. Lately, the conversations with him brought uneasiness. Sometimes it felt like he was older than her, the way he asked questions or said something to her.

"I am doing things I like." said Mia, assuring her son that the choice was hers before he asked anything further.

Pierce was staring at the transparent plastic folder with Glen's drawing inside lying on the table.

"What's this?"

"One of your father's sketches that I am planning to frame." Mia said smiling.

Pierce looked at Mia with an air of surprise. "After so many years?"

"It has been lying in a drawer for a long time. It was his last sketch. He woke up early that morning and opened the window blind to sketch the view. There were striking shades of orange, yellow and amber against the sky lightening up, unusual colors. He got excited and quickly took out a blank paper and the colored crayons to get the view down on paper. It's strange how he said he might not see those colors in the sky again. Your dad left us the following Monday."

There was a brief silence. "Strange that you want to frame it after all these years."

Mia did not say anything.

Pierce looked at her and waited, wondering if his mother would have anything to say. He didn't think they would suddenly talk about a picture that his father drew years ago; he didn't want to talk about what his father did years ago now. He wanted to ask how she was doing at present, and what kind of life she was having aside from work.

"Any new people in your life?"

Pierce rarely talked about Mia's friends with her. The question at once felt awkward; she looked at him questioningly. "I meet new people every so often. I have my regular friends, you know them."

Mia took out the baking sheet with the freshly baked chocolate chip cookies from the oven.

"I know. The same women friends of yours," he said in a disinterested tone.

"I have known them a long time. We like each other's company."

"What about Kyle?" Pierce abruptly asked as if he was not interested in speaking about the women friends.

A silence befell for a few minutes before she responded. She was puzzled by the question. She looked at Pierce.

"Kyle? Your dad's tennis buddy? I see him every so often at the farmer's market. We talk a little. Why?"

"Just asking."

Mia suddenly felt conscious. It sounded strange.

"He comes forward to talk to me. He played with your dad for a number of years. You know that," she said casually.

Mia put the second baking sheet with the oatmeal cookies. She could not tell where their conversation was leading. There was a short pause.

"I could be wrong but I think he feels something for you."

The comment immediately made Mia stop what she doing and stare at her son in a questioning manner.

"Really, Pierce! What are you saying!" Mia thought his words sounded direct and uncomfortable.

"I am saying what I think could be true."

"What makes you say that?" Mia said accentuating the words forcefully.

"Just the way he stopped by when I was visiting last time. The way he asked about you. You were not at home."

"And why are you suddenly bringing it up now?"

"Just wondering if you had felt anything or had anything to say."

Mia did not say anything. She resumed putting the chocolate chip cookies in the jar. She instantly felt ambivalent about what her son said. It was not a topic she ever imagined to expand on with him.

"He was just being nice," Mia answered quietly.

Pierce did not comment immediately. He sensed the hesitation in Mia's voice.

"May be. But I think it's more than that."

The conversation was awkward. She was surprised at Pierce's sudden openness about the feelings for Glen's friend.

For many years she had kept her distance from his thoughts, thinking that there would be unnecessary confrontation. She would blame it on herself for not keeping her control as she was his mother. But, now, she wanted to converse, and not let the guessing game continue.

"What are you saying?" Mia asked impatiently.

"Maybe he likes you?"

"Why would you even think that?"

"I can sense something mom." Mia stopped briefly what she was doing and stared into Pierce's face.

"You can sense what you like. It's not what I think."

"It's normal, mom. You have been without dad over seven years."

"Let's not get into that…."

Mia suddenly became quiet, out of discomfort. She started to wash the things in the sink.

"Just so you know, it would be alright with me and Grant." said Pierce casually almost making the situation difficult for Mia to tread over and forget.

Mia did not say anything. Something in the way he answered, it bothered her. It sounded like both her sons had compared notes on the subject.

"Don't you miss your dad?" Mia blurted out with emotion disregarding what he said. It was as if he or his brother had no right to come up with such thoughts. She even wondered if anyone had influenced them to think that way.

"I miss dad, of course I do! But he has been gone a long time and you are alone!" Pierce's voice sounded assertive.

Mia was glad she did not bring up the subject of meeting Kyle at the farmer's market recently, that he gave his name card to her. Anything she said, would give the impression that something was developing between them.

"I like my life the way it is now," Mia said forcefully.

Pierce looked at his mother's face in a steady gaze. "What's there to like? You have been living alone!"

"I am getting used to living differently. It's not perfect, but I look forward to it."

There was silence. Pierce never expected her to give such a straightforward response; he never thought she would react so adversely to the idea. He immediately rose to his feet without saying anything and noticed the handwritten 'Things to do' list lying on the table. There was one that read, "Make Pierce's favorite dish for dinner."

Mia was at the sink, her back turned, washing the glass mixing bowls. He gave a quick glance at his mother and walked out of the kitchen.

Mia did not wish to speak. She felt a kind of relief listening to his footsteps leaving her presence. It was strange that Pierce brought up the things that he did, the things she had never expected. It was somewhat bold on his part, she thought. Till that moment, he had never been upfront with Mia concerning her life. It wasn't the idea of a second relationship that distressed Mia, nor was it that she felt dreary in her current life. It was that she did not expect Pierce to start steering the conversations to matters that only Mia should have been thinking about, not anyone else. He should not even be connoting the idea that the time had come for her to move on with someone else. How could he! She had never given thought to a second relationship in the last seven years; the idea of living her whole life alone was agreeably acceptable. She understood what was harping on Pierce's mind. He wanted his mother to begin the kind of life she had in the past. The idea of someone like Kyle was a likable choice.

It was the tutoring day.

Mia sat in front of the twelve years old girl, Rachel, gazing into her eyes, and wondering what was going through her mind. In the past three months, since the girl had begun tutoring with her, she had continued learning rancorously, angered about why she had to learn when she didn't want to.

As she was already falling behind the sixth-grade academic level, the teacher had recommended extra tutoring for all subjects, but Rachel was not progressing in either remembering or completing the assignments.

Mia looked over the form with her profile details: her parents' names, the town she lived in, her siblings' names and the school she attended. The father was forty-four, he had been a driver of storage trucks for some years. The mother, two years older than the father, worked at a gas station shop. Rachel was their first child, the second was a boy eight years younger. What she understood from reading the few lines scripted on the form was that Rachel's parents were divorced. Her father remarried few weeks before the girl began tutoring; his new wife or supposedly Rachel's stepmother, was now the woman who replaced Rachel's mother.

The years before the divorce, Rachel had lived through distress at home. Her stepmother had moved into the house the day after the divorce was finalized, even though she also made frequent visits to the house when Rachel's own mother was living there. She immediately took the role of an established family member, and Rachel's father expected a total appreciation from Rachel for the woman he remarried. But it was not till the girl spoke out candidly about her feelings that Mia realized how degraded and hopeless the girl felt inside.

"Everyone takes care of their own life and expects me to do the same," the girl said in a soft voice.

"What do you mean?"

"I mean I am not old and I don't know what to do."

"You can tell me what you need and maybe I could help you."

"You won't understand."

"I will try. You can tell me."

Mia could sense the girl was trying to overcome some injured feelings. She spoke in a soft tone.

"I don't feel like studying or doing homework."

"Do you know why you feel that way?"

"It doesn't matter. My feelings don't count."

Mia gave a pause, looked at her compassionately.

"What do you feel like doing?"

She shrugged her shoulders. "Nothing. I don't want to live in my home anymore."

"Why is that?"

The girl kept quiet. A disheartened expression came onto her face. "I don't like my father's new woman. She can never be my mother, never!"

The girl paused, lowering her eyes looking down at the table.

Mia felt the resentment at the core of her heart. What could she even do at her age other than to express her frustration distressfully.

"She orders me around the house like she owns me. She gives me work every time she sees me. I get tired."

Mia stared at her uncertain eyes. Tufts of brown hair fell over her forehead, and her face was pinched and sullen from tiredness. She clearly appeared uncared for by the ordinary, wrinkled t-shirt she wore along with the worn-out shorts.

"Have you ever told her that you feel tired?"

"Every time I tell her, she complains to my father and he yells at me."

Her eyes watered; she looked almost as if she would break down. She stared dully at the table, keeping her eyes low, her arms stretched on the table. Mia took Rachel's hand and squeezed it gently.

"I am very sorry." Mia kept holding her hand.

"The woman's sister stops by for meals at my house. They laugh boisterously, chatter sipping beer at the kitchen table. I want to live with my mother. Please let me live with her."

The girl uttered, misty-eyed, almost in the verge of tears. She repetitively called her stepmother 'woman.' She was a stranger with no connection to her.

Mia was not going to ask further questions about her family. She could clearly comprehend what was going on. She had now come to know the details of the girl's home life; there was nothing on the form about how Rachel felt about the new family member or about the home environment. It only said Rachel was under performing in school.

"She gives me very little to eat. I miss my mother."

At her words, a wave of throbbing pain came over Mia.

Mia closed the math text book that was open in front of her. This was the first time she realized how little the school textbooks meant for Rachel. She lived in one kind of world and was made to learn in another, carrying the emotional burden with her.

"Do you like to draw?"

Rachel gazed at Mia's face. "Depends on what it is."

"How about you draw me a picture of things that make you happy. Be ready to describe what you have drawn."

Rachel nodded still staring at Mia. Mia's words definitely surprised her.

"I have only three colored crayons."

Mia bent down to take out the one crayon box she carried in the bag; she had kept it in case she needed it while tutoring. She gave the box to the girl.

"For me?"

Mia nodded smiling. The girl looked at the box in her hand. "Okay."

She shoved the box inside her backpack. Mia noticed the torn pockets without the zippers.

Mia ended the conversation just as she noticed a young woman standing at the door, her back turned and looking the other way. She curiously asked Rachel who the woman was.

"The woman's sister," Rachel responded.

"Make me the drawing, okay?" Mia told her as she started to walk with Rachel towards the door.

"When will I see you again?" Rachel asked.

"Again on Friday."

Rachel nodded as she walked past the woman without even looking at her. The woman followed from behind.

Mia checked for a voicemail from her mother at the time she was getting dinner ready. The call was expected; every two days her mother called to find out how Mia was doing. This time she had left a message saying, "Call me after you are done working. I have some things to ask you." She knew it was not urgent; her mother's voice sounded that way. She had been her soul support even since Glen was gone. She used to visit regularly in the first three years after Glen's demise, but Mia had told her not to worry about her, a few calls during the week were just as good.

She had fifteen more minutes till the chicken casserole was done, she sat down at the dining table and opened her laptop. She felt she needed to send an email to Rachel's school counselor and her teacher. There were some things that she wanted to convey in her message about Rachel. Mia was convinced the girl was losing direction as a result of being away from her mother and being dejected at home by her father and her stepmother. Her unhappiness had everything to do with the home situation, and it was affecting the girl's mental condition, and her academic learning and progress. Mia wanted an examination on the matter even though she was not part of the school Rachel went to.

Mia would wait for their reply on how they would undertake the matter. She signed her name at the end of the message.

She closed the laptop and sat staring out the window for a few minutes. She didn't believe for a minute Rachel's intellectual inability was the reason for her underperformance.

A child pays the price for adults' insensibility. She recognized there were many things happening in the lives of students beyond the classroom. Rachel's case was a challenging one.

Mia dialed her mother's number. The phone rang a few times before her mother answered.

"Mom? Is everything okay?" Mia spoke just as she heard 'hello' from the other side.

Her mother answered. 'Just fine sweetheart.' She did not waste a minute to tell her that she had stopped by the house to give the cherry pie she made for Pierce. It was the same time when Kyle stopped by to see if Mia was at home.

He said he was returning back from the sports store and wanted to check how things were with Mia.

There was a short pause, Mia disturbingly felt all the focus was on her for some reason. She had no idea what to say or how to react to what she heard; she did not know Kyle had stopped by.

"Why didn't you tell me?" Mia's mother's voice sounded surprised.

"Tell you what, Mom?"

"About the new friendship in your life."

"No, mom! It is not what you are thinking."

"There is nothing wrong even if there was."

"Kyle is a good friend. He has always been friendly even when Glen was there."

"Whatever. But don't be hard on yourself."

"I am not, Mom!"

"Is there anything you wish to tell me yourself?"

"There is nothing."

"Call me when you feel like talking about it."

Mia heard the phone turn off from the other end; her mother did that when she sensed uneasiness in her daughter. She left her cell phone on the table.

She instantly felt doubtful about how things were turning out without her being present or even without her feelings even being taken into consideration.

First, for no good reason, Pierce had brought up the subject just because Kyle had happened to stop by to meet her, and now, just when she had been out tutoring, Kyle had happened to visit when her mom came. Both Pierce and her mother seemed to find a bright side to Kyle's visits, and Mia wanted to avoid the subject. Other than meeting Kyle a few times at the farmer's market, she had never thought of him in any special manner.

Now suddenly, she oscillated between what they were assuming and how she had always known him....as Glen's tennis partner.

Pierce returned from visiting his long-time high school friend.

At the dinner table, Mia was not inclined to say anything at first after what she had heard from him. It was one of the downfalls of discussing one's personal feelings with a grown-up child; there would be misunderstanding at some point. She had to weave her way out of conflicting topics.

"Have you ever given a thought to your life after retirement?" Pierce asked casually, as if he just wanted to make a conversation.

"A few choices have crossed my mind; I still have time."

"Tell me about one."

"Travel to another country for a few months and do some volunteer work."

Pierce did not say anything at first. He looked at Mia stunned. He had never imagined his mother would talk about traveling alone far from home; it was definitely not something he had anticipated or even thought his mom was capable of. He silently took the pasta salad on the plate, and then sipped some water.

"Really? You would do that?"

"I have not decided on anything at this point. But it is a plan on my mind."

"I never imagined you would actually think something like that."

"People progress in their thinking." She took a bite of the sourdough bread and looked at her son.

"But, why go far away to volunteer?"

"For cultural experience. We traveled a lot with you dad. Don't you remember?"

Pierce nodded. "But now you are alone."

Mia gave a quick glance at him and started cutting the salmon piece topped with mushroom sauce.

"I know…so?" Mia responded.

"Would you like that?"

"If I make the choice, then wouldn't that tell you that I wanted that?"

Pierce didn't say anything for a short moment.

"I would rather that you go with someone than by yourself."

"That's too complicated."

"Why?"

"The person has to like the choice I made."

Pierce looked at his mother's face. He wasn't thinking about her woman friends but he didn't want to tell her that.

"Would you date someone?"

Mia looked at him. The abrupt question took her by surprise. She immediately knew she had again reached the arena she was trying to avoid.

"I have not given thought to that. Besides, I don't see why that matters."

She had no desire to instill the picture of skepticism to the feelings of love, she had had her share. She felt certain it would never be the same, she had been much younger when she met Glen. Besides, every phase of life gave opportunity for a new purpose, she had started to believe in that.

"There is a freedom we attain when we let go of things that do not reflect our true self…something good, something motivating."

"That's deep!" Pierce said quietly. "What true self are you talking about?"

"Think profoundly, act meaningfully."

"What about the life you had with dad?" Pierce kept his eyes on his mother, she was wiping off the bread crumbs on the table.

"He was with me then. It's different now."

"You could have the same with another person."

"I was younger then, everything new. Now, it will be different. The mind alters as life moves forward."

"What about Kyle?"

Mia got up and took the dishes to the sink. She felt a little anxiety in her, her throat felt dry. She poured a glass of water from the jug and drank the whole glass of water. She hesitated, choosing her words carefully.

"He is a friendly person, but I don't think about him."

Pierce did not say anything. He didn't like her indifferent attitude and the way she explained like she trusted herself a great deal.

"Time changes people in different ways, sometimes the external things influence people, other times, the internal feelings speak to people. It is why everyone does not follow the same course," said Mia assuredly wiping the kitchen counter as she looked fixedly at her son at the table.

She spoke about the eighty-six years old woman at the senior center where she volunteered once a week. The first time Mia saw the woman, she thought she was a perfect example of positivity and hope, her amber eyes sparkled with a kind of enthusiasm and energy that Mia did not often see in women her age. The woman was a widow; she was noting down a widower's name and number from the message board. The woman told Mia that she was eager to call and meet the man, she was open to a long-term relationship.

"Age is unrelated to how people think, talk or do things. Sometimes we generalize expecting a person to behave or do things in a certain manner. It doesn't always happen that way."

"Well, that's some enthusiasm at her age!" said Pierce grinning.

"Yes and I admired her for what she was. If she felt that way, it was her choice."

Pierce grinned and did not say anything.

"As many are the people in the world, as many are the ways of thinking," Mia said as if to assure her son that however a person decides to fulfill the personal wishes, without harming anyone, it should not concern others; it is the person's choice."

Pierce watched his mother empty the dishwasher and stack the clean plates in the cupboard. He hesitated to say what he had in mind; he worried it would end their conversation. He sat without saying anything and played with a spoon on the table. He knew he was wasting his time.

"Don't get me wrong, Mom! A second chance is not a bad thing," Pierce quickly uttered.

Mia had anticipated that the conversation would take a turn towards what exactly Pierce had in mind.

"It's not a bad thing if the person wants to."

"Would you date Kyle if he asked you?"

"I would not call it 'a date.' A dinner sounds fine."

"I have the feeling you have decided not to change."

"If that's what you think, let's keep it that way."

"It's true, isn't it?" Pierce pressed.

"There are many ways people change." Mia answered in a decisive tone. "It just hurts that you see it one way."

Mia understood that Pierce wanted to see his mother in the similar life she had in the past. She also knew that every relationship was different; a person had to be prepared to begin new with no certainty to how it would turn out afterwards.

"In the last seven years, I have come to learn things about myself. I don't need anyone to sympathize with me because I am living alone. If I had felt differently, I would have acted long ago."

There was a sudden uncomfortable silence.

Pierce did not respond. He thought he saw a glisten of tears in his mother's eyes.

"May be you will understand one day," said Mia in a low voice.

She walked over to Pierce with the cup of green tea in her hand and sat down near him. She saw the side of him that she had not seen before…a grown up one, a different one. She stretched her arm forward and clasped his hand.

"I seem different to you because I have been living alone."

"You are alone, Mom."

"What you don't see is that I am comfortable with myself. I am not lonely."

Pierce kept quiet, failing to find the right words to say anything further.

"Your dad may not be with me, but I had twenty-seven years of memories with him. They will remain fastened to my heart. His absence has also made me reflect on the kind of life I want to have for myself. Tangling myself with threads of emotions is not on my list."

Mia felt a relief to get the words out; she wished she didn't have to explain so much. There were hundreds of ways she could explain to him, still, they would not sound as meaningful to him as they were for her. The ideas of acceptance, contentment, sacrifice were not valid reasons at his age; sometimes, they were beyond the understanding.

Pierce got up and took his plate to the sink and began washing it.

"You are just so unassuming and unmovable about everything that it bothers me," Pierce said with a steady voice.

"I see no reason to be pretentious. It hampers realistic thinking."

Mia kept sitting at the table responding to what Pierce was saying. She sensed that their talking was not going anywhere except that Pierce was dissatisfied with how she lived her life.

She felt a kind of sympathy for her own self, and how much she had to endure the mental burden of raising her two sons at an age when she was also young; she could have done many other things that she wanted to. But she never felt any kind of remorse because her sons came first. They had lost their father, they were also hurt. The well-being of her sons, their education and future mattered more than her life of enjoyment. But she did not want to elaborate those thoughts to Pierce. He was an adult now; he knew how much his mother had managed on her own. Now, he should try to understand her feelings and let her do things the way she wanted to for herself.

But Mia did not sense Pierce thought along those lines from the conversation she had been having with him.

Suddenly a clinging sound came from her phone; it was an email. She checked the email. There was a message from Rachel's school counselor. She wrote that Rachel's father and his new wife would meet the counselor at school. The counselor requested for Mia to be present, as Rachel wanted her there.

Mia hoped that meeting the father would give her the chance to explain him how Rachel's learning was being improperly affected. She reflected that she would request for the option to have Rachel live with her mother for three months to see if the change of place altered her spirit towards learning.

"I gladly accept the offer to join the meeting. Let's hope for the best alternative for Rachel."

Mia sent the reply.

The summer morning was cool and pleasant when Mia stepped outside to the patio with her cup of coffee. The mix of floral fragrances wafted through the air as she walked over to the flower beds to admire the colorful blossoms that she had added to her garden. She liked the leisurely morning hours. She reflected on her upbringing as a young girl; an easy going positive living was ingrained in her. Perhaps, it was why her calm steady ways never lured into feelings of boredom, persistent worries or expectation of others. Now, surprisingly, as an adult, she seemed to find a young girl in herself who wished to make her own dreams; independent from the typical expectations of the world. She felt strength in the thought that it takes courage to be different.

The packet from India had arrived in the mail the previous day. It contained the two school pamphlets and a few photographs of a school in India with its students and teachers.

Mia had learnt about the school on a message board at her local public library that read 'English Teachers Needed' amongst the many bits of information posted. There was a local contact name, but the message said to directly email or phone the school director, Mrs. Seshadri for further enquiries. Mia had called her first time to get the initial impression of the school on the phone. Mrs. Seshadri confidently spoke in a clear Indian-accented English, she was cordial and willingly answered her questions.

"We have two American teachers already working with us. We welcome more teachers."

She had described how the classrooms had basic learning resources and minimal materials. The children came from underprivileged families though they demonstrated enthusiasm for learning. She told that the accommodation arrangements were made for teachers visiting from outside of the town. She would mail Mia a packet with the school details.

Mia sat down on the patio chair and opened the packet. There was a separate letter in a white envelope. Mia opened the white envelope and read the content. She described why she wanted to establish the school. It was a school for girls.

She wrote that, a shop owner known to her, had his twenty- year old daughter married to a suitable boy that matched his daughter's horoscope. The boy was college educated and had a job. He lived with his parents. In the eight months of living with the boy and his family, the girl was harassed for not bringing in sufficient dowry for his family. Anguished in pain, the girl told the boy and his parents that her father emptied his savings to give whatever he had, and her mother sold her wedding jewelry to give as much as she could.

Neither the boy nor his family accepted her words even though they were true.

The girl left her in-law's home early one morning saying that she was going to the market. She never returned. She choked herself with a scarf. Her body was found near the riverside. A note was found in a shoulder bag lying next to her.

"Forgive me, dear Mother and Father. I could not bear the painful torment anymore. If I returned to you, you would have to endure the ridicule of others rest of your life. I will stay with God instead. Yours forever, Prakashini."

Mia suppressed her emotions while reading the letter. She did not know what to think of that kind of a social situation—it was painfully agonizing and deplorable. She wouldn't have even known unless she had enquired about the school. She sat quietly for a few minutes reading the letter again, reading the lines of the note the twenty-year old girl wrote to her parents, Mia imagined her face—her eyes watered.

She looked through the materials inside the packet. She saw the pictures of the school building, a one-floor structure with four rooms. The name of the school Prakashini was written on a board fixated on the wall in front of the school. A significant amount of land with a few banana trees surrounded the one floor brick structure. A paved road led from the school to the guest house where the teachers lived, and the staff who managed the place.

Looking through the materials, the few pictures, the idea of spending a few months in a different cultural environment felt inspiring. Strangely, she did not feel apprehensive about the place being outside of her cultural understanding and completely unknown to her. There was something about Mrs. Seshadri's cordial letter and her reason for starting the school. Mia thought she would regret if she disregarded the opportunity. She thought reading from books or watching documentaries on television, did not always make a person connect personally, with one's senses. There was more to being in the place.

The last long-distance trip was to Greece and Rome for two weeks with Glen, she never made trips afterwards.

Surprisingly, it was in one of her trips to the local library to drop off books that she had stopped to check the notice board. That was when she saw the message about the school. At that moment, she had dismissed the notion of traveling far away, it had seemed unlikely she would even contemplate on such a venture—except for the fact that she did.

Mia sent an email thanking Mrs. Seshadri and praised her for the institution she had created for girls in the community. She told her that she would await to receive the teacher's application forms and the required materials she needed to complete.

The tire rotation was going to take an hour. Mia decided to wait in the car dealer's lounge instead of finishing the errands, she wouldn't have been able to achieve much in an hour driving through the traffic. She checked her phone and found a missed call from Kyle and a voicemail. She understood he called to let her know he had stopped by the house and missed meeting her. Mia waited briefly to listen to the voicemail. An awkward feeling emerged in her because of her conversations with Pierce and her mother; she felt uneasy about the impressions they had created. She could wait and call back later, but it seemed a better choice to do it while she waited at the dealer; she could make the conversation brief.

"Hey, Mia! How are you doing?" Kyle's voice came from the other end just after the second ring.

Mia imagined a smile on his face as she listened to his tone. She told him she got his phone message and heard about his visit to her home.

"It was great to see Pierce and your mom! I haven't seen your mom in a while!"

She told him about how her mom stops by to see Pierce when she is out working.

"I must say your mom looked great!" Kyle sounded spirited. "So, what are you up to these days?"

"Just the usual. Teaching, volunteering, exercising, working in the garden."

"I see no bad habits in the list." He laughed.

"I keep them out."

Mia had nothing to say. If she said something, it would be like she was trying to force the conversation with superficial statements.

"So, how does a dinner sound?" Kyle suddenly asked.

Mia had somehow anticipated the question. She controlled herself not remarking with any kind of excitement.

"I need to check my calendar. I am at the car dealer now."

Mia paused and thought for a moment. She felt awkward that the conversation had fast- forwarded without her giving more thought to the matter. She scrolled through the appointment calendar on her phone thinking about what she should do. She saw most days were out. She had a few evenings marked with her women friends. A few were free after six in the evening.

"How about this Friday. How does it look?" Kyle suddenly asked before Mia could reply.

There was a pause, Mia hesitated at the suggestion— *It's too soon!* she told herself. But she wanted to respond quickly instead of lingering on the matter for a later decision. She didn't have anything marked down for Friday, why would she delay to tell him?

She remembered what she had told Pierce: 'just a dinner, not a date.' It was exactly how she wanted to maintain the friendship.

"Friday looks fine. I have nothing marked."

"That was easy!" Kyle laughed again. "I am not bold enough to attempt cooking a good meal for you. I figured eating out is the best choice."

"Sure, thanks!"

He enthusiastically spoke about the dinners she and Glen had hosted; he thought she was an excellent cook.

"I haven't done that in a while." Mia said.

She noticed the mechanic walking towards her, the car was ready.

She apologized for the interruption and told him she would see him on Friday.

Driving back Mia evaluated the phone conversation with Kyle, word for word. It was as if she had allowed herself to fulfill his wish of spending an evening with her, something she would have otherwise hesitated to do. What felt unsettling was that Kyle was Glen's tennis partner, someone she and Glen had known for years, and socialized with on a few occasions. He was now divorced from the woman who had been his high school sweetheart, with two grown-up children.

She pictured him as a decent man. His unsuccessful married life did not bar him from doing what he desired… meeting people who interested him and pursuing to establish an advanced digital technology education in schools. Then there was a side of him that puzzled Mia. Every summer he would leave his wife and children and go off to Shasta Lake for four weeks. He would rent a fancy houseboat with hot tubs, satellite TV, and entertainment systems and he would spend time by himself, every year.

"Two people are never made from the same mold," Kyle had once told Glen jokingly.

He appeared more restored after the divorce, though he never spoke about his personal challenges. She formed a mental image of him: independent, discreet, forthright. Mia reflected that there were advantages to entering new relationships. One could distance oneself from the past; the present becomes meaningful. What is visible in front of the eyes, is what tends to get focused on. But the ambiguities remain; they are never completely discernible. At the end, everything becomes commitment and responsibility.

Mia stood in front of the mirror in her bathroom vanity with a housecoat on and stared at herself in the mirror. The avocado cream smudged on her face felt cool; she wanted the moisture to penetrate her facial skin while she soaked her feet in the warm water of the bathtub.

Sitting on the edge of the tub, she applied the rosemary and peppermint oil on her arms, neck and shoulders. This was her own therapy that she did once a week, carving out time for herself. The jasmine-fragranced candle flickered at one corner of the counter; on the other side was a green plant in a ceramic pot. Both evoked a mood of tranquility inside the bathroom space. She had nothing planned in the evening; Pierce would be out with his friends. She wanted the quiet relaxation to break away from the daily thoughts. Even doing the minimum on herself, she often drew attention from her friends; her vibrant light-brown eyes on her soft complexion made her appear younger than her age.

Her phone buzzed on the bathroom counter. Mia looked at the screen. It was Kyle.

She preferred texts to phone calls, but she still answered, clearing her throat. He sounded animated and responsive on the phone; he wanted to check if Mia reached home all right after the tire rotation. She was amused, thinking...*Really? I am certain that was not the reason you called!*

"All good! The car drove great! Thanks!" she said.

"Great! Look forward to seeing you on Friday!"

Immediately after, she noticed a voicemail left on her phone. It was from a parent of one of her past students. Mia recognized the student's name as the mother spoke about her concern; she was unhappy her son had group projects with average-performing students in class, and she wanted to speak to Mia about it. She did not feel comfortable speaking to the current teacher. Mia remembered that the student was a diligent high achiever who was in accelerated programs in all subjects. She particularly recalled his quiet, well-mannered persona and appreciated his well- prepared assignments. What concerned his parents was that the current teacher had informed them that the group activities always had a mix of students with different skills and abilities, but the parents were overwhelmingly displeased with the current teacher's decision. It was the reason the student's mother had phoned Mia.

There was a week left before the start of the upcoming new academic year. Mia agreed to meet them in teacher's room during the teacher's preparation week.

"Your child is one of the seven students who are placed in the accelerated programs. He will follow, like the other seven students, most programs of a higher academic level as a result of the fast progress. However, the group projects are not part of the program," Mia told them politely.

The parents sat quietly, startled to hear the last part of Mia's statement. They worried their child would go down academically if he had to do group projects in mixed groups. They preferred that their child work solely with the six high-achieving students.

"Group projects are meant to reflect how a real-life situation works. Diverse ideas develop when the student interacts with students possessing a mix of skills." Mia explained them.

The words did not resonate much with the parents, Mia thought. Situations like this stressed her out more than she wanted them to, considering that the student made no complaints and did not react adversely to the group projects.

"How does your child feel?"

Both parents looked at each other. Clearly, it is what they wanted, not the child, Mia thought, following their facial expressions. She explained to them that learning to work with various kinds of students was an opportunity, not a handicap for the child.

"In real life, there exists all kinds of people with a variety of skills and thinking. The group projects are a good beginning for experiencing the real-life work situation."

Mia ended the brief conversation.

Mia's long-time friend from college, Stella, was moving to a town sixty miles from where Mia lived. A part-time interior designer, Stella found a reasonable amount of free time to do things she liked as well as doing her hours at work. Her husband's job as a graphic designer in an advertising firm kept him late at his office, developing the layouts and production designs for magazines and corporate reports. For the past one year, he spent the weekends working to build the new home, toying with ideas and partnering with Stella and with the construction company. Mia was not surprised when Stella suddenly stopped by at her house. She had kept the interactions with Mia consistent, no matter how occupied their life was. It was how their friendship was as good and close friends.

The bright, sunny morning was a good time to sit outside on the patio. For many years, the patio was the socializing place where she and her family spent evenings and weekends together or with guests for desserts and coffee in the evening. In the years, after Mia's sons left for college, it became the place where Mia spent in solitude; reading, writing her journal or lying quietly with her eyes closed. She had become accustomed to the quietness, but at times, she wanted company...someone to talk to, someone who knew her.

Stella sat down on the lounge chairs and instinctively moved to the subject that she had heard bits and pieces about: Mia's plan to travel abroad. She could not imagine her friend making a plan of that sort; she had never known Mia to be the over adventurous kind.

"So, when are you leaving me?"

Mia did not comprehend the comment momentarily, but quickly laughed when she understood what Stella meant.

"It's strange how my interest in the school in India started just around the time I was tutoring a young girl who was having serious learning problems."

Stella stared in Mia's face with a confused look.

"Obviously they are not related."

"I see neglect in both cases. The girl in India probably faced anguish, pain and ended her life. No one cared how she felt inside. And the girl I was tutoring was struggling in class and falling behind, but no one knew why till I started to understand her. She lived in a troubled home."

It took a moment for Stella to take in everything Mia was saying. "Sounds like you are now taking the responsibility of problematic social issues."

"I can only try."

Stella looked at her dazed. The conversation did not make her enthusiastic, in a sad way. To her, Mia seemed to be in an unusual mind set.

"You are a changed person, Mia."

"Oh, no! Not you also!"

"You were so socially involved at home—cooking, decorating, hosting big dinners, and even those dancing parties on Valentine's Day. It was amazing how much people loved your home."

Mia smiled. "I enjoyed too. I loved doing those. But my life has changed and I don't want to go back to them again. They are now good memories."

"Even your beautiful relationship with Glen…"

Mia became quiet and pressed her lips together.

"But he is not with me now and I am at a point where I don't want to stand and stare at the scenes I have left behind. They just hurt you."

Stella gazed at her face. "I never heard you speak like that."

Mia smiled. "Well, now you do. I want to look forward to different moments awaiting to be experienced."

"What moments are you talking about?"

"Meaningful, different and inspiring."

"Haven't you always done that? All your life you taught children of other people, counseled, advised, encouraged them."

"Sure. A rewarding profession it has been, too."

"Then?"

"Extending the boundary is another choice."

"That means what?"

"Experience a new place, a new culture. A teacher should not be bound to one place."

Mia poured coffee in Stella's mug and slid a plate of homemade brownies in front of her.

"It's what I have been feeling lately, more intense than before."

"Well, you have traveled to distant places with Glen. It's not surprising."

"That was different. I was like a tourist. I was with my family." Mia took a sip of the camomile tea.

"And now what do you foresee?" Stella looked curiously at Mia's face.

"A new kind of teaching experience will bring me closer to a different community of students, learn about their life, their dreams and about the culture....."

Stella did not say anything. She could not imagine doing the things Mia was mentioning. She never traveled outside the country, she had no desire to either.

"Do you think you will do well handling the surprises?"

"If I could handle a devastating, shocking situation that happened to me at a younger age, I think I will do fine."

"You are stronger than you look, Mia. It amazes me sometimes."

"It is probably why surprises don't take me by alarm....We become so wrapped into our small world that everything outside of it seems troubling. Why should that be?"

Stella listened calmly. Everyone had their own way of thinking, even more so Mia. She had managed her life so far with her boys without openly revealing how she thought or felt, but right now, the things she reflected on amazed Stella about her friend.

"I cannot imagine you are same Mia that used to be so active with doing things with her children, socializing with parents, going to family events, movies and vacationing with family."

Mia grinned. "It's like a window inside of me has opened which was shut tight before because there was no need to open it."

Stella smiled and became quiet briefly. Mia could tell from her friend's face what she was thinking.

"I know exactly what you have in mind." Mia smiled giving a playful grin.

Stella laughed. "Well, tell me more then. I want to know."

Mia had mentioned about the dinner invitation from Kyle, but she had never spoken anything further about it. Stella somehow felt Mia would never bring it up again unless she asked her.

"He invited me for dinner," Mia said smiling.

"That sounds like a good beginning." Stella said nodding her head.

They both looked at each other and laughed realizing how entertaining they sounded.

"Seriously, I like how I am now." Mia got up from the chair and brought out a fresh pot of coffee for Stella. She sliced a fresh piece of banana bread and put it on Stella's plate.

"I know you like to keep relationships away," said Stella.

"How do you think it will end?" asked Mia glancing at Stella's face while cutting a piece of bread for herself.

Stella gave a questionable look at Mia. "And you are asking me?"

Mia was quiet for a few minutes.

"Yes."

"I don't know. It's you who needs to tell me."

"Good. Then listen to me……" Mia took a sip of her tea and cleared her throat.

"The most painful part of life got revealed to me in the midst of happy times when I was under the impression that the saddest phases of life come at a later age, and that I still had time on my hands. But I learnt that it was not how life works all the time. I found myself suddenly standing on an unusual stage…shocked, perplexed, hurt. I started to reflect on myself and on the life I was placed into without my choice."

Mia paused and looked away from Stella's face.

"But, all that time, something didn't let me disarray. It took me away from unavailing, bleak thoughts. I remember I quietly started telling myself to let go of emotional thoughts, stop worrying about things that did not help me, and to put trust in the strength that was still alive within me. I felt good because of those motivating words coming from myself."

Stella listened engrossed looking at Mia's face. She nodded gently as she took a bite of the banana bread.

"Change comes first in the heart. Till it is felt, everything stays the same…the old feelings, the behavior, the thoughts, the attitude…." Mia stopped and looked at Stella, gazing at her face.

"Are you still with me?" Mia asked smiling.

Stella nodded. 'It's deep. But I like it."

"I am going out for a dinner with Kyle because he was Glen's friend. He invited me. That is all."

She put light makeup on her face: she applied a shade of mauve lipstick, highlighted the contour of her cheeks with blush, applied some concealer under her eyes to smoothen the insipid look. Under ordinary circumstances, when she had been with Glen, she would have taken time to look her best. Now, she did not have those urges; she wanted to keep the appearance subdued.

Mia took out the light mauve dress from the closet to wear to the dinner with Kyle. She had bought the dress three years after Glen's demise for her niece's wedding. She spotted the dress because of the color, Glen had liked the color on her. He told her that how the colors mauve, coral, fern green and aqua suited her personality. The design was plain, unsophisticated in style. Mia paired a thin pearl-and-gold necklace around her neck with its matching earrings; they had been gifts from Glen for her fortieth birthday. She kept her light-brown hair loose, she had brushed and curled it to give it a little style. She hadn't been out with a man since Glen's passing. She did not wish to be too forthcoming.

"You look charming, Mia." Kyle made the first comment after she opened the front door. He was dressed informally, in a half-sleeved plain beige shirt and brown pants. His physically fit body-built and a well-groomed appearance on a sweep-back, dark-brown hair style had not changed through the years from how she had seen him with Glen. He was about the same age as Glen would have been, mid-fifties though taller and appeared older than Glen. Mia thought he had a more sociable personality than his wife when he was married to her which made him more approachable in social situations.

He handed Mia a large bouquet of coral-and-red roses and a box of Godiva chocolates.

Mia smiled looking at the flowers and the chocolate box, and thanked him telling that there was no formality needed.

There was still light outside when they walked out the door to the car. The late summer evening air was pleasant. Mia was self-conscious despite her outer calm, she was momentarily hesitant to embrace the situation, though, she reflected how indifferent from her part it would have seemed, if she had declined the invitation. Kyle was eager to have a dinner out with her.

Pierce had intentionally left the house before Kyle arrived; he wanted his mother to begin the evening alone with Kyle. His fastidious act was thoughtful yet felt quite unnecessary to Mia.

She took the passenger seat next to Kyle trying to make herself feel at ease. He asked her politely if she was comfortable in her seat and she said that she was fine. He told her how he wanted to get rid of his car and was hoping to buy a new one before he asked her out for dinner. Then, he thought Mia would not mind if he waited.

"What car are you thinking?"

"I don't know." Kyle grinned. "I like German cars."

Kyle slowly maneuvered out to the main road.

"Do you have any favorites?" asked Kyle glancing at Mia.

"All good cars are similar in their performance. I drive a Ford Fusion.

"The tough and reliable." Kyle gave a laugh.

"Sturdy and safe over fancy appearance. I can take that."

"That's for sure." He paused. "The fancy appearance has its own issues."

Mia did not say anything. She clearly understood the comment was not just meant for vehicles. Even Kyle realized he was too close to what he did not wish to imply so soon in their conversation.

"So, how has the past few years been for you?" asked Kyle turning his head to glance at Mia.

"All right. I have my job, my boys, my interests."

"What about Zumba?"

Mia shook her head, laughing. "Not really. I prefer a few laps in the pool."

"A swimmer? Were you ever in a team?"

"In high school. I love water."

"You know what they say…People who love water are compassionate, are good listeners and make great therapists."

Mia smiled. "I guess I am in the right profession, then. What about you?"

"I played basketball….. May be air and earth." Kyle burst out laughing.

"That's quite a contrast."

He nodded hard, grinning. "I have to admit that I have more 'earthly' qualities…realistic, understandable. I don't hold the abstract features that 'air' tends imply—. philosophies and all that."

"Glen and I were both basketball fans. We went to a lot of games together. Of course, I also had the garlic fries on my mind."

Kyle looked at Mia's face, smiled, not bothering to hide that he was interested to hear what she had to say He liked how she talked. He held the steering wheel with his left arm and kept the right arm on his leg. He seemed the type who believed in living the way he wanted, would not reconcile to differences if they went against his choices. Mia was surprised when he opened up about his ex-wife very soon into their conversation. It was almost like he wanted to gain her trust regarding the life he had, but now, on a different road.

"I lost the attraction for my partner early." Mia was surprised that he referred to his ex-wife as partner.

Mia was briefly quiet. "Do you know why?"

"I was a teenager in high school. I liked her a lot then. But, later…." Kyle paused, "I blame myself for getting too close to her without thinking. The only reason we didn't leave each other sooner was because of the children."

"Strange how that happens. I always think that when you know someone from early years, the relationship lasts."

The comment took Kyle by surprise. It was as if the idea had never occurred in his mind.

"Why do you think that?"

"I feel it is easier to mold to each other's habits, tastes, likes, and dislikes at a younger age."

"You forget, the reality is frolicsome at that age," Kyle said in an assured manner.

"True. Then again, the youthful feelings are untainted. They are what they are," Mia responded back.

The car entered the parking lot of the restaurant. Mia recognized the place, she had come here with Glen for a night out without the children. It was a Mediterranean seafood place. Kyle laughed and told her that he somehow felt Glen would have brought her to the same restaurant.

"I knew what kinds of food Glen liked," he said in a pleased tone.

Mia walked towards the restaurant with Kyle, she quickly realized how different it felt; Glen would have immediately held her hand as they walked through the parking lot towards the restaurant together. It always happened. She missed the stability in her life with him. She kept her composure with Kyle, though she felt unsettled at times knowing that Kyle had feelings for her. She did not know for how long he had been feeling that way. She walked in silence feeling like a novice in this kind of situation.

At the restaurant door, a woman greeted them and lead the way towards their table in a private location at the back. The table was set with a candle center-piece flickering, wine and champagne glasses ready. Even though she hadn't known what to expect, it certainly was not the romantically decorated table in front of her.

"A beautifully decorated table!" she exclaimed.

"I am glad you like it." He pulled out the chair for Mia and waited till she sat down.

"I have not treated myself to a formal dinner in a while."

"Really? I am sorry to hear that."

Mia didn't tell him that she did not focus much on formalities anymore. So long as she had the right companion of friends to enjoy a good meal together in a nice place, that was all what mattered for her. She did not feel the need to have a man take her out, she was not ready to go through the formalities of dinners and dates. Perhaps, it was why she never went out singly with anyone in the last seven years; instead she missed Glen.

The waitress brought the champagne, and he wine bottles and showed Kyle. He gave his approval with a smile; she poured the champagne into the glasses. They both toasted, and took sips. Mia thanked him again for the wonderful evening he had planned, staying aware of the fact that she was not going to give him the impression that she was on a rebound.

"Trust me, this is new to me," said Kyle.

Mia nodded in an understanding manner.

He began to tell her about a hikers' club he belonged to. The second Saturday of every month, his group of eight hikers left home early morning taking snacks and water to explore nearby places. They hiked a few miles, and then found a beer joint and had lunch there. It was usually his most eventful weekend other than watching college basketball games on TV. He had begun the activity just as his relationship was nearing its end.

"I guess the challenges of the home demand a life outside," he said.

He continued to describe how much he valued both home and the outdoors. He thought everyone thought like that until his wife showed him another side; she disliked the outdoors. She enjoyed neither trips to the beach nor a walk inside the woods. He felt fortunate that his children did not turn out like her; he encouraged them not to spend indoors all the time.

The waitress came to take the orders. Mia told the waitress she wanted the salad, angel hair pasta with seafood. Kyle ordered salad, green beans, and steak.

Kyle sipped from his glass, took a bite of the tomato and garlic bruschetta.

"My alone time used to be in Mount Shasta living inside my entertaining boat in those days when things were going downhill at home," said Kyle.

Mia found the comment a bit absurd, but realized he was telling about all the things he did when he probably had no communication with his wife. He told her how his ex-wife preferred a life with herself, taking care of her appearance and clothing. The fact that he abruptly offered to speak about her without Mia asking anything about her, startled Mia. What's more everything was about how different she was from him.

"You never had common interests?" asked Mia curiously.

"We both liked going to clubs, dancing and all that—but we were still separate individuals." He took a sip of his champagne, and did not comment anything further.

"Life, people—they teach you all kinds of lessons."

He said he grew up watching everyone in his family do their own things. No one felt it was important to extend their hand to others. He was taught that in order to do well in life, he needed to think about himself first, and put himself first in line. That kind of mindset carried him through school and college. Then, when he quickly decided to marry the girl he really liked, he realized much later that she was different from him in many ways. It was his first biggest lesson, he said.

Mia did not comment anything. It was his personal story. Perhaps, he felt her presence reassuring and just wanted to provide something to her that she may not have known.

A message flashed on Mia's phone. It was from Rachel's counselor. Mia excused herself politely to read the message. It said a decision had been made to place Rachel with her mother for three months with the consent of her father. The counselor thanked Mia for conscientiously taking Rachel's side to change her circumstances. She especially appreciated her patience to get through the challenging conversations with Rachel's father in a poised manner. He was a difficult man to convince, adamant in his ways. Mia smiled and put the phone back on the table.

"Good news?" asked Kyle immediately as he noticed a smile on her face.

"Just jumped the first hurdle."

Kyle looked at her in an inquiring manner, waiting to hear more.

"Teaching is not just about filling students with information. Arduous situations emerge in their personal lives that affect their learning. The teacher has some responsibility."

"It must be overwhelming."

"I would say it certainly makes my own problems less significant in the scale of difficulty, at least momentarily."

Kyle leaned towards her, bringing his face closer, as if he did not wish to miss a word she said. Obviously, he did not know anyone who spoke like Mia. He stretched his arm and gently patted her hand, a fond expression on his face. Mia didn't want to say anything, she smiled acknowledging the gesture politely.

"I am surprised that you have been without someone for so long," said Kyle in a passionate tone.

Mia looked at his face, analyzing his words.

"Actually, I never gave much thought to that."

The light of the candle fell on Mia's face. Kyle looked at her with tenderness, and then instantly and then instantly conscious, he dropped his eyes looking at the candle. He has started to have the kinds of feelings that surfaced in the beginning of relationships, Mia thought. She thought she was in control, though, something surged inside her suddenly. She felt the blood rush to her face, warm. She restrained from saying anything that he might interpret as inviting.

"In all the years I saw you with Glen, never did I imagine I would be having dinner with you alone," she said softly in a guarded tone.

Kyle nodded. "Change is inevitable."

"When Glen was taken away from me, I told myself I would always hold onto the good memories in my heart, amend myself to the new conditions and not sink into dismal thoughts."

"That was it? You never thought further about the life ahead?"

"I did. But not the type of life I had with Glen."

"I think you had an extraordinary life with Glen. Why would you not wish for that?"

"What I want to say is...I want to preserve those feelings, and the experiences just how they were. I feel no desire to expand those types of feelings and experiences anymore. Time has moved me forward. As you said, change is inevitable. It is what happens to people too."

Being Friday, all the tables were occupied. The waitress came and placed the food in front of them.

Kyle sipped the champagne. "I am glad for this evening."

They said *"Bon Appetite"* and started with the food. She ate quietly keeping her face focused on the food. She commented on how good it tasted, and that she liked the restaurant. Kyle added that he thought about her, how she preferred a healthy seafood place even though he liked meat as his first choice.

"I wait for the boys to come home to grill meat."

"I must say you have kept up well with your selected style." Kyle grinned and paused. He cut a piece of the steak and put it in his mouth. "I need a meat every day."

"Everyone is different," Mia said softly.

Kyle wanted the conversation to continue and Mia could clearly tell he had things in mind that he wished to express. But he kept delaying and switching to general topics.

"So, I suppose life has been treating you good so far?" Mia asked.

Kyle laughed. "It depends what you mean by treating good."

"Generally good, no headaches and distresses daily."

"You can say that."

Mia nodded smiling. She did not wish to hear more.

"Do you go to San Francisco with your women friends?" Kyle immediately asked.

Mia understood a subject of that sort would start sometime.

"We have done day trips. We enjoy the Ghirardelli Square on every visit."

"What about the dinner cruises over the bay?"

"A few times with Glen….. champagne and music included. Not with my women friends." Mia laughed.

Kyle listened and nodded smiling. Then he politely asked if she wanted to meet every so often for a dinner out, may be a movie, a night stroll or a dinner cruise in San Francisco. He thought, maybe, she would interpret the gesture as moving forward. At their age and situation, many people searched for companionship, it was normal. He had no idea how she was thinking.

Mia wanted to give herself a moment to respond. She did not wish to be misunderstood, she had never contemplated on a regular companionship with someone in the years without Glen. Nothing was going to change so soon, she knew that.

"I am thinking of experiencing a new culture."

There was a sudden silence. Glen raised his eyebrows as if he had not anticipated such a response.

"Really? I wouldn't have imagined you thinking like that," he said wistfully, and took a sip of the champagne.

"You are not the first one. It's kind of how I have been feeling," Mia said openly.

"Boredom of a place, is it?'

"Definitely not." She understood that people tended to interpret things in their own way or did not bother to go deeper into others' thoughts.

"I have been imagining myself teaching in another country to students with different needs. May be I will learn something and share in return." She took a sip from the glass and looked at him.

"How does your family feel?"

"They all have their own thoughts, I have mine."

She told him that feelings change with harsh experiences. The person who experiences, understands more than others. Not everything can be explained.

She sipped a little water, and wiped the mouth with her napkin. She thought Kyle was honest about what he said or felt. Despite this, she recognized that she was on the opposite end of his situation. Kyle had a discontented past, a part of life he regretted. Maybe he was looking for a second chance. Mia was not looking for that; memories with Glen were too close to her heart.

"The more I reflect on what others say or comment about my plans, the more I realize it is what they want. It has nothing to do with me, my feelings or my wishes."

She told Kyle how she had been feeling in the past years. She promised herself that she had suffered enough internally, she would not allow herself to continue that or let others mold her thoughts. She would now like to live her life on her terms—as a mother, as a widow of a man she loved and as a woman who wanted to bring some meaning and purpose to the life she was living.

Kyle took the last piece from his plate, putting the put his fork and knife together, he sighed as one does after a satisfying meal. He waited for Mia to say something about spending more time together, but she did not say anything.

"Whatever way you respond to me, it will not change my feelings for you," he said softly, faltering, as he leaned towards Mia, taking her hand and giving a gentle squeeze.

Mia blushed looking at Kyle." Please don't wait for me."

There was a brief silence. Mia knew it was exactly what she wanted to tell him, but it was not what he wanted to hear. Kyle quickly took out his wallet as if to hide the feelings that instantly hit him hard. He didn't like what she said, but he didn't show any kind of distress at her words. Perhaps he still wished to keep the door open, slightly.

He hurriedly pulled out a picture of the boat to show Mia.

"My best days of the summer are spent here," he said appreciating the picture.

Mia glanced at the photo. "Impressive."

He laughed continuing to show Mia the pictures on his phone…. a 65" colored television screen, his music system and the large three-room living space with a luxurious kitchen, bar and a hot tub.

"When I am there, I feel I can shut out the world."

"If that's what makes you feel happy…."

He gave a witty grin. "Happy…that can take up a few more hours to talk about."

Mia did not say anything. She was not going to enquire about his life…and about the subject, everyone had their own opinion. She had heard enough.

"At the end, it all comes down to how you feel about the life you made for yourself. That is what matters."

He looked at Mia's face as if he was about to say something, but waited—he had to be sure about what he wanted to say.

"I believe you made the most obvious statement, but also the most difficult one. I don't know —I feel I am still searching."

Mia thought the evening ended on a good note even though she did not commit any future meetings with Kyle. But she sensed that Kyle didn't want the dinner to be their last meeting. She didn't want to go into the subject knowing how she felt about dating. They walked through the half-empty parking lot towards the car without saying anything. Mia felt tense thinking what kinds of thoughts could be going through Kyle's mind; she wouldn't be surprised if he thought her to be a 'heartbreaker'—she wanted to bring up something light-hearted, but she decided not to say anything at all.

"I had a wonderful evening, Mia."

Kyle broke the silence and told her how comfortable he felt spending the few hours with her.

"It was great! I am glad we could catch up with the news of our lives."

He opened the car door for her, and apologized to her for taking her out in his old car. But he knew Mia would never think along those lines.

"I had known Glen a long time so it was not surprising that I felt I have known you just as long," Kyle said as he exited to take the highway.

Mia did not say anything. It was one of those moments she wanted to watch every word she spoke or how she acted. She felt it was wrong to put hope to his thoughts. The music kept playing on the radio. At one point, Kyle asked her if she had any preference for the radio stations. She told him 'country music' was a good choice.

"Really?" Kyle instantly gaped at her with wide open eyes, grinning.

Mia nodded with a glowing appreciation on her face. She said she had loved the guitar and the rhythm of country music since she was a young girl. She introduced Glen to the music; he got into the dancing part quickly.

"Glen danced?" Kyle asked laughing as he eyed Mia with interest.

Mia nodded and suddenly became quiet. Then she said softly, "He couldn't dance long. Life kept it short for him."

Kyle entered the driveway and stopped the car. He looked at Mia, she was taking the keys out of the purse. He waited gazing at her for a long moment as if to gain strength. His senses overpowered him. He stretched towards Mia.

"May I?"

Mia glanced at his face, waited, to let time pass briefly. She leaned towards him shifting in her seat. She conceded. He kissed her on the cheek.

"I hope you didn't mind," said Kyle.

"To be loved is a good thing." She paused briefly and smiled at him appreciatively before getting out of the car.

This was, of course, not how she had expected the night to end. She felt the throbs of her heart-beat, her hands were moist and warm. An intense restless aura overtook her. It was anything but easy. She stood for a few minutes as Kyle backed the car from the driveway feeling relief that she was in control as best she could be. Kyle gave a wave as he turned on to the road. Mia walked hastily to the front door.

She knew Pierce was back at home, but she used her keys to open the door. The lamp next to the door was on, Mia glanced at the clock on the wall; it was eleven-fifty. She put the purse on the coffee table, plopped down on the arm chair, taking a deep sigh. She leaned her head back and closed her eyes. The few hours with Kyle had felt like she was in a theater rehearsal with him, without an audience, turned away from the past, waltzing to the present. It finally came to an end.

She liked the quietness inside the house, it calmed the vigor that had restlessly risen inside her. The stair lights were on, but dimmed, also the kitchen light. She knew Pierce was in his room, on the computer or reading. Mia got up and went to the kitchen.

The kitchen looked meticulously clean. The dishwasher had been emptied, the clean dishes were neatly organized on the cabinet shelves when she opened to see them. The flower bouquet that Kyle brought was arranged nicely in a crystal vase on the center table of the family room. Even the kitchen towels were neatly folded and hanging.

"I must have done something right." Mia smiled.

She saw the vase of maroon and orange chrysanthemum flowers at the corner of the kitchen counter, the same place she had been putting the vase ever since she had moved in to the house, and the same place Glen had set his eyes every time to compliment the flowers. The chocolate box from Kyle was lying on the counter.

She knew everything was the work of Pierce. She wondered what was going through his mind to take charge of the kitchen.

Suddenly, she heard the door open upstairs. Pierce came walking down with the phone in his hand.

"How was your evening, Mom?" He asked in an enthusiastic tone.

"Nice!"

They both looked at each other, and smiled.

"Did you have dinner?" asked Mia.

Pierce nodded. "I was going to make something myself, then I saw the dinner ready in the oven. Thanks, mom!"

Mia looked at his face. Things were not perfect between them and she wished she could bring him back to the days when Glen was there. He was different then, of course younger, he changed over the years in Glen's absence. She wanted to ask if he could stay two more days, but she didn't.

"Thank you for taking care of the kitchen," Mia said in a caring tone.

Pierce smiled. "Looks alright to you?"

"Of course! It's like the cleaning service came and did the job." Mia said smiling at him.

"I guess you taught me something."

Mia did not say anything. She smiled.

"What time are you leaving tomorrow?"

"Early morning. May be around six."

"Do you need anything?"

"I am good."

"Should I pack sandwiches for the road?"

"Don't bother. I will get something on the way."

"What about before you leave?"

Mia thought she sounded obtrusive, but she was not troubled. It was the right thing to do as his mother, no matter how old he was or how the relationship was between them, she reflected.

"I will decide tomorrow. By the way, the envelope from India is on the dining table." Pierce gestured towards it.

Mia looked at his face. She was surprised he mentioned it. Knowing how he had been feeling about her plans, she thought that he wouldn't have cared, at least, not bring it up at that moment.

"Thanks for telling me!" Mia said smiling.

He drank a glass of water, said good night and went upstairs. He didn't ask for any details about the dinner with Kyle.

"I will be up to see you off when you leave tomorrow morning," Mia said as she watched him going up the stairs.

"Okay, thanks!" He stood on the stairs, smiled at Mia before heading up.

An oversized envelope with the stamp 'first-class mail' was lying on the dining table. Mia looked at her printed full name and address, also the sender's name, Mrs. Laxmi Seshadri. She noticed the four postage stamps on the envelope, pictures of lighted earthen lamps. She instantly recalled what the Indian lady, Ruma, at the health club told her.... Diwali was the festival of lights when the country was lit up with earthen lamps and candles to celebrate joy and peace. Mia had gone home and read about the festival. She liked the fascinating mythological story connected to the holiday. She started looking up the significance of the characters and learned a few things she did not know before. It was a good feeling.

"A brief encounter with you, took me a long way." She had told Ruma afterwards.

She picked up the envelope, held it to her chest and took a deep breath.

Things in life exist to be experienced. Change has a good side.

She glanced at Glenn's photo on the table in the family room and smiled.

Mia turned off the lights.

CPSIA information can be obtained
at www.ICGtesting.com
Printed in the USA
BVHW031110170419
545535BV00033B/298/P